THE HERETIC'S CREED

THE HERETIC'S CREED

Fiona Buckley

CRÈME de la CRIME

This first world edition published 2016
in Great Britain and the USA by
Crème de la Crime, an imprint of
SEVERN HOUSE PUBLISHERS LTD of
19 Cedar Road, Sutton, Surrey, England, SM2 5DA

Trade paperback edition first published 2018
In Great Britain and the USA by
SEVERN HOUSE PUBLISHERS LTD
Eardley House, 4 Uxbridge Street, London W8 7SY

British Library Cataloguing in Publication Data
A CIP catalogue record for this title is available from the British Library.

ISBN-13: 978-1-78029-091-1 (cased)
ISBN-13: 978-1-78029-574-9 (trade paper)
ISBN-13: 978-1-78010-823-0 (e-book)

PROLOGUE

I t was midnight and cloudy and the room at the back of Stonemoor House would have been dark even with the shutters wide open. They were however firmly closed, not to keep light out, but to keep it in. No late-night wanderer on the moor, no shepherd guarding his sheep, no poacher out after illicit game, no prowling insomniac who had left his bed in the village of Thorby must realize that the inhabitants of Stonemoor were anywhere but respectably in their own beds.

The room was large and the darkness so intense that even four triple-branched candlesticks couldn't hold enough candles to overcome it and Abbess Philippa Gould (who was not an abbess at all, but had merely appropriated the title) could not tell, when looking at the huddle of cowled and black-robed figures before her, whether or not they were all there. Therefore, she called the roll.

'Bella Yates.' Bella was a senior in the household because she was Philippa's natural sister. Otherwise, she would have been near the end of the list. She had been reared by her mother, an unlettered woman on a remote farm. Bella was literate now because Philippa herself had taught her to read and write, though Philippa had sometimes had cause to regret it. Bella was still essentially as ignorant and superstitious as her mother had been. She was also both opinionated and truculent. Her 'Yes, I'm here,' was spoken in a broad Yorkshire accent and also in an uncooperative tone that made her sister frown.

'Angelica Ames.' Angelica was as dignified and as well-educated as Philippa herself. She could read Latin and Greek as easily as English and also spoke both French and Italian. Her parents had made a poor job of naming her, however, for she in no way resembled an angel, being tall, gaunt, and unsmiling, with watchful eyes, as dark as the thick waves of her hair, which continually escaped from under her veil.

'Present,' she said, in her deep voice.

'Margaret Beale.'

'Yes, my lady.' Margaret was small and timid but the equal of Philippa and Angelica in her accomplishments. She, Angelica, Bella, and Philippa were the original founders of the household. All the rest had come later.

The roll call went on, the choir nuns (as Philippa insisted on calling them, though they sang only in this back room and only when they didn't think they could be overheard) being named first, in alphabetical order.

'Marie Chartley . . . Susanne Leblanc . . . Jean McNab . . . Eleanor Overton . . . Daisy Pendlebury . . . Katherine Trayne . . . Jane Wellingdale . . .'

Then those who were regarded as lay sisters. 'Katy Greene . . . Mary Haxby . . . Cat Marshall . . . Annie Peel . . . Annette Turner.

'Good. We are all here.' Philippa stepped into the pool of light cast by the candles, which were all on a table in the middle of the room. Also on the table were a small knife with a silver handle and a gleaming blade, a little phial of what looked like water, and a box made of walnut wood, about eighteen inches long by ten inches wide and six inches deep. Philippa undid its brass clasp and put the lid back, revealing that the box held a book, beautifully bound in white leather with a title and an intricate pattern on the front in gold leaf.

'Our purpose tonight,' said Philippa, 'is to strengthen the protection that a past generation, so it is said, has already placed upon this book. For who is to know what really, truly happened or was done in a vanished century? I propose to make sure that it *has* really, truly happened, so as to defend this remarkable thing from the harm that *some* people undoubtedly wish it . . .'

'It's evil.' The protesting voice was Bella's. It did shake a little, because she was at one and the same time defying both her abbess and her stately and dominant elder sister Philippa, whose cool grey eyes could, as Bella had sometimes resentfully said, freeze the very blood in one's veins with a single glance. But passionate feeling could overcome that and Bella did indeed feel passionately. 'It is full of strange lore from the infidel lands in the east!' she said fiercely. 'About stars and planets and arithmetic, which is close to witchcraft! And it talks of the Earth circling the Sun, which is wicked heresy according to the teaching of our mother Church, and worse, there is a drawing, disrespectful to the Holy Father. Insulting him! Making fun! Nothing in that book is decent reading for Christians! It's heathen and . . . and blasphemous! It should be destroyed!'

There were some murmurs of agreement, most, though not all, from among those who were classified as lay sisters. Philippa sighed.

'This volume contains most valuable lore,' she said, with determined calm. 'During the short time I spent at home with my father, after I was widowed, he talked to me about such things. He was interested in matters of science and he had learned of the theories of a man called Nicolaus Copernicus, who claimed that the Earth does indeed circle the Sun, and by means of diagrams, showed that this theory made sense. My father would have liked to correspond with him, but Copernicus died over thirty years ago. However, with my father, I studied the theory and concluded that it is probably true. Our Church, our priesthood, no matter how much we respect them, are not always in the right, can at times be very much in the wrong, blind to proven facts . . .'

'They are never in the wrong. They can't be in the wrong!' snapped Bella.

'Our mutual father,' said Philippa, 'considered it wise and right to keep the laws of Elizabeth as far as possible, even though the Pope has told us not to obey her. Are you saying that Father was wrong to say that?'

'Yes!' said Bella.

'Well, this is not the time or the place to argue about it.' Philippa could see them all being sidetracked when it was vital that they should concentrate on the matter in hand. 'Many of you simply do not understand these things and therefore cannot pronounce on them, and that, Bella, includes you. I repeat, it is said that in the past, because this book needed to be defended against those who thought as you – and some others here – apparently do, a wise Christian priest laid a curse on anyone who harmed it. He did so at the request of the family who then owned it. He did it because he, like the family – your family, Eleanor – recognized that it was valuable, whatever it might contain, because it is an exquisitely made medieval manuscript book, delicately illuminated, a wondrous example of the skill of monkish scribes.'

'And what kind of monks were they, who copied and illustrated such a book, and drew that wicked picture?' demanded Bella irrepressibly.

Plump, fair Eleanor Overton, who had joined the community only two weeks before, said: 'It is true, Mother, that in my family, there is a tradition about that curse. It is said that it was laid, though no one knows when. I for one believe it.'

'You may well be right,' said Philippa. 'But I wish to make it certain. Here, this night, in this place, I shall renew the curse.'

There was a silence. An October wind, blowing across the moors, rattled the shutters and a draught crept into the room, making the candle flames quiver and lean sideways, and stirring the shadows that the gathering cast on the panelled walls. Someone caught a nervous breath. Philippa let the tense moment grow yet more tense. Such an atmosphere was precisely what she wanted to create. It was imperative that somehow she must generate belief, compel a shuddering acceptance of what she was about to do. Only then could it have the desired effect.

The trouble was, she had no idea at all how to do it. Some of the priests of Holy Church knew but she did not. She had to invent.

When she felt that the silence had lasted long enough, she took the book from its box and laid it on the table. Then she picked up the phial, holding it up so that the candlelight shone upon it.

'This is water,' she said. 'But it is holy water. Our good priest, Walter Cogge, whom all the world believes to be our bailiff and groom, has blessed it for us. He knows what I am about this night. He is a learned and a wise man. He did not wish to officiate – he has never pronounced a curse, he said, and does not wish to do so – but he understands why I think it necessary, and is leaving the task to me. I have summoned you all here to be witnesses.'

Someone said: 'Shouldn't it be done by bell, book, and candle? We have candles but no bell, and what about the book? It can't be that one. Shouldn't it be the Bible?'

'I'm not exorcizing anything,' said Philippa irritably. 'I am cursing. That's different. Quiet, please!'

There were more murmurs, a mingling of surprise, approval, and disquiet and once more, Philippa let the tension grow for a moment or two, before continuing.

'I lay this curse,' she said, in the resounding tones of one whose voice had been trained in both singing and speech, 'on any who would do harm to this book, on any who would destroy or deface it. Cursed you shall be, firstly by water . . .' she poured a little from the phial into the palm of her hand and then splashed it on to the white-leather cover of the book '. . . and secondly by fire . . .' The gathering gasped as she lifted the book and put a corner of it into a candle flame. She withdrew the book at once and set it down. The burned corner glowed faintly and then went out, leaving a tiny blackened tip behind.

'And thirdly, I curse you with blood drawn by steel,' said Philippa. She held the little knife up in the candlelight. It shone softly on the silver hilt but flashed flame-coloured and sinister on the small sharp blade. With evident difficulty and a shiver of dislike, she drew the blade across her left thumb, firmly enough to draw blood. Now it was the thumb that she held in the candlelight so that they could all see the dark line across it. She lowered her hand and smeared blood on to the top edge of the cover, transferring a little stain.

Then, laying her right hand on the cover and raising her left in the air, she said, in yet more ringing tones, 'I hereby declare that by holy water and fire and steel-drawn blood, I dedicate this book, *Observations of the Heavens by John of Evesham*, to the care of God. From this day forth, it is His, and may His wrath will fall upon on any that wilfully harm it. In His name, I call upon water, fire, and steel to exact vengeance on such a one and I seal the curse with my own blood. In the name of the Father, the Son, and the Holy Ghost, I curse any who touch this book with intent to injure it!'

As she fell silent, she wiped her left thumb quickly on her dark-blue robe and then she lifted the book once more and held it high, letting them see it clearly, letting the curse resound in their ears, letting the air quiver with it. To her satisfaction, she heard a few jittery whimpers and even – excellent! – a frightened sob from someone. Then she laid the book gently back into its box and closed the lid. The brass latch clicked home with a soft, final sound.

'This work is now complete,' she said in her normal voice. 'Our good priest Walter Cogge is waiting to say Mass for us, before we retire to our beds. He will be here very shortly. No matins will be sung tonight. My daughters, make no mistake! There is a curse now on any of you who harm this most precious volume of lore and I would advise you, all of you, not even to think about harming it, let alone carrying thought into action. Who knows how far the curse will stretch? Remember that God knows the secrets of all hearts.'

Her eyes, by now, were well adjusted to the bad light. She scanned their faces, so many pale countenances, oval, square, or triangular, framed in wimples and veils, shadowed by the dark cowls. She was pleased to see fear in many of the eyes that looked back at her, and, in some of them, tears.

It would do. She did not think that anyone here would dare to touch this precious volume.

The curse need not hold for too long, anyway. She had plans for John of Evesham's *Observations of the Heavens*. The illicit little community at Stonemoor House was always short of money.

ONE
Spectre at the Wedding

I t was a happy wedding and a wonderfully successful marriage breakfast, and it all took place on a beautiful day. Early February in that year of 1577 was pretending to be May, with dazzling sunshine and soft winds, a glorious contrast to the January storms just behind us.

My ward Kate Ferguson, who had that morning become Mistress Eric Lake, was seated beside her new husband at the top table in the great hall of Hawkswood House, and she was as lovely as the day. Her cream silk gown and the amber and topaz jewellery that she and I had chosen together suited her dark hair and her brown eyes so well, and subtly flattered her smooth young skin. I sighed a little, looking at her. I had once had a skin as good as that, but I was now approaching my forty-third birthday and my mirror told me, all too clearly, that time and trouble had left their marks.

At Kate's side, young Master Lake also looked splendid in his blue velvet doublet with its big puffed sleeves and cream slashings. Eric Lake had a Norwegian grandmother, which accounted not only for his Norwegian Christian name, but also for his looks. He was as fair-haired and blue-eyed as the Vikings were said to have been and had the permanent bronze of a man who spends time out of doors. He was a handsome fellow altogether and a cheerful one. The blue eyes sparkled as he whispered something into Kate's ear, and Kate laughed as she replied to him. They had liked each other from the moment they were introduced.

The feast was satisfactory too. My large and opinionated cook John Hawthorn had, as usual on special occasions, managed to take most of the decisions over what to serve, and with the help of his second in command, Ben Flood, he had created wonders. We were dining on roast mutton, capons stuffed with chopped and highly spiced liver and kidneys, and duck in a citrus sauce, as well as fresh fish from our own lake, preceded by a rich vegetable soup and hot fresh bread, with elaborate desserts to follow. Hawthorn and Flood had done marvels with spun sugar and marchpane.

Since the death of my husband Hugh a few years ago, John Hawthorn had sometimes complained that we didn't entertain often enough. His skills weren't being fully used, he said. In preparing this feast, he had had the time of his life and he and my steward, tall, silver-haired Adam Wilder, were further enjoying themselves by bringing in each course in style, leading the way and playing fanfares on bugles, while my manservant Roger Brockley, together with Ben Flood and the maidservants Phoebe, Margery, and Lucy, bore the dishes in behind them.

The crowd pleased me, too. We had a gratifying number of guests. My married daughter Meg and her husband George had come all the way from Buckinghamshire to be with us here in Surrey, while Kate's parents had ridden from Dover, along with her sister Sheila, the husband that Sheila had recently married, and her brother Duncan, also with a newly wedded wife. I was very pleased to see Duncan. He had had to leave the country for a while after killing his adversary in a duel but his name had been cleared and I was happy to see that he had been allowed to marry the girl he had already been in love with. Bessie was the daughter of a Dover innkeeper and Mr Ferguson senior had once objected strongly to the idea of an innkeeper's daughter in his family. Evidently, he had given way at last and with good grace, for at this very moment he was talking animatedly to his daughter-in-law and both of them were smiling.

The guests also included Eric's parents, who had gallantly made the journey for the second time (the first was when they brought Eric to meet Kate), even though neither was young. Their marriage was the second one for both of them and I had gathered that Eric had arrived in the world somewhat unexpectedly, when his mother was in her mid-forties. Fortunately, it was not so very far from my home at Hawkswood to the Lakes' farm near Guildford, and the couple had come by wagon rather than horseback. In addition there were many friends of my own from round about, and one very prestigious guest indeed: Lord Burghley, Sir William Cecil. He was seated beside me, at the top table, to the right of the newly wed pair. The hall hearth had a good fire in it, but the hall was too big to be easily warmed and Sir William had kept his fur-trimmed cloak on. It was made of thick russet velvet and the fur was white miniver. He was a splendid figure, an ornament to any big occasion.

'They're a fine-looking couple,' he remarked. 'I think they're well matched. I like to see a bride look so happy.'

Sybil Jester, my gentlewoman, friend, and to some degree chaperone (for she was now well into her fifties), was seated on my other side. Leaning forward to address Cecil, she said: 'Yes. A frightened bride must be a difficult problem for the groom! Kate clearly won't be that. Of course . . . we don't know . . .'

The reason why Kate had become my ward was because she had once fallen in love with a most undesirable man and run off to him, only to find that she had run herself into terrible danger. I had become involved in her troubles and when Kate's outraged father rejected her, I had offered to take charge of her. He had consented, and now, forgivingly, he had come from Dover to lead her to the altar himself. But none of us knew, and probably would never know, just how far Kate's unsuitable affair had gone. Fortunately, Eric Lake was not censorious. He had been told about her previous history before he agreed to meet Kate, and had said from the start that he had an amour or two in his own past and he wasn't one to throw stones. He reckoned, he had said with a grin, that he was capable of keeping his wife content and he wasn't going to trouble himself about her girlish fancies.

But of course, if the undesirable Captain Garnett had been her lover, then she probably had no fears about the night to come and I couldn't regret that, because I had had wards before and I had once had to cope with one to whom marriage, at least at first, had been a nightmare.

But for Kate and Eric, all the omens had been propitious, from the start. I remembered that beginning very well, and with pleasure.

*   *   *

My good friend the Queen's Messenger Christopher Spelton, who had once offered me the chance of being his wife instead of just his friend, had first brought Kate and Eric together. He had visited us the previous November and while he was there, I had confided to him that I was anxious to find a husband for Kate. I spoke quite casually, but he at once looked interested.

'I may be able to help you there,' he said. 'I have a younger cousin living with his parents quite near Guildford. Eric is my Aunt Anne's son. He's twenty-five, a very suitable age for marriage, and he wishes to find a wife, and my aunt has actually asked me if I know of anyone. She married a yeoman farmer; they're comfortably off, goodhearted folk. Suppose we arrange for the young people to meet? Just to see if they take to each other. Lake, that's the name of the family.'

Accordingly, I asked Christopher to bring his aunt, his uncle by marriage, and his cousin Eric to dine with us one day. Kate and I, attended by other household members, received them in the great hall of Hawkswood. I remembered how nervous we all were. I know that when we heard the guests arrive, I had to restrain myself from rushing out to inspect young Master Lake straight away.

I did restrain myself, however. We all stayed where we were while the guests dismounted in the courtyard and were escorted indoors by Adam Wilder. The two elder Lakes came in first and then, behind them, came Eric. They entered the hall through a door that led straight into the open air of the courtyard, and as he stepped over the threshold, a shaft of low December sunshine caught him, revealing a young man, tall and looking even taller than he really was because he held himself so well.

He was clean-shaven, with tanned features and his fair hair, though cut short, was thick and vigorous. His blue eyes had small laughter lines at the corners. His doublet was of tawny velvet with blue slashings on his sleeves and matching blue stockings, and the blue hat which he had taken off and was carrying in his right hand had a jaunty golden-brown feather in it and a topaz brooch. He had a tawny cloak, airily tossed back from one shoulder and he was smiling.

He looked, in fact, like a young god, Balder perhaps, the son of the Viking god Odin and the goddess Frigg. As a child, being brought up by an uncle and aunt, I had shared my cousins' tutor, a man of wide learning. He had told us tales of the Viking gods. Aunt Tabitha and Uncle Herbert didn't approve when they heard about it and after that, there were no more of what my aunt and uncle called pagan tales, but we had already heard a good many. Balder, the tutor said, had been splendid to behold, wise and gentle. Eric Lake could have played him in a masque without needing to act. Just for a moment, despite my mature years, I felt the visceral jerk that is the instinctive female response to beautiful males. But he barely glanced at me. He was looking about him and taking in all who were present, and when his gaze lit on Kate, it stayed there.

Christopher Spelton came in behind the family party, but once in the hall, took charge and performed introductions. From the very first, Eric and Kate seemed to look only at each other. There was general conversation for a while, during which the two of them exchanged a few commonplaces with the rest of us and then dinner was served, but throughout all that, their eyes constantly sought one another. I remember how keenly Christopher had watched them, and how impressed he was with Kate. He was seated beside me at the table and whispered his admiration to me.

'She looks so beautiful! I think you have taught her how to dress well.'

'I was once one of the queen's ladies,' I said. 'In that position, one *has* to dress well, and of course, there are examples of fine clothes all around. I suppose I learned a good deal myself. It's true that I've advised Kate. I think that rose-coloured damask suits her and I would have recommended it, but she chose it herself.'

'A good choice. She is a most elegant young lady now. I can hardly take my eyes off her. And I can hardly believe that she is the same girl who, according to you, was so brave when you were in danger together, and actually struck an enemy with an oar!'

'Well, it's true,' I said, remembering the occasion with a shudder.

'My cousin Eric is going to be a lucky man, if she takes to him,' said Christopher.

After the meal, I spoke a word in Kate's ear and Eric's father spoke a word in the ear of his son, and the young pair left the hall. Kate led her companion to a parlour, the smaller of the two that Hawkswood boasted, a comfortable little room where I had ordered a fire to be lit in readiness. When they emerged, a good hour later, they were hand in hand. It was as easy as that. They met, I think, as simply and trustfully as Adam and Eve in the lost Garden of Eden, and now they were wed, and everyone in the hall smiled to look upon them, and heartily wished them joy.

The dessert course was being carried in. Between blasts from Adam Wilder's bugle, I remarked: 'I'm delighted to have you here, Sir William. It's a great honour for Kate.'

'I am glad I was able to attend,' said Cecil. 'I have many commitments, as you know. I've had a talk with the bridegroom. I fancy he'll be good for Kate. For all his spectacular looks, he strikes me as a sensible, practical young man. The kind to settle down and settle her down as well. She has had a wild past.'

'She just fell in love,' I said indulgently. 'And now she's done it again, and more safely.'

In fact, on closer acquaintance, Eric, despite his spectacular looks and evident good humour, had struck me as slightly dull and I knew that Kate had in the past annoyed her father by refusing suitors that she said were dull. But I knew that they had also been much older than she was, probably chosen by her father for that reason, thinking that they would curb the wildness that he knew was in her. Eric was young as well as handsome and that must make a difference. Yes, the auguries were good, I thought.

I had one regret. 'I wish Christopher Spelton could have come,' I said. 'After all, he is Eric's first cousin and it was he who arranged to introduce him and Kate to each other. I sent him an invitation and he sent back word that he had an errand to Scotland – Edinburgh, I think he said – but expected to be back in time to be here. There's been no sign of him and no word from him. I suppose his errand, whatever it was, has taken longer than he thought it would.'

'No doubt.' For some reason, Cecil looked troubled, and changed the subject. 'Where are Eric and Kate going to live?' he enquired.

'They're leasing a house and farm a few miles the other side of Guildford. It's ready for them now and they will be moving straight in.'

Cecil smiled. 'And no doubt, by the end of the year, they will be inviting you to a christening! Mistress Jester!' He leant forward a little to speak to Sybil. 'I believe you are to be congratulated on once more becoming a grandmother? The mention of Edinburgh reminded me. Is it not true that you have a married daughter there and that she has lately had a little girl?'

I was well aware that for various reasons, Lord Burghley kept himself informed about me and those close to me, and that his main source of information was our local vicar, Doctor Fletcher, but it always startled me when he revealed the extent of his knowledge. It made me feel that I was under constant scrutiny. It was for my own good, but I disliked it.

Sybil, meanwhile, was answering the question. 'Yes, the little girl was born in January. A courier arrived soon after the snow had gone. All went well, it seems, and the baby has been named for me! They have called her Sybil!'

'I see.' Cecil seemed oddly distracted. He had a slice of fruit pie on his platter – made from Hawkswood's own apples, kept from last autumn's harvest, sweet as honey and encased in rich, buttery pastry – but instead of eating, he seemed to be crumbling the pastry with his fingers and had apparently not noticed the jug of cream that someone had set on the table near his place. Abruptly, he said: 'You must long to see your new grandchild. Are you considering a visit to Edinburgh?'

I was suddenly and uncomfortably alert. I knew Lord Burghley so well. 'Well . . . no,' I said. 'It's a long way. Though, of course, I'm sure that Sybil . . .'

'Would you not like to go?' asked Cecil, addressing Sybil and me both at once. Sybil said, 'Well . . .' and stopped and I adopted a light tone of voice and said: 'Hardly at this time of year. We're only just into February!'

Cecil was a serious man. Above his pointed beard, his face was grave and lined, especially between his light blue eyes. That line had deepened suddenly and I knew that he was thinking of something solemn. 'Lord Burghley?' I said, questioningly.

'When the feast is over,' said Cecil quietly, 'when the dancing starts, I would like to talk to you, Ursula. In private.'

My pleasure in this successful day was dimmed at once. I felt alarmed and with good reason. Many years ago, when my first husband, Gerald Blanchard, died suddenly of smallpox, he had left me with Meg, then a small child, and with very little money, for my marriage to Gerald had had a somewhat scandalous beginning and neither his family nor mine showed any inclination to help me out.

I had scandalous origins on my own account, anyway. My mother had been at court, as one of Queen Anne Boleyn's ladies, but she had been sent home, disgraced, carrying an unlawful child and refusing to name its father. That child was me.

Home for her was that of my Uncle Herbert and his wife Aunt Tabitha. They had sheltered us, but reluctantly and grimly. After her death, they continued to shelter me, but they never loved me. Probably they suspected that if not watched, I might go the same way as my mother. I more or less proved them right, eventually, when I eloped with Gerald, who was at the time betrothed to their daughter Mary.

When I was widowed, my position might have been desperate but I was rescued from penury because Gerald had been an aide to Sir Thomas Gresham, who worked in the Netherlands in the financial interests of Queen Elizabeth. Through him, I obtained a position as one of the queen's ladies, which meant that I was housed and fed and paid a stipend that enabled me to settle Meg in a cottage with her nurse.

Even so, however, I hadn't much left over. My thirty pounds a year not only had to cover the rent of the cottage and pay the nurse, it also had to cover the cost of dresses suitable for a queen's attendant, and the various gratuities one always had to give pages and other servants for this or that service.

So, because of my difficult financial state, I let myself be led into doing secret tasks, for money. I had done well out of it; that could not be denied. My circumstances had changed over time, bringing me two further marriages, a house of my own – Withysham, in Sussex – and, after my last marriage, to Hugh Stannard, this Surrey house, Hawkswood, with its accompanying grounds and farm.

But now that I was past forty, I wished to be done with the court and political affairs and the danger into which my various assignments had at times led me. Meg was grown and married; I had taken on the wardship of Kate Ferguson and now seen her safely married as well; henceforth, I desired only to be let alone.

The trouble was, that I had been too successful in the tasks I had been set. The court – and the queen – kept coming back for more and I usually agreed, for a very special reason.

My mother had consistently refused to say who my father was, but the truth came to light in the end. Henry the Eighth had not been faithful to his unhappy queen, Anne Boleyn. He had fathered me and therefore, I was half-sister to the queen.

She knew it. She accepted me as a sister. There was a bond between us. So it was no wonder that when she called on me to undertake duties for her, I found it hard to refuse. These two facts were the reason why Doctor Fletcher consistently kept Cecil informed about me and my household. Now, after seeing that line deepen between Cecil's eyes, and hearing him ask to speak to me in private, I took fright. Here, in the midst of all these happy wedding celebrations, he had ceased to be a valued guest and turned into a spectre.

The feast was over. We had risen from our places and stood back while the tables at which we had dined were pushed aside and the musicians that I had hired, who had played softly throughout the meal, had taken some refreshment and then resumed their places. They now struck up a lively tune for a galliard. Eric was leading Kate out on to the floor to start the first dance. And Cecil had appeared at my side. 'Shall we go now? Where would you wish us to talk?'

'Hugh's old study is best,' I said. 'I've had a fire lit there.'

I led the way without demur. Sir William Cecil, Lord

Burghley, was a friend in a sense, to the point that I thought of him and sometimes spoke of him as just Cecil, but in fact he was very much a lord of the land, a member of the queen's council, and also her Lord Treasurer, noble and powerful. I therefore said nothing of my fears, or my reluctance. Before the feast was over, I had beckoned to Phoebe, Hawkswood's senior maid, and told her to get the study ready for use. Now, as I walked towards it, I hoped that Cecil had not guessed that my feet were dragging.

TWO
A Perfectly Innocent Errand

The galliard music faded behind us as we crossed the vestibule outside the hall and went into the small room that Hugh had once used as his study and where I now did my household accounts or wrote my letters. It was ready for us; Phoebe had not only seen to it that a fire was kindled in the small hearth but had had the candles lit in the three-branched, elegantly fluted silver candlestick on the desk. The light of fire and candles played pleasantly over the handsome linenfold panelling, most of which was visible, for there was only the one long shelf to accommodate the accounts ledgers, along with a stone jar of ready-prepared ink and Hugh's books, which were mostly about travel, political history, and agricultural matters, especially rose-growing, which had been one of his hobbies. There was a pile of maps at one end of the bookshelf, and on a little table below, stood a globe showing the known world.

The desk, which I kept polished, had on it just the candlestick and a writing set consisting of inkpot, sander, two paperweights, and a quill-holder, all in green onyx. I had given the set to Hugh as a Christmas present, two years before he died. I felt a pang whenever I used it. The rest of the furnishings consisted of three stools with padded seats covered in green damask, and an oaken settle with cushions. There were no rugs or rushes; the room wasn't used enough to warrant such things, but the floorboards were polished. It all added up to a business-like place where work could be done, but where one could be comfortable as well. I led us to the settle, where Cecil sat down, eased himself against the cushions and hooked a stool towards him, to use one of the crossbars between its legs as a rest for his right foot. Cecil suffered a great deal from gout. I seated myself beside him.

There was a silence and then I said: 'I think you want me to take Mistress Jester to Edinburgh. Am I right?'

'Yes. I had it in mind as soon as I heard that Mistress Jester's daughter had had a child.'

'Doctor Fletcher told you?'

'Yes. I saw at once that it might be the answer to a problem. Ursula, don't look so worried. I am not going to send you into danger, not this time. I only want you to undertake an errand. I think you can help us and by *us* I mean me, Sir Francis Walsingham, and the queen. The birth of Mistress Jester's grand-daughter has presented us with a good opportunity to get a perfectly innocent errand safely performed.'

They were always perfectly innocent errands, according to Cecil and Sir Francis Walsingham, the saturnine, fanatically Protestant, and utterly ruthless Secretary of State. The trouble into which these harmless tasks had led me into the past was almost past belief and I didn't think this one would be any different. *Safely performed.* That said it all. If it needed to be done safely, then danger was lurking somewhere. It always did. It was a miracle that I was still alive.

I waited.

'Yours would be quite a large party of travellers,' said Cecil. 'That would matter. There would be yourself and Mistress Jester and no doubt you would wish to take the Brockleys, and perhaps one of your grooms, to help with the horses. You could use your coach. The road to Edinburgh by way of York is in regular use even in winter; the chances are that your journey wouldn't be too hampered by bad weather. You might even take Harry and his nurse.'

My little son Harry, who had just had his fifth birthday, had thrown a tantrum because he wasn't allowed to attend the wedding feast, and because of this, his nurse Tessie hadn't been able to join us either. I had had some choice dishes sent to the nursery to make up for it. He was a lively youngster, but I didn't like the idea of taking him on a lengthy and tiring coach journey. Least of all when it involved an errand for Lord Burghley. 'Harry is still too young for long journeys,' I said. 'Lord Burghley, what is the purpose behind all this?'

'It's simple enough. We would like you to take a letter to

Edinburgh and deliver it to James Douglas, Earl of Morton, who is likely to be found at Holyrood Palace. It's the culmination of an exchange of letters between him and Queen Elizabeth, and it bears her signature. The gist of it is a firm undertaking that in *no* circumstances will the English court and government ever facilitate the return to Scotland of Queen Mary Stuart, even as a private person and certainly not for the purpose of regaining the Scottish throne.'

'Why can it not be taken by a Queen's Messenger, in the usual way?' I asked.

'It was,' said Cecil. 'Twice. It didn't get there, and neither of the Messengers have returned. No one knows what has happened to them. *That's* why we want, this time, to send the letter by means of a harmless party of private travellers, going to visit family in Scotland. No one will be suspicious of such a group.'

'But . . .' I hardly knew how to put my feelings into words. They were a mixture of alarm at the possible risk and indignation that I should be expected to accept such a task as innocent and safe. I stared at Cecil, and waited for him to go on.

'You look horrified, but you need not. Listen,' he said. 'There have been several plots to reinstate Mary. They weren't well planned and we stopped them short, but Walsingham fears that others will follow. There are people, especially in the north, who cling to the old religion – and to Mary. Douglas has become nervous. The letter that we are asking you to deliver contains details of two recent plots that have been discovered and crushed, and it also explains how we did it, and what precautions are being taken to ensure that Mary remains our . . . guest, as the queen insists on calling it. Our captive would be more accurate. We don't want details like that to fall into the wrong hands and we fear that some of them already have – the disappearance of the first two Messengers points to that. However, this third one – the one I want you to carry – contains more confidential matter than either of the two that went before it. It gives details of the most recent conspiracy, and describes the latest and very stringent precautions we are taking to keep Mary under control. We certainly don't want *those* to become known to Mary's supporters. I may say also that part of the importance we attach to this letter is in the assurance that it offers to James Douglas. That is a very desirable part of the good diplomatic relations we are trying to create between England and Scotland. We are most anxious that this time, nothing shall go wrong.'

'But what *happened* to the first two Messengers?' I said. 'Does no one know anything at all?' My pulse was thudding. Innocent errand, indeed!

'The first letter,' said Cecil, 'was despatched just after Christmas. It was carried by a man called Bernard Hardwicke. I handed it to Hardwicke myself. He winked at me, put it in a wallet, and thrust the wallet down inside one of his riding boots. That was where he always put confidential documents when he was asked to carry them. No one would be likely to find them there, he said. He was putting on a show for me, I think.'

He laughed a little, ruefully, and said: 'There is – or was – something of the strolling player about Master Hardwicke. He actually started out in life as a player, until he made friends with a Messenger, who got him a post in the messenger service as a junior. He did well and won promotion, working mainly for Walsingham. According to Walsingham, Hardwicke likes having steady employment and a steady income. He finds it an improvement on living hand to mouth as a travelling actor. Not that any of that matters now. We think he was intercepted, and the letter with him, but all we actually know is that he didn't come back. We put it down at first to the snowstorms in January, but the weather cleared up before the end of the month and still he didn't come back; nor did we receive any acknowledgement from the Scottish court, though we expected one. We became concerned. We started a search for him, and we despatched another Queen's Messenger with a copy of the letter. That would have been in late January, just after the snow cleared. The second Messenger was Christopher Spelton, the cousin of today's bridegroom . . .'

'Christopher!' I said involuntarily.

'I fear so, yes. He had instructions to see if he could learn anything of Hardwicke's fate as well as to deliver the letter. As you know, Spelton isn't just a royal courier, he also under-takes tasks as an agent, just as you yourself do at times.'

'*Christopher!*' I said again. I knew nothing of Bernard Hardwicke but Christopher was my friend. I hadn't accepted his proposal of marriage but I had a fondness for him. 'I knew he was going to Edinburgh,' I said. 'He said he hoped to be back to attend the wedding . . . and he has vanished as well and that is really all that anyone knows?'

'I'm afraid so,' Cecil said. 'Both men are being most energetically sought, of course they are – every county sheriff and local constable in the districts the two men must have crossed is aware that they are missing and is looking for them, and I have also asked various people in the north that I happen to know – landowners, merchants, other agents who are based there – to be on the lookout. So far, no trace of either has been found. And still there has been no acknowledgement from James Douglas. He is presumably still waiting for that letter, hoping – expecting – that it will give the assurance that it does give. He needs that confirmation. And that's not all. We have a suspicion that somewhere at court, there is a leak – that there is a spy working for Mary Stuart or some of her friends. I have mentioned plots. A few plotters managed to escape abroad just in time, as though they were warned, which they should not have been.'

I was thinking rapidly. 'So – you mean that perhaps Hardwicke and Spelton were intercepted because someone who shouldn't have known anything about that letter had nevertheless heard about it, perhaps was told by this unknown spy, and wanted to get hold of it, thinking it would provide information useful to Mary's supporters?'

'Yes. The first two letters wouldn't have told them as much as all that – though more than we would like! – but the third one, the one I want you to take, could be much more useful to them. It has got to get to Douglas safely.'

'You have no idea who the spy could be?'

'I believe that Walsingham has but he hasn't confided the name of his suspect to me yet,' Cecil said. 'He told me he wasn't sure but was planning some kind of trap, to confirm his idea or dismiss it. When he does lay hands on the man, I could almost pity the fellow. Walsingham will send him to the Tower and hand him over to Richard Topcliffe, his Rackmaster. Have you heard of Topcliffe?'

'Yes. He has a fearsome reputation,' I said, shuddering.

'Ah, well, none of that need concern you. I simply want you to deliver the message. There is no reason why you shouldn't be able to do so in perfect safety. Your journey will have a completely innocent purpose, and no one at court knows of it, for the very good reason that until now, it wasn't being planned! The only courtier who knows of the idea is me and I didn't know of it until today. I assure you that I am not the traitor.'

'Of course not,' I said.

'That's all you have to do,' said Cecil, watching me. 'Take Mistress Jester to Edinburgh to see her daughter and her grandchild and while you're there, slip off one morning and go to Holyrood Palace. I will give you a letter of authority carrying my seal. Present the letter to James Douglas. Preferably in person. You must do your best about that. Then come away. Your task will be done.'

'You're not sending me to find out what happened to Bernard Hardwicke and Christopher Spelton?'

'Certainly not! That really would be overburdening you! I said, they are being sought, by every means available. None of that need concern you. All *you* have to do, I repeat, is go to Edinburgh with Mistress Jester and pay a call at Holyrood Palace while you are there.'

'I see.' I said it with a sigh. It was always the same pattern. The quests I undertook usually started out as innocuous and then changed their nature when it was too late. 'I suppose I must agree,' I said. 'As you knew I would,' I added with more than a tinge of bitterness. 'And despite all your sheriffs and constables, I somehow think you will want me, shall we say, to keep my eyes open?'

'If you wish but take no risks. No one wants you to take risks.'

'You mean,' I said, dragging the monstrous thing out into the light, 'that for all your talk of an innocent errand, Master Hardwicke – and Christopher – may never be found. May have been murdered, their horses stolen and sold at the nearest fair.'

'Very likely,' said Cecil. 'Both men were using the royal remount service, of course, and the proprietor of the Yorkshire stable which is the last one that they used – they both went there – is very angry. In particular, the horse he gave Hardwicke was one of the best in his stable, according to him. And easy to identify. Three parts Barb, nearly sixteen hands, golden chestnut with a white mane and tail, a white star and a white sock on the near fore. I have had that description cried through the streets of York. The men who are searching for Hardwicke and Spelton are on the lookout for the horse as well.'

'It would be a clue to Hardwicke's fate if they find it, I suppose,' I said.

'Yes, it would. But you are not required to look for it. You must maintain your air of innocence at all costs. You are part of a group of people travelling north for a family reunion. As long as you maintain that appearance, you will be perfectly safe. That you are part of a group will be an added protection, too. Hardwicke and Spelton rode alone.'

He fell silent and I found a moment to absorb the hideous fact that Christopher Spelton, who had once asked me to be his wife, with whom I was still on the most amiable terms, who had helped me to find a husband for Kate Ferguson, might be – probably was – now dead. I had not chosen to marry Christopher, but I had liked him very much. He was a little younger than I was, but slightly worn by a hard-working life, and by no means good-looking. He was stocky of build, unremarkable as to his face, and balding, with a ring of scanty brown hair round his pate. But he had the most friendly, good-natured brown eyes in the world and a curiously calm, reassuring presence. I could not bear to think of him as dead. Tears pricked my eyes. Then, through the fog of shock and sorrow, I heard Cecil clear his throat. He said: 'There is one more thing.'

THREE
Physician and Magician

I might have known. I had been about to rise. Now I sat back once more and prepared to be patient. Instructions emanating from either Cecil or Walsingham usually turned out to have – I suppose *complications* would be the right word. This time I was at least being warned in advance instead of being left – as had happened in the past – to find out too late. I saw that Cecil was looking at me with something like compassion. 'What is it?' I asked resignedly.

'The news about Spelton has given you a shock,' he said. 'I'm sorry. Shall I call for wine? Perhaps you should . . .'

'Presently,' I said. 'Please tell me what this extra thing is.'

'I can assure you that it has nothing to do with the letter. There is nothing secret about it at all! It's nothing more than a little commission for Doctor Dee, the queen's Magician. Both Hardwicke and Spelton were to have undertaken it along with the task of delivering the letter to Scotland but presumably were prevented from doing so. The queen herself is interested in the matter.'

I knew about Doctor Dee, of course. He was an adviser to Her Majesty on all manner of esoteric subjects, some more worthy than others, at least as far as I had heard. He was known for his researches into map-making and mathematics, but also concerned himself with trying to transmute base metal into gold and attempting to materialize angels and forecasting the future. I had heard that he wished to revise the calendar. I had never met him and didn't feel I wanted to.

My face probably showed something of this, for Cecil said: 'Dee is just a man with an enquiring mind and wide interests, which have sometimes led him into trouble. He was arrested once, for casting horoscopes – of Queen Mary and Princess Elizabeth, as our present queen was then.' Cecil looked amused.

'He talked himself out of it, but ever since then, although he is fond of cats, he says he daren't keep one: people are suspicious of anyone who has esoteric interests and also keeps pets. They remember the superstitions about demon familiars and cats are especially suspect! He doesn't want to lay himself open to a charge of sorcery. He makes a rueful joke of it. I rather like him, myself.'

'What sort of commission does he want?' I asked.

'On the north York moors – you could divert to the place on your way either to or from Scotland – there's a house called Stonemoor, where a number of middle-aged ladies are living together. They're all ladies who for some reason don't have proper homes, have no relatives or at least no relatives willing to look after them. They're unmarried women, or widows without much money.'

'I can sympathize with that,' I said, remembering my own predicament after Gerald's death.

'Quite. Well, this little community started with a widow called Philippa Gould. She isn't quite without family; her father's a cloth merchant in York. She is his only surviving legitimate child. She has no children herself. Her late husband owned a dyeing shop in York, but not a very successful one. When he died, the shop had to be sold to pay his debts. She was virtually penniless and went home to her father. Her mother was dead by then, though, and her father had just remarried. The two women didn't get on. So Philippa's father bought Stonemoor House for her and got a natural daughter of his, Philippa's half-sister, to join her for company. The two sisters already knew each other though only slightly, it seems. Philippa herself brought in two more friends. So to begin with there were four ladies, but over the next few years they were joined by others, their own acquaintances and then *their* acquaintances, and now there are sixteen of them.

'The thing that makes the Stonemoor household special,' said Cecil, 'is that the ladies are all Catholic. They all come from known Catholic families. It's no secret. It isn't illegal to *be* Catholic, as you know, as long as there is no attempt at making converts. Sir Francis Walsingham would like it to be illegal, but so far, the queen won't agree to that.'

I nodded. I knew Walsingham's fanaticism very well.

'It is known,' said Cecil, 'that the ladies of Stonemoor have organized themselves into a . . . a kind of unofficial convent. They have no communication with Rome and as far as anyone is aware, they don't actually take vows. Nor do they accept novices. But they are said to live very much as though they are Benedictine nuns. The household is careful to keep the law, however, and two or three of them turn up each week at St Mary's, the Anglican church in the village of Thorby, which is close by. The vicar there doesn't approve of them but he can't complain that they don't attend church, even if they don't all do it together. They don't have servants; some of them are apparently regarded as lay sisters and they do most of the domestic chores. They all dress in the same dark-blue gowns and yes, they sing the office in what they fondly believe to be secrecy, although they're wrong about that. The singing has been overheard and reported by Thorby villagers, who are mostly respectable Protestants though I understand that there are one or two Catholic sympathizers.

'In Thorby, there's some division of opinion about the Stonemoor ladies and not along religious lines, oddly enough; it's more that a few of the villagers – and the vicar too – suspect them of witchcraft. Mostly, though, the Thorby folk are tolerant, even amused by the ladies. The blacksmith, who was the one who overheard some chanting and reported it, was one of a minority. He complained to the vicar, who informed the High Sheriff in York, who informed Walsingham but Walsingham didn't act on it. The ladies have a tame priest who presumably says Mass for them but neither they nor he have tried to convert anyone and so haven't broken the law. A farm goes with Stonemoor House and the ladies keep some horses, and the man who is known to be their priest is outwardly their bailiff and groom.'

'I see,' I said, in the tone of one who doesn't see anything clearly at all. 'But what . . .?'

'I want you to understand the background because you'll need to call there and you'll find Stonemoor confusing if you don't know what it's all about. We've taken the household there seriously enough to discuss it in council. It is known that on the Continent there are seminaries where Jesuit priests are being prepared for a kind of secret invasion of England, to raise money for Mary Stuart from her sympathizers, and seek converts, all of which makes Walsingham nervous, not to mention angry and very suspicious of any house where the Catholic religion is openly practised, but the ladies of Stonemoor seem innocent enough, and the council agreed with that.'

'But how in the world was Walsingham persuaded to put up with them?' I was surprised. 'He'd surely want them suppressed on principle!'

'The council talked him out of that,' said Cecil. 'Even Sir Francis Walsingham didn't really care for the idea of turning a whole lot of middle-aged women out on to the moors with no means of support and no roof to call their own. Philippa's father might rescue her and his other daughter but he can hardly take in fourteen other indigent ladies as well! As I said, the ladies do keep the law of the land, more or less, and they aren't genuine nuns. Walsingham growls about them but so far he has left them alone.'

'I wonder how long that will last,' I said.

'I wonder, too. I know Walsingham. Though lately, I've wondered if, now, he is leaving Stonemoor alone for some devious purpose of his own. Well, there the ladies of Stonemoor are, dubious but tolerated, and they have something that Doctor Dee wants. It's a book. It was written by one John of Evesham, back in the reign of Henry the Second. John of Evesham sounds like a thoroughly English name, doesn't it? In fact, he was born in Italy to a Jewish family, but converted to Christianity and came to England as a young man. He settled in Evesham, in Worcestershire, and was a successful physician, in fact, so successful that once, when King Henry fell ill while he was travelling in Worcestershire, the king consulted him.'

'Didn't the king travel with his own physicians?' I asked, surprised.

'The story goes that King Henry, who was always in a hurry, had outdistanced his entourage and his own physicians, and then, finding himself unwell, broke his journey at

Evesham Abbey and demanded the services of the best physician they knew. They called John, who apparently gave good advice and was well paid for it. Later, when he had completed his book, he sent King Henry a copy. Made by himself, so the story says, as the monks of Evesham disapproved of it and were not prepared to have it copied by their scribes. I imagine John's own efforts were just text and charts, without decoration.'

'The book was heretical?' I asked.

'Yes, it was! John of Evesham was interested in astronomy and related subjects and had done some travelling on that account. Also, before he left Italy, he had met and talked with Arab scholars. Among other things, his book – it's called *Observations of the Heavens by John of Evesham* – puts forward the theory that the Earth circles the Sun and not the other way about. You have heard of the theory, I expect?'

'Nicolaus Copernicus,' I said. 'Yes. Hugh was interested in that theory. He thought it made sense. But yes, the Catholic Church would call it a heretical creed.'

'The theory does make sense,' Cecil remarked. 'It makes the movements of the planets much more comprehensible. I understand that the book also contains details of various astronomical events – comets, conjunctions of planets, and so forth – and relates them to events in the history of the Christian nations. For instance, there was a comet in the sky at about the time of the Norman Conquest. There are calculations about when certain celestial occasions, such as eclipses or unusual conjunctions of the planets, are likely to occur and links them to possible future happenings, makes prophecies, in fact. It's all backed up by complex mathematical tables about the movements of stars and planets in time and space, set out in Arabic numerals. In fact, wherever numbers are mentioned, they're in the Arabic style. John of Evesham was clearly at home with that. Some of the occasions he foretold have come and gone since he wrote the book, of course. According to Doctor Dee, who once saw a copy, John was quite good at forecasting the appearance of conjunctions and comets, though the events he thought would go with them mostly didn't happen . . .'

'Did he foretell the end of the world?' I asked mischievously.
'Yes, but the world hasn't reached that point yet. The date
he gave was the year 2000. Let me continue. There is one
more thing of interest about that book. It is said to contain an
amusing drawing that makes fun of the Pope for resisting the
heliocentric theory. Another reason for regarding it as heretical!
King Henry, though, was interested in the book and its theories.
He received it, it seems, in the year 1175, which was after the
killing of Thomas Becket and Henry's subsequent penance at
the hands of the Canterbury monks. Henry the Second,' said
Cecil thoughtfully, 'is supposed to have had a violent temper.
Outwardly, he is said to have accepted that he was guilty of
Becket's murder and to have accepted the flogging that he
received from the monks, but his private feelings may have
been quite different. A man like Henry might well have been
very angry.

'At any rate, he evidently didn't object to the book's contents.
He ordered illuminated copies to be made. No one knows who
made them. It wasn't the scribes at Evesham, who refused.
Virtually all scribes capable of producing illuminated manuscript books were monks, so the king must have found a
complaisant monastery somewhere, probably just by paying
well for the work. Monasteries never were immune to venality!
Also twelfth-century monks might not have been as shocked
as you would expect. The Catholic Church of today regards
the theory of the Earth going round the Sun as extremely
heretical, but back then, things were less rigid, at least in
England. And it's possible that the drawing which is said to
be so scandalous might only amuse unsophisticated men. At
any rate, somewhere, King Henry found scribes who were
willing to undertake the work and four copies were made. One
was for King Henry. That one vanished long ago but the other
three were made for John of Evesham, and survived.'

'And?'

'Doctor Dee has seen one of them. He came across it when
he was travelling abroad years ago. I believe he stayed in the
house of its owner, whoever that was. Dee is a great collector
of books. He has an immense library and after seeing that
copy he began to want one of his own. I understand that he

did find another last year but it was in bad condition, with pages missing and a binding that was coming to pieces.'

'But the ladies of Stonemoor House have the third one and it's in good condition?' I hazarded.

'Yes. They got it from a Gloucestershire woman whose family had a copy. It must have been handed down through centuries. One of Dee's friends is the lawyer who was the executor for the will of the last but one member of the family – a man called Ralph Overton. When he died, his unmarried daughter, Eleanor Overton, aged about fifty, was the only surviving Overton. The family were of the Catholic faith, and this woman decided to join the Stonemoor community. According to the executor, she took the book with her.'

'As a kind of entrance fee?'

'Yes, precisely. It really is valuable. The executor had seen it and described it to Doctor Dee. It's bound in white leather, with the title and the name of the author on the front in gold leaf, and a gold-leaf pattern of some kind as well. Eleanor Overton presented it to the community and Philippa Gould is willing to sell it – for a high price. I think the ladies of Stonemoor are short of money. Philippa's father gives them a small income but he probably can't afford much more and he's known to be a warm man, anyway. He probably chose Stonemoor House for his daughters as it was cheap, no doubt because it's so isolated. Apart from Thorby village, which really is very small, there's nothing else for miles, except for one tumbledown cottage about two miles away, where there's a man who keeps sheep and makes his living from them. He's practically a hermit except that he goes to York once a year to sell wool. Doesn't like his fellow creatures.'

'Do the ladies just rely on an allowance from Master Gould?' I broke in. 'Didn't you mention a farm?'

'Yes, though not a big one. There are smallholdings dotted round the outskirts of the village – most of the villagers have a little bit of land; some are craftsmen but they don't have enough customers to live by their crafts alone. The one fair-sized farm goes with Stonemoor. It gives employment to some of the villagers and helps the ladies to maintain themselves. Village and house and the surrounding cultivation amount to just a little dot in a vast expanse of uninhabited moorland. Thorby and Stonemoor are maybe among the loneliest places in England and *that's* probably what gave the ladies the idea that they could get away with pretending to be nuns. In accordance with Benedictine tradition, however, the ladies don't travel, so the book must be collected.'

'And you wish me to collect it.'

'Yes. Both Hardwicke and Spelton were asked to call at Stonemoor on their way to Scotland, pay for it, and take it with them. It seems that neither of them ever got to Stonemoor any more than they got to Scotland. Sheriffs' officers from York have called at Stonemoor twice, making enquiries, but the ladies hadn't seen either of the missing men and the book is still there, awaiting payment and collection. That has helped us to concentrate our search a little, by the way. We do know one thing about the journeys made by the two missing men. We know that they both passed through York because they changed horses at the remount stable there, as I told you. So they were presumably stopped between York and Thorby, a distance of around twenty-five miles. But we haven't been able to narrow it down any further than that. Well, Ursula, that's it. I will provide you with the necessary money and perhaps you could pick the book up, either on the way to Scotland or on the way back. You are *not* required to do anything more. The ladies accept guests and will take you all in for an overnight stay.'

'But if I discover a golden chestnut horse with a white mane and tail in the Stonemoor stables, I report to you. Yes, I see.'

'Well, there is that. Look, Ursula, I'm sure you can deliver the letter to James Douglas in complete safety. If by any chance he is not at Holyrood Palace, I fancy someone will be there to whom you can legitimately pass it, as long as you do so in the presence of witnesses – bear that in mind. I don't want you to step outside the protection of being on an innocent family visit. And there's no risk at all attached to calling at Stonemoor House.'

He paused and then added: 'I mean it when I say I don't want you taking risks. I have come to value you highly and I now regret the dangers I have sent you into in the past. I tremble when I think of the peril you ran into last year, when you were trying to get to France to warn Christopher Spelton that he was in danger.'

'I tremble, too,' I said. 'I and my companions were lucky to escape. But for that good luck we might all now be slaves in North Africa or Turkey, forced to work against our will and compelled to worship Allah or die.'

'I trust,' said Cecil drily, 'that you would have had the good sense not to become a martyr but to pretend and await a chance of getting away.'

'You would advise that?'

'I did it myself, more or less, during the reign of the late Queen Mary,' said Cecil. 'I adopted her Catholic faith, kept my head down and hoped that one day Elizabeth would replace her, which is what happened. But it has been on my conscience that you were in that appalling danger and ran into it because the queen asked you to do something for her, and things went amiss. The queen was angry when she heard of it, believe me. No one wants you to take any chances now. I don't think you can possibly be in danger because of carrying that letter. No one will suspect that you have it. Nor is there any danger in going to Stonemoor to buy a book! The queen would not wish you to undertake either errand, if she had any fears for you. I assure you.'

'I believe that assurance,' I said, pushing the words out, though my heart was heavy. But I could not refuse because, as ever, I wished to please the queen. Even though she had been angry when I had run into such peril in the previous year, it was also true that on that occasion I failed to do something she wanted. The failure had been a relief to me, but not, I thought, to her.

I was, however, making a decision. Too often I had stumbled headlong into disaster when undertaking what should have been harmless tasks.

Therefore, I would take what precautions I could. It was hard to think of many, but I could change the pattern set by my ill-fated predecessors. I would not do things in the order that they had chosen. I would call for the book on the way back from Scotland rather than on the way to it. Christopher and Bernard Hardwicke had apparently gone about things the other way round, but as the letter was the more important task of the two, I would put that first. I would get it into James Douglas' hands as quickly as possible.

FOUR
The Raven's Prophecy

We stayed in the study for some time. Cecil had a few extra things to impart. Having assured me all over again that I was not expected to look for Bernard Hardwicke or Christopher Spelton, he then proceeded to tell me that if I did by chance cross the spoor of one or other of the missing men, I would have a better chance of realizing it if I knew this or that detail. If such a thing should happen, I must report at once to the sheriff in York. Then he enlarged upon the details he had mentioned.

'You know what Spelton looks like. You may as well know what Hardwicke looks like, too.'

Quite right. I had never heard of Hardwicke before, let alone seen him. I looked at Cecil enquiringly.

'Unfortunately,' said Cecil, 'he doesn't stand out. He looks like ten thousand other men. Nearing middle age, of middle height, nondescript hair beginning to thin. Eyes of no special colour. You'd never pick him out of a crowd.'

'That's not very helpful!' I said.

'Well, never mind. But there's one extra thing you should know about Spelton. Hardwicke is – or was – simply a Queen's Messenger but as you know, Spelton also doubled as an agent. He has a way of leaving traces of himself if he wants to – if he feels he is in danger and might disappear, or wishes to warn someone else that there's danger about. He would want any friends who search for him to have a chance of finding him or at least a chance of finding out what has happened to him. He has used the sign to good effect at least twice to my knowledge. Once, it helped a friend to trace him and assist him out of trouble; once, it warned another agent that a so-called safe house wasn't safe at all. This is the mark.'

Cecil reached inside his doublet and pulled out a piece of

folded paper, which he opened and handed to me. 'If you come across that anywhere, Christopher Spelton has been there.'

'I knew nothing about this!' I said, looking at the paper. On it was a red circle, about four inches across, quartered by a cross. 'If I find this anywhere, done in red chalk, then Christopher Spelton must have left it?'

'Yes, but be careful, for the love of heaven. Don't get caught out, peeping and peering!'

'I won't,' I promised.

'Enough of that,' said Cecil. 'Now, more to the point, you will need to know how to get to Stonemoor House. If I remember rightly, Hugh Stannard had maps here. Do you have them still?'

'Yes,' I said. 'Those scrolls there on the end of the bookshelf.' I got up and fetched them. Cecil went rapidly through them, picked out two and compared them. He unrolled one on the desk, weighing it down at the corners with two paperweights and the sander and inkstand from the writing set. 'This will do. It's more detailed than the other.'

The map he had chosen showed a good deal of eastern Yorkshire. Rivers, tracks, and villages were marked, including Thorby. After a moment's thought, Cecil put a cross to show exactly where Stonemoor House was. Just behind the house, he said, on the upper part of the slope on which it stood, there were numerous stone outcroppings. They had given the house its name and probably contributed to the stone the builders had used. At any rate, the house was a noticeable place. 'Once you're actually within sight of it, that is,' he added drily.

Eventually, because I wanted to compare the two maps at leisure, he left me to it. When I had finished, I put the maps away and came out into the vestibule. To be confronted at once by three worried-looking members of my household: my manservant Roger Brockley, his wife Fran, who was my personal tirewoman (though Sybil shared her services), and was still usually known by her maiden name of Dale, and an aged hanger-on of mine called Gladys Morgan. The sound of dance tunes and prancing feet still continued in the hall, but this trio had abandoned the merriment to lie in wait for me.

Roger Brockley was well into middle age now, though he had excellent health. He had a high forehead, dusted with pale gold freckles, light brown hair in which a good deal of grey was now mixed, very steady blue-grey eyes, and he did not approve of my secret calling at all, though time and again, when we were in the midst of an assignment, a latent adventurousness had appeared in him and proved immensely valuable.

Dale, a few years younger than he was, hated my assignments too, because they were dangerous. Dale didn't like danger and had no latent adventurousness whatsoever. When she was frightened, which was often, her blue eyes would bulge and the marks of childhood smallpox would become noticeable. She had suffered a good deal in my service, mainly because when I went off on a secret errand, I always took Brockley with me and Dale didn't like him to be alone with me. There had been a time, long ago now, when Brockley and I almost became more than lady and manservant; when we slid near to becoming lovers. It hadn't actually happened, but the feeling was still there, quivering now and then in the air between us, there in the private jokes we still, sometimes, exchanged, in the way we sometimes read each other's minds, and Dale knew it.

Gladys Morgan was a Welshwoman who had become attached to me, also many years ago, when Brockley rescued her from a charge of witchcraft. She had fallen foul of the same charge a second time, after we had brought her to Hawkswood, and was very nearly hanged for it. Gladys was an unprepossessing old woman (one couldn't possibly refer to her as a lady), whose teeth were like brown fangs, with gaps in between them. She disliked washing, though I did insist on this as far as I could, and she had a horrible turn of invective if someone upset her. She was good at hurling curses, which had annoyed a vicar or two, and she was gifted with herbal medicine, which had annoyed a physician or two. These things explained the second accusation of witchcraft. She was in my house because there was nowhere else for her to go. She also had an uncomfortable knack of forecasting the approach of catastrophe, and being right.

The three of them stood in a row, in my path, and brought me to a halt. Brockley cleared his throat, evidently preparing to be their spokesman, and then said: 'That was Lord Burghley, madam. You've been shut in the study with him for a long time when everyone else was dancing.' His tone of voice bordered on accusation. 'Madam, what's afoot?'

'Yes, has he asked you to do something for him? Again? Ma'am, what did he want?' Dale's voice was full of anxiety.

Gladys said: 'Whatever it is, it'll mean trouble. It always does, indeed.'

'No trouble,' I said firmly. 'He wishes me to visit Edinburgh, and to have a harmless pretext, so the plan is that Sybil shall travel there to see her new grand-daughter, and we will go with her – at least, I will, and so will you, Brockley, and Dale. Not you, Gladys.'

'Couldn't stand the journey, at my age,' said Gladys. 'So, what are you *really* going to Scotland for?'

'We're going there to deliver a confidential letter to the Scottish court. It is a letter from the queen. On the way back, we are to pay for and collect a valuable book, which is just now in the hands of some ladies in Yorkshire. The queen's adviser Doctor Dee wants it. That's all. There's nothing dangerous about it and no need for you all to look so worried.'

'Why you, madam?' asked Brockley. 'Aren't those tasks for Queen's Messengers?'

Three pairs of eyes were fixed on me. I explained the circumstances, emphasizing the harmless appearance of family parties and houses full of pious middle-aged women.

'So we're to deliver a confidential letter that has already been sent twice, only it apparently didn't get there and the couriers haven't returned,' said Brockley, fastening on the most ominous part of my assignment.

'But there's nothing dangerous about it?' said Gladys, her snapping black eyes boring into me like gimlets.

Dale said: 'I don't like the sound of this at all.'

'You needn't come if you feel doubtful,' I told her. That was sheer cunning on my part, for I knew what the answer would be.

'I know you wouldn't leave Roger behind,' said Dale stiffly, 'and you will also need my services. So will Mistress Jester.'

Which meant, essentially, that Dale wouldn't want Brockley to go without her.

'Splendid. Then that's settled. And we shall all be perfectly all right,' I said.

'Now, how many times have we all heard *that*?' remarked Gladys.

'Be quiet, Gladys!' I snapped. 'How you love to croak like a raven! You're always prophesying trouble. All will go well and we'll be home again in a month. Wait and see.'

'Reckon you'll be the one as does the seeing,' Gladys said.

I brushed them all aside and walked on into the hall. The fire had warmed it through by now, aided by the flames of the numerous candles stuck in the holders round the wall, and from the perspiring bodies of people who were still exerting themselves in the dance. The atmosphere was merry.

I didn't feel like joining in. I was sorry about the disappearance of Bernard Hardwicke, as one might be sorry to hear of such a thing happening to anyone, but where Christopher Spelton was concerned, I was horrified, and it wasn't just on my own account. He was Eric's cousin as well as my friend. For the moment, I thought, I must keep that piece of news to myself and let the young couple enjoy their day, and their wedding night. They would have to be told, but not now, not here.

If only that female raven Gladys, in her uncanny way, hadn't forecast disaster so often before and been proved correct.

I pasted a smile on to my face and walked steadily forward. A moment later, one of the gentlemen guests came up to me, holding out a hand. I took it and joined the dance.

FIVE
Just a Family Party

I finally decided not to tell Eric and Kate of Spelton's disappearance. There was still the possibility that he might reappear and meanwhile I chose to let them enjoy the first days of marriage. They looked so happy when they came to breakfast that I couldn't bear to do otherwise. I waved them off to their new home, with a determined smile on my face, and then got on with the preparations for travel.

At heart, the members of my household were all against my new assignment but they helped, all the same. A journey of any length needs careful planning and when it is to be made in winter, through the wild north, it needs to be prepared very thoroughly indeed.

Brockley went over the coach inch by inch, cleaning, polishing, and making sure that the wheels and shafts were sound. Gladys, because I have a tendency to migraine, gave me a bottle of the herbal mixture with which she treated it. It worked with varying success but it was sometimes effective. She made her potions in the kitchen, rather to the annoyance of John Hawthorn and Ben Flood, but they tolerated her, on my orders, and I allowed her to keep a number of preparations in my still room, where they were always in readiness.

'What are these other things?' I asked her, as she filled my bottle from one of the jars on the shelf.

'That's to help a body sleep,' said Gladys, pointing. 'And that's for loose bowels and that's for bowels as won't work, and that little one's for pain but I'd only give that to someone as was half dying anyway. Smell it!'

She handed me the jar and I unstoppered it and sniffed. 'Ugh! Whatever is it?'

'Smells like cats' piss, don't it?' said Gladys, with her

horrid, gap-toothed grin. 'One of our kitchen cat's best efforts, wouldn't you say? Reckon even she never managed to produce anything that stank *that* much. Hemlock, that's what it is. It's dangerous. Only for desperate things. There's a safer one there.' She pointed. 'Got chamomile in it, that has. Soothing, if you've got colic or rheumatics.'

I took a phial of that, as well. A journey to the north, in winter, might well induce rheumatics.

The last thing of note that happened in the house before we set off was the death, to our dismay, of the kitchen cat that Gladys had mentioned. She was a big sleek tabby with a white front and four white paws and her name was Huntress, because her prowess at catching mice and rats was legendary and her kittens always took after her. We never had to drown Huntress's progeny; there were always homes eager to welcome them. On this occasion, annoyingly, it happened that we had just found homes for all of her last litter so that for the moment the Hawkswood kitchen was without a cat.

'If you find a likely stray in the streets of Edinburgh, madam,' said Hawthorn, 'please bring it back with you.'

'Somewhere in Hawkswood village, or in some household we know of, there must be a cat with expectations!' I said. 'Keep on enquiring while we're away. We need a cat. I saw mouse droppings in the kitchen this morning.'

'I dare say. Holding a celebration dance, I expect, madam,' said Hawthorn.

I had no time to pursue feline enquiries myself. The letter I was to deliver to James Douglas and Cecil's accompanying letter of introduction had just arrived, by courier. I gave my prospective travel companions a last chance to withdraw from the expedition.

'I will understand if you don't want to come. No one is forcing you. But I really am just going to deliver a letter and collect a book from a household of ladies.'

'You're not supposed to be looking for the missing Messengers?' Brockley enquired.

'No, though I shall naturally keep my eyes open.' I explained about Christopher's secret signs, which I had not mentioned before.

There were pursed lips and eyes that rolled upwards as if to plead with the heavens for protection. But no one accepted the invitation to stay behind.

It took us a fortnight to reach Edinburgh. I had had Hugh's coach, which was originally designed to be drawn by two horses, adapted for four. I had lately added some extra horses to our stable, all of them accustomed to both harness and saddle, and could provide a four-horse team. Sybil, Dale, and I travelled in the coach, and one of my grooms, Joseph, a taciturn but good-natured young man who was a very competent driver, took the reins. Brockley rode alongside on his sturdy cob Mealy. Brockley regarded himself as a bodyguard and carried a sword. I suspected that under his doublet he also had an ancient breastplate!

It was Brockley who insisted that we should bring four sets of saddlery with us, in boxes, tied on the coach roof.

'You never know with coach travel,' he said. 'Winter weather, lonely places. What if the thing gets stuck somewhere, miles from any habitation? We would have to unhitch the team and take to horseback to seek for help and shelter. Well, it would be better if no one has to ride bareback! And the long reins you need for driving won't do for riders. We need to take some spare tack with us. And saddlebags. If we have to take to riding because the coach is mired, we'll need to take our belongings as well. There are brackets for extra luggage on the roof. We can put what's needed into crates and strap the crates on.'

'Aye.' Our head groom, Arthur Watts, who had been checking the team's harness, joined in. 'I always keep useful oddments handy. I've got straps and boxes.'

We were several miles from home when I remembered that what we hadn't packed were leggings for the ladies, though if we did have to take to the saddle we would miss them, as stirrup leathers could pinch. Brockley and Joseph had riding boots, but we did not. However, it was too late to turn back. I held my tongue.

Driving conditions were actually good. The weather was cold, but it remained dry and above freezing, if only just, and the skies were mainly clear. As on previous occasions, we went by way of Lincoln, as far as York on the well-used main road that was first created by the Romans. During my long talk with Cecil in Hugh's study, I had thought to ask him the name of the remount stables that Hardwicke and Spelton had used in York, and when we reached the city, I visited them, taking the others with me.

The proprietor was a Master Maxton, who was large, ginger, and bearded and had a way of standing with his feet apart and his hands on his hips. He looked, in fact, so astoundingly like the portrait I had seen at court that the court painter Hans Holbein had made of King Henry the Eighth – who was my father – that I almost gaped at him, and found myself trying to remember what, if anything, I knew of any visits King Henry might have paid to York. Until Master Maxton himself grinned at me and said: 'I know who I look like. No need for your pop eyes, mistress. I've had many a comment from Queen's Messengers who've been at court and seen portraits. One of the older ones had even seen King Henry himself. It's all just an accident. My ma's dad came from Wales and there's Welsh blood in the royal family, or so I've heard. Maybe that accounts for it.'

Embarrassed, I pulled myself together, stopped gaping, and enquired after Hardwicke and Spelton. Had they indeed used the stable; had any word of them been heard since; did they say where they were bound?

They had used the stable, they were bound for a godforsaken place called Thorby, where there was said to be a house called Stonemoor, they had ridden off on two of the stable's best horses, and nothing had been heard of either of them since and *where*, demanded Master Maxton indignantly, were the well-bred brown mare that he had given Master Spelton, and the beautiful part-Barb chestnut that Master Hardwicke had taken? Neither hide nor hair of either of them had been seen anywhere, and Master Maxton would very much like to know why.

It seemed that both men had got into their saddles, nodded goodbye, and ridden off into eternity. I debated whether to change my mind and travel towards Stonemoor at once, but so much time had gone by since the two men vanished that it probably wouldn't matter if more time was lost, and meanwhile, to divert from the direct road to Scotland might look suspicious – if anyone should be on the watch. We were a family party bound for Edinburgh. We would do best to go on looking like one.

We went on our way later that same day. After York, the road became less good and we had to take care because of the ruts. However, the only problem we encountered was when the nearside wheels of the coach ran into a muddy verge and stuck because we had moved over in a narrow place to let a wagon carrying sackloads of something and half a dozen farm labourers, noisy fellows who were having a singsong, pass us going the other way.

However, the labourers realized what had happened, stopped singing, and came to our aid. With eight stout men to help push and our four horses tugging nobly, the coach was safely back on the track in a few minutes.

Considering the difficulties that could sometimes attend travel into the wild and barren north, our journey to Edinburgh was as smooth as cream. No one was lying in wait for us, no one assailed us. Brockley's sword remained peacefully sheathed all the way. Wherever we stopped, we all kept our eyes open for Christopher Spelton's chalk signs but never discovered any.

We never even needed to consult the two maps I carried. We arrived in the city in good order on the fifteenth morning, with the horses still brisk and glossy in their harness.

Though we ourselves could not have been described as brisk or glossy, for we were tired and travel-stained by then. Still, as we came into Edinburgh and entered the main street, we looked up at the castle on its hill above the city, and at the tall houses with the arched alleyways here and there between them, and we all had a sense of familiarity, for we had all, except Joseph, been there before. This was the end of travelling for a while, and we were thankful.

We found Sybil's daughter Ambrosia, and her sensible, likeable husband James Hale, in the best of health and full of good cheer. Somewhat noisy cheer, in fact. Sybil's new-born namesake had a fine pair of lungs which she exercised frequently, and also Ambrosia's spirited twins by her first marriage, five-year-old Paul and Tommy, and her two step-daughters, Lucy, aged eight, and May, who was four, had the run of the house and kept it in a state of mainly good-natured tumult. On arrival, after we had first been shown (and nearly deafened by) the infant Sybil, we went to sit in the pleasant parlour and partake of wine and oatcakes, and the children bounced round us without ceasing, demanding to know all about our journey and bubbling with excitement because of the new addition to the family.

In the midst of all the jolly uproar, Brockley, who was helpfully handing the oatcakes round, leant towards me as he offered the dish, and said quietly: 'When do you intend going to Holyrood, madam?'

The precious letter was on my person. It and Cecil's letter of introduction were both folded safely into a pouch that was stitched out of sight inside my open over-gown. I always wore the open style, with a decorative kirtle beneath. It had never gone out of fashion and it allowed me to have such pouches in nearly all my outfits. In them, I carried a variety of useful things. Such as money, and a small dagger in its sheath, and a set of picklocks. The tasks I performed for Queen Elizabeth sometimes required some curious and unfeminine tools. I always took these things with me when I set off on an assignment.

Even when Cecil had insisted that there was no danger.

I said, also quietly: 'I felt that to start with, I should look as though we really are – just a family party. If anyone has been paying attention, I hope they're now satisfied of that. I mean to go tomorrow.'

'Fran and I will accompany you, madam,' Brockley said.

SIX

Holyrood

We went to Holyrood the next morning. Sybil did not come with us, but stayed behind with Ambrosia and the children, not wanting to miss a single hour of their company. 'Who knows when I shall ever visit Edinburgh again?' she said. But Brockley and Dale walked with me, one on each side. Brockley, his sword at his side, was on my right as an armed guardian should be, leaving his own right arm, his sword arm, free play, while Dale, on my left, kept a respectful half a pace behind.

We had all dressed with care. I had brought a suitable dress for court, a pale-green damask sprinkled with little pink roses over a cream kirtle dotted with the same pink roses. My sleeves were puffed at the shoulder, with slashings to match the kirtle. And, naturally, inside my open overskirt, I had my usual hidden pouch, in which Cecil's letter of introduction and the letter for James Douglas were concealed, along with the other items that I had transferred from the much less fashionable dress I used for travelling.

I also had a smart pale-green hat and a necklace and earrings of freshwater pearls. My green shoes had silver buckles. While I was outdoors, my finery was hidden by a warm brown cloak with a glossy, deep-brown marten-fur trim. Dale was in blue, hat, dress, and cloak alike, while Brockley was all in soldierly buff. We were making it clear that we were people of dignity – who were also prepared for anything.

We went on foot, for Holyrood Palace was only at the end of the main street, the opposite end from the castle hill. It didn't take us long. To the gatehouse guards, I presented Cecil's letter with his distinctive seal. This was examined with care and then returned to me, and a guard escorted us through the gatehouse and presented us at one of the palace doors. Here, we were passed to a higher-ranking guard and taken into an entrance hall, panelled and decoratively paved, with a fine ceiling of carved beams. Our escort then handed us over to a still more senior guard, and at last to an usher, who politely but firmly relieved us of our cloaks and hats and Brockley's sword.

After that, we were handed over to a yet more high-ranking usher, who led us up some stairs and across a lobby to a pair of double doors, heavily carved with a criss-cross pattern with what looked like thistles dotted here and there. The doors were flanked by more guards, armed with halberds. They saluted our guide, who led us through into an anteroom. It was already full of people, all men. The usher spoke to a clerk, who hurried away through a further pair of carved doors, similar to the ones by which we had entered and similarly guarded.

'Your arrival has been reported. You now wait until you are called,' said the usher, and disappeared. James Douglas was evidently receiving, but we would have to take our turn.

We waited for an hour, standing together. From time to time, a clerk emerged from the further door, which presumably led to the earl's audience chamber, and called out a name, whereupon one of the crowd would be shown in. None of them showed any interest in us beyond a glance at me and Dale, probably because we were the only women there. Many of them clearly knew each other, so there was a low hum of talk, from which we were excluded. The place was gloomy, since the glass in the small panes of the leaded windows was thick and a dark shade of greenish-blue, admitting little light. There was nowhere to sit down, and the panelled room was bare. The darkly polished wooden floor had no coverings; there was no hearth, and the day, though bright, was cold. I think we all longed for our cloaks.

Dale muttered to me that perhaps it was a ploy to discourage people from waiting. 'If some of them give up and go away, my lord will have fewer folk to trouble him.'

'Hush,' I said. 'We're representing the queen. We must keep up an air of dignity and guard our tongues.'

Finally, my name was called and we all went forward, only

to have the guards bar the way for Brockley and Dale. The clerk who had summoned us, a thin, black-gowned fellow, said testily: 'I was only bidden to call Mistress Stannard,' and I had to leave my attendants behind. I followed the clerk inside on my own.

I had expected to find the Earl of Morton seated in a chair of state, but instead, he was standing behind a littered desk, turning over sheets of paper and conferring with several other gentlemen and a couple of clerks. This room, which was sizeable, was better by far than the anteroom, for its tall windows had larger panes and thinner glass and let in a certain amount of sunlight, and there were tapestries on the walls and paintings on the ceiling. But it was wildly untidy, with more documents strewn carelessly on side tables and window seats and on an uncushioned settle, and there were crumb-strewn plates and used goblets here and there amid the paperwork. It was also nearly as cold as the anteroom, for although there was a hearth with a fire in it, the place was too big to be easily heated.

Everyone there was in fact warmly clad, many of them wearing their cloaks. For a moment, I had a comical vision of these noble gentlemen and their no doubt highly qualified confidential clerks, when arriving to attend to their business, resisting the ushers and clinging to their mantles.

James Douglas was recognizable at once, because although his doublet and hose were plain brown and his ruff plain holland, the cloak he wore slung round his shoulders was a rich black velvet with gold embroidery and an ermine trim. Not that I would have needed that to identify him, for he stood out of the crowd in any case. He possessed that unmistakeable aura of power that defies definition but is instantly obvious, and the attitudes of those around him were visibly deferential. He was tall, with a long chin, and had hair and beard of pale ginger, though there were grey streaks in them. He was over fifty, I thought. He had light eyes which fixed their glance on my face immediately.

'Mistress Stannard. An emissary from Queen Elizabeth. You are welcome. A message from her majesty has been long expected.' He had a strong voice, the kind that could thunder commands above the sounds of fighting, and his Scottish accent wasn't too heavy; he was easy to understand.

'I have it here, my lord,' I said, making my curtsey and proffering the introductory letter and the missive from the queen both together. One of the attendant gentlemen stepped forward to take them and hand them to the earl.

'We do not often have ladies to deal with,' said Douglas, as he unrolled the letter of introduction. 'We are gentlemen and must remember our manners. Madam, you may be seated. Clear a space on that settle, someone. Mistress Stannard has come to us all the way from London. John, bespeak some refreshments.'

One of the humbler-looking clerks bustled away through a small side door, and somebody shifted a stack of files and boxes off the settle so that I could sit down. A small table was pushed close to me and similarly swept clear of oddments, and a moment later John reappeared with a servant bearing a goblet of wine and a wedge of pie on a tray. The pie, by the taste of it, contained pheasant meat. It and the wine were of excellent quality and although I had lately had breakfast, I consumed them to be polite, and found that I enjoyed them, while James Douglas read the introductory letter, set it aside, and began upon the other.

It was lengthy and he took his time, showing it to some of his companions. They discussed it, in voices too low for me to hear. Then he turned back to me, holding the queen's letter in his long, pale fingers, and gave me a wintry smile.

'I am indebted to you, on behalf of our young King James and on my own behalf too, since I have to keep this realm safe for him until he comes of age. This is the undertaking I have hoped to receive and I am grateful to her majesty of England. It seems that there has been trouble in getting this to me. According to Lord Burghley, this is the third attempt.'

'That is so, my lord,' I said.

'You have some knowledge of what the message from your queen contains?'

He was precise, speaking to the point without wasting words. The pale eyes were penetrating. I remembered hearing that he had been among the men who, many years ago, had murdered

Queen Mary's secretary David Rizzio, virtually in her presence. He had never been her friend even then and he was now her very powerful enemy. I felt thankful that he wasn't mine.

'I know some of it, my lord,' I said carefully.

'Then you know why it is important and no doubt you are aware that some of the contents are highly confidential, but all the same . . . I cannot understand why it should have been intercepted. Even once, never mind twice. If Mary has spies at Elizabeth's court – and this letter says that she has – I would expect them to be capable of learning the details of the security that surrounds her, without murdering messengers and stealing the correspondence they carry, in such a public fashion! Any message your queen wished to convey to me, would be got to me eventually somehow. Stealing letters wouldn't prevent that, as indeed it hasn't. Spies are supposed to work in the dark and *keep* in the dark. I myself wouldn't dream of employing men who were likely to use such crude tactics. Mary, who is a foolish and unworldly woman, might do so, but her spies are not chosen by her but by her friends, who mostly have *some* common sense, though not much,' he added cynically, 'or they wouldn't be her friends.'

'It does seem strange,' I agreed, since he seemed to want a reply. 'However, my task was simply to bring it safely this time, and I am glad to have done so.'

Still holding the letter, he moved away from the desk and beckoned me to follow him, drawing me aside. None of the other men in the room gazed after him, but began quiet conversations among themselves. This, no doubt, was James Douglas' way of having private conferences.

'I have heard of you, Mistress Stannard,' he said, dropping his own voice to a level that only I would hear. 'And the note from Lord Burghley in any case tells me who you are. It also tells me that you have a second task to carry out during your journey – either to or from Scotland. Have you done so yet? I refer to the collection of a book from, apparently, a house full of Catholic ladies in Yorkshire. Tolerated by the English, it seems, though I wouldn't tolerate them. I would call such a house a vipers' nest.'

'My second errand is mentioned in one of the letters, then?'

I said. 'I haven't been there yet, my lord. I propose to call on the ladies on the way home.'

'The letter mentions the book in case you already have it with you when you reach me. It says that my Lord Burghley thinks I might be interested to see it, as indeed I would be. However, if you have not yet been to Stonemoor, I must do without.' He looked regretful. 'A pity.'

'I would have collected it first had I known you wished to see it, my lord,' I said. 'As it was, I decided that the first thing I ought to do was to get the queen's letter into your hands, and worry about the book later.'

'Yes, well, I agree that that was good sense. I approve.' James Douglas pulled at his beard and the light eyes searched my face. 'Lord Burghley says that the book still awaits collection because the two messengers who preceded you never got as far as Stonemoor House although they did get as far as York. I wonder . . . has it occurred to you that perhaps one or both of those earlier messengers did actually reach Thorby village and Stonemoor House and that danger may have overtaken them, not at the hands of Mary's spies, but in that nest of snakes at Stonemoor?'

I stood quite still and for a moment did not answer, as an unease surfaced in my mind. Though hitherto unacknowledged, it had been present within me from the very beginning. In fact, from the moment when Cecil admitted to me that the search for the two missing Messengers had been narrowed down to the space between York and Stonemoor. It had been strengthened by the encounter with Master Maxton in York, when he confirmed that both men had indeed used his stable. And though I had never put it into words even in my own head, never contemplated it directly, I had instinctively acted on it when I decided to deliver the letter to James Morton first, and collect the book afterwards.

At length, I said: 'I had thought of that, my lord. That was why I came to Scotland first, meaning to go to Stonemoor later, whereas the two men who went before me seemingly intended to do the reverse. But I must go to Stonemoor before I go home. I have undertaken to do so.'

He frowned, staring at the letter he was still holding. 'You are conscientious. That is a virtue, no doubt. And I myself can't really see why this household of women should want to harm Queen's Messengers. They would risk ending the toleration they have so far been shown and bringing catastrophe down on their heads. But all the same . . . one never knows, with snakes. Take care as you journey on, Mistress Stannard. Still,' he added, 'you are a sizeable party. They might find it difficult to do away with you all!'

'But it's ridiculous!' said Brockley, when we had left Holyrood and were on our way back to Ambrosia's home. For the Brockleys' benefit, I had been recounting my interview with James Morton. 'Here we have a house of middle-aged ladies pretending to be nuns,' said Brockley. 'They're timid by nature – well, Cecil apparently told you that they keep within the law and send representatives to the village church! They obviously want to keep out of trouble. They are short of funds and want to sell a valuable book to help their finances. And they've been knocking Queen's Messengers on the head and stealing the scrolls they carry? I never heard of anything so absurd!'

'They might have been paid by Mary's people,' said Dale. Dale had in the past had a terrifying experience in France, when she was arrested as a heretic and barely escaped a horrible death. She did not like Catholics and was ready to believe anything of the Stonemoor House ladies.

'Mary's adherents are perfectly capable of intercepting messengers themselves, if they want to,' I said. 'They wouldn't need to seek help from a lot of respectable, God-fearing women. James Douglas says it's hard to believe that Mary's spies would want to attack messengers in any case. It makes no sense.'

My own doubts and fears throbbed in my mind like twinges of toothache but I mustn't frighten Dale. I must not admit that I was anxious. Anyway, my errand had to be completed. I put on a brisk manner.

'It's all very mysterious but we have no choice. We are bound next for Stonemoor and that's that. If we time our journey with care, we might not even have to spend a night there! Then all we have to do is travel home. We haven't found any of Christopher Spelton's signs anywhere and I don't suppose we will.'

'I've gone on looking,' Brockley said. 'Mostly in the stables and tackrooms, wherever we've made a stop. They're the likeliest places. If he put chalk signs inside houses, or even on the outside walls of houses, someone would very likely clean them off, but on stable premises, they might not arouse much interest – grooms and stable boys often scrawl graffiti here and there. But there's been nothing.'

'I'll be glad once we've been to this Stonemoor place and then got away from it,' said Dale, with feeling. 'I can't abide trouble,' she added with pathos, 'and time and again, whenever we go on an errand for the queen, trouble is what we get.'

'I hope not this time!' I said, with determined cheerfulness.

Though in the depths of my mind, anxiety remained.

SEVEN
No Bigger Than A Man's Hand

We spent a week in Edinburgh, which was what we had planned, though the wet weather which suddenly set in would in any case have kept us from leaving sooner. We paid a visit to Kate's relatives in Edinburgh, to tell them about her marriage. They made us very welcome, but getting there and back involved hurrying through rain-swept streets with our cloak hoods pulled over our heads, and taking dry indoor slippers with us, in a bag which Dale carried.

However, the day before we wished to leave, the rain obligingly stopped and on the morning of Monday the 6th of March we woke to find the clouds gone. There was frost on the roofs of Edinburgh, but the sun was out again and there was no wind. We could start for Stonemoor at once.

There were tearful partings, for who knew when any of us would make the four-hundred-mile journey from Hawkswood again? Brockley and Joseph fetched the coach from the stables where it and our horses had been kept during our stay, and loaded our baggage. There was much embracing and a good deal of weeping. The children howled, Ambrosia and Sybil sobbed in each other's arms, and Brockley, busy stowing hampers inside the coach, shook his head at the uproar.

'It hardly seems worthwhile to have family reunions,' he remarked, somewhat cynically, 'since they have to end in such a display of grief!'

'They'll all be all right once the wrench is over,' I said encouragingly. 'We shall have plenty to occupy our minds once we're on the road. There's a good seventy miles to go to reach Stonemoor. I've been studying the maps.'

'So have I. It'll be rough travelling,' said Brockley glumly. 'We've got to go across the moors this time.'

We both had vivid memories of previous journeys in the north. I nodded, having been worried about the same thing. The road ahead was unknown to us and could be much rougher than the heavily used Roman road which was the direct route to the south. However, the first two days of our journey went well enough. The track was bumpy but wide and despite the recent rain, not too muddy. We made quite good speed. By the second nightfall, we were on the edge of the moorland and could hope to reach Stonemoor the next day.

There are few inns in the north, except on the main road. Off it, we had to seek shelter at farms. The one we found this time, though it was isolated, was quite big, lying in a shallow vale, encircled by heathery hills. The soil in the vale was evidently fertile and the place looked prosperous. The fields that spread round the farmhouse had well-tended drystone walls, and we saw three or four labourers' cottages, each with its own patch of land for vegetables and chickens. The farmhouse itself was sturdily built of grey stone, with a fair-sized stable adjoining it. When we led our horses in, we found that the farm boasted three horses of its own: a grey cob, a big, hairy-heeled workhorse, and a brown mare.

At this farm, and at the one where we had spent the previous night, Brockley and Joseph followed what had become a habit and looked sharply round the stable in case Christopher Spelton had left his red chalk sign there, but he had not.

The farmer's name was Master Thwaite and he and his wife made us very welcome. Mrs Thwaite was lame, which I suppose limited her movements and explained why, unusually for a farm wife, she was fat. There was a maidservant, a lively, bonny lass, who probably had to do most of the housework on her own, but was clearly not downtrodden. Master Thwaite, in contrast to his wife, was wiry and active. Neither of them had many teeth and were apt to shoot out spittle when they spoke, and as with their maidservant, their northern accent was strong. Communication with any of the three was difficult but they were all kind.

We were offered one room with a wide bed for the ladies and a straw-filled barn for the men (though the Brockleys looked depressed at this arrangement). We also searched our indoor quarters for signs in red chalk, just in case, but were not unduly surprised to find that there weren't any.

'And bedchambers wouldn't be a likely place for them,' Dale remarked, echoing Brockley.

We were excellently fed. The Thwaites, most hospitably, slaughtered a couple of chickens for our benefit. After supper, we gathered round our maps to discuss the route for the final stage of the journey to Stonemoor. Evening was falling and the Thwaites' living room was both dark and smoky but there were candles on the table and by their light we could follow the maps well enough.

The Thwaites were puzzled by them; clearly they were not used to such things. However, they knew their district, and they knew how to get to Stonemoor. Despite the difficulty of talking to them, we managed to establish that the track which had brought us from the north continued straight on southwards for some miles and then forked, and that we should take the left fork. The right-hand path went eventually to York, 'Though it be a roughish track,' Master Thwaite said. The left-hand way would take us in a south-easterly direction and led to Thorby and Stonemoor. But we should start early and press on hard, because there were no habitations along the way.

'Do you often get travellers who want to break their journey here?' I asked. 'Have there been any recently?'

They didn't understand me. 'You get a muckle folk passing through?' said Brockley, in an attempt at a Yorkshire accent.

'Muckle's a Scots word,' said Sybil, not very helpfully. Brockley fixed the Thwaites and their bonny maidservant with a quizzical eye.

Whether or not muckle was really a local word, they did understand it, and shook their heads. No passing travellers had sought shelter with them since the previous autumn, they said, though oddly enough they had been visited twice by the county sheriff's men, from York, who had asked after two men who had gone missing.

'But we could tell them nowt,' said Master Thwaite. 'We'd not seen their lost men, any road. Only guest we've had lately, except for thee, is a horse, only she turned up later, after the men from York were here.'

It was our turn to be puzzled. After a little to-ing and fro-ing, however, it turned out that the brown mare we had seen in the stable wasn't theirs. They had found her straying on their land. No, she had no saddle or bridle and no halter. She had been in poor condition and seemed forlorn. She was easy to catch. They were keeping her, feeding her well, and making use of her, until someone should come in search of her.

We all exchanged glances. It didn't seem that either Christopher Spelton or Bernard Hardwicke had passed this way, but a stray horse did suggest that something untoward might have happened in this district, and this one matched the description of the horse that Christopher had hired in York. 'When did the mare first appear?' Brockley asked.

They couldn't remember exactly. One day was so like another. But it had been some days after the second visit from the sheriff's men. It evidently hadn't occurred to them to send word about the mare to the authorities. When Brockley had conveyed to them that we were wondering about this, they looked surprised. 'She's nobbut a stray horse. Happen she wandered off from some other farm somewhere . . . there are places west and east of here, though there's a good lot of miles of moorland in between, either way, and in winter, we doan't travel much. Might do come the spring,' said Master Thwaite. 'Then us might do some asking about.'

He then changed the subject, and presented us with a problem. 'How'll thee travel when thee goes on, come tomorrow? Thee'll not get there in that great lumbering coach thing.'

'But the track's good,' said Brockley. 'Rough, but broad enough.'

What Master Thwaite said next amounted to the fact that however broad the track might be to the north, towards Thorby and Stonemoor it would deteriorate within two or three miles until it ended up little wider than a sheep path. 'Thy wheels'll be on the heather and there's stones sticking out of that all over the place. Coach is no good for that. It's ride or walk.'

'Aye, and I'd not say it's any trudge for a lady,' put in Mrs Thwaite.

'Well, we've got enough horses,' Brockley said, grasping the situation and pointing out the only solution. 'Lucky we brought saddlery. But do we all need to go? Wouldn't it be simpler if I just rode to Stonemoor and fetched the book on my own? How far is it?'

We sought the opinion of the Thwaites, who estimated twenty miles.

'I might get there and back in one day, if I start early,' said Brockley briskly. 'If not, I can stop the night in Thorby and be back by midday the next day. I should think . . .'

I opened my mouth to protest but Dale was ahead of me. '*No!*' She said it passionately. 'I can't abide the thought of it. Don't, Roger, don't. *No!*'

We were guests in someone else's house and could hardly ask our hosts to leave their own main room so that we could confer in private. I said: 'Please excuse us. We must talk of this outside,' and although the Thwaites stared at us as though we had suddenly gone mad, I rose and my companions trooped after me, out of the living room, into the little farmyard, and there, in the chilly dusk, with hens pecking round our feet, we held council.

'Now what's all this, Fran?' Brockley demanded.

'You'd be on your own! So were *they* – that man Hardwicke that madam has told us about, and Master Spelton! They were both travelling alone! I think that brown mare is Master Spelton's!'

'So do I,' I said. 'That mare is a fine strong animal with sloping shoulders and good round haunches. Very much the sort for a remount. Buyers for remounts don't pick weedy animals with goose rumps. She could well be Christopher's. She isn't Hardwicke's – he was riding a chestnut.'

'But I *don't* see how there can be danger at Stonemoor,' Brockley said. 'Hardwicke and Spelton *must* have been attacked because of the letter they carried – Stonemoor is a household of ladies with no possible reason to harm a messenger who is bringing them money and just taking a book away! The ladies *want* to sell it, apparently.'

'There's no question of you going alone anyway,' I said. 'The task is rightly mine and I must go as well.'

'Then I must attend you, ma'am!' said Dale, grimly. Dale might not be a good horsewoman and she certainly wasn't getting any younger, but she had a determined streak. 'Bronze is a quiet horse,' she said valiantly. Bronze, on the journey, had been the offside wheeler. 'I can manage if I ride him.'

What Dale really meant, and I knew it, was that she didn't want me and Brockley to go off together. I understood. I also felt quite sure that Cecil and James Morton had been right to feel that safety lay in numbers. It would be best for us all to stay together. If there *was* any kind of danger in Stonemoor, we would protect each other.

'You're not perfectly sure that Stonemoor is . . . all it should be, are you, Ursula?' said Sybil.

I met her eyes and knew that she was reading mine. But Dale was looking anxious and I wanted to ease her mind.

'I am sure there is nothing to worry about at Stonemoor,' I said, untruthfully, 'but I prefer that we don't separate. In any case, I am in a way the queen's representative and I should be properly attended. We will all go to Stonemoor and that's that.'

The taciturn Joseph now joined in. 'The mistress is right. She should have folk with her. That's *proper*.'

'We will have to leave the coach here and come back for it later,' I said. 'I hope the Thwaites won't mind. We leave tomorrow morning, on horseback.'

We did of course have to sort out who was to ride which horse. Bronze was the quietest and therefore he was the best one for Dale. The others who had made up the four-in-hand were Rusty, another quiet bay, very like Bronze, and two of the new horses I had recently bought. They too were bays; my team was nearly a matched set though not quite, for Blaze had a broad white stripe from brow to nose, and Splash looked as though he had started out to become a skewbald but had changed his mind. He had a white patch on his near shoulder, another on his off haunch, and a small one on his off foreleg, above the knee. The two of them had been bought as a team and were used to being together.

We settled that Sybil, since she was nearly as uncertain a rider as Dale, should take Rusty, because he was almost as placid as Bronze, while I chose Blaze. Joseph would have

Splash and Brockley of course had his own cob. We left at daybreak, warmly dressed, with hooded cloaks, and with us we took food, flasks of water, and spare clothes and other necessities in the saddlebags that Brockley had so providently insisted on bringing. My saddlebags were heavy, because I was carrying the purse containing the three hundred pounds in angels and sovereigns which were the price of the book we had come to buy.

The track was good to begin with and to save both Dale and Sybil from the tiring business of constantly rising to the trot we alternated between the walk and the canter. Within half an hour we found the fork that the Thwaites had told us about. As instructed, we took the left-hand way. After that, however, the path began to narrow and we saw how right our hosts had been to say that the coach would be useless. Even riders could not travel two abreast and we had to settle for single file. Then, after a while, the path began to be bedevilled by stones. We slowed down.

'This is the most desolate country I've ever seen,' Sybil said, awed.

She was right. All around us, there was moorland, rolling hills of it, covered with heather and thin winter grass, with grey stone outcrops here and there. The morning frost had gone, but the wind was bitter, moaning dismally across the bleak expanses. There was no trace of humanity in any form. We could see no prints of feet or hooves on the path and there was no sign, in all the surrounding empty miles, of any dwellings, no homely spires of blue chimney smoke, no cultivation. Once we saw a few sheep in the distance and once a raven flapped, croaking, across our path. Apart from these, we seemed to be the only living creatures there.

We came in due course to a river ford where we stopped to let the horses drink, and then we dismounted to use some outcrops as seats while we ate a meal of bread and cheese. It was probably the only ford for miles, Brockley remarked, since to our left, which was upstream, the river flowed swiftly in a deep, narrow bed, and downstream, to the right, where the land rose abruptly, it entered a channel like a knife slash through the hill and ran between banks that were almost perpendicular, dropping fifteen or twenty feet to the water, which in their shadow looked as black as ink. The ford, in between, was a place where for a few yards the river slackened speed and spread out over a patch of flat, low-lying ground, and didn't look as though it were more than a couple of feet deep. It still appeared cold and unwelcoming.

As we finished our meal, Sybil stood up to survey the scene once more, and again, commented adversely on it. 'I *don't* like this country. It's so *wild*. Why would people – why would these ladies we're going to visit – want to live in such a district?'

'Maybe it won't be so wild where they are,' I said. 'We're not there yet. Let us remount and ride on.'

We did so, not too cheerfully, for apart from the cold, none of us ladies were very comfortable, because we had no leggings. We all had to ride astride in bundled-up skirts, which was awkward anyway, and we had nothing to protect our calves from the stirrup leathers, which soon began to bite. Also, the track now began to wind, finding its way round hills and avoiding steep gradients. I suspected that the twenty miles we had heard about referred to the flight of a crow and that the distance for travellers on legs was a good deal longer. However, after we had been riding for about four hours altogether without seeing any habitations, we came to a long rise which brought us up to the crest of a ridge and here we drew rein to survey what lay track ahead. 'Look!' said Brockley.

He was shading his eyes and pointing. 'We've covered more than twenty miles, by a long way,' he said. 'It's high time we saw where we're bound – and there it is!'

And there it was, indeed. He pointed and with relief we saw that at last, in the distance and a little to the left, there was chimney smoke and from more than one chimney.

'Surely that must be Thorby,' Brockley said. 'It's in a dip . . . that's why we can't see the houses.'

'There's more smoke, from behind that hill there, next to where the village must be, look.' Sybil had risen in her stirrups. 'That might be Stonemoor House. Well, the end is in sight. Thank God. I never imagined such a barren land could exist! I'll be thankful to get under a roof again. It was cold enough when we started, but I'm sure it's worse now.'

I thought so too. The sun still shone in a clear pale-blue sky, but there was no warmth in it. Then Brockley looked round and pointed. To the west, above a hump of hill, a small brownish cloud had appeared.

'I don't like the look of that,' he said.

'It's just a tiny cloud,' said Sybil.

'No bigger than a man's hand,' Brockley agreed. 'But I've seen weather change, many a time. That's often the way it starts. A little cloud. And then another. And then an army of them. That is a snow cloud, or I have never seen one. Come on. We'd better make what haste we can.'

EIGHT
The Uneasy Sanctuary

'Are we still on the track?' I asked, leaning down over
Blaze's shoulder to talk to Brockley.
         We were no longer travelling in a wide landscape
with clear visibility. There was nothing around us now but the
silent, bewildering dance of falling snowflakes. Heather, grass,
and track were swiftly disappearing beneath a white blanket.
A little way back, we had passed through a dip where a few
trees grew and by then their branches were already carrying
an inch of white on their upper sides. We had been riding
from the start with our cloak hoods over our heads but now
we had pulled them forward as far as possible, to keep the
cold out of our ears. Brockley had dismounted and was leading
Mealy, using his feet to brush a way along the edge of the
track and thereby to keep us on it. The path was slightly sunk
between its tufty heather verges, which helped.

'We're all right so far,' he said.

I wasn't so sure. As long as we didn't stray from the path,
we would probably arrive at Thorby eventually, but if the track
were to branch again, unseen, and we made the wrong choice,
we could find ourselves hopelessly astray. Also, although Dale
seemed to be enduring her discomforts with fortitude, I was
seriously worried about Sybil. She was riding just behind me
and a glance back showed me that her face was as white as
the snowflakes that were gathering on her hood. She was sitting
awkwardly and I suspected that her stirrup leathers were
pinching her badly.

We went on in silence, for what I estimated was another
fifteen minutes, and then I said: 'Surely we should be near
Thorby by now.'

Brockley didn't answer. He had come to a halt. I couldn't
at first see why, and then realized that out of the haze of falling

flakes a large grey outcrop had appeared in front of us. Brockley, kicking at the snow, was trying to see how the path negotiated it – on the left, on the right, or did it split, go past on both sides, and come together beyond it? Joseph dismounted and led his horse forward, and by what seemed to be tacit agreement, he tried the right-hand side of the outcrop and Brockley tried the left.

After a moment, Joseph came back and Brockley called to us to follow him. The rest of us did so. Just here, the path seemed to turn from earth to rock, for the horses' hooves first crunched as they trod on the snow, and then rang on whatever was beneath it. The two men continued on foot, leading their mounts. Then Rusty stumbled and Sybil cried out. I twisted quickly in my saddle, to see that although Rusty had almost come down but was just recovering, Sybil was not. She was in the act of tilting sideways and falling from her saddle.

I was down in an instant. Joseph and Brockley came beside me. The snow had given Sybil a soft landing, but she seemed dazed as we helped her to her feet, and leaned heavily on us. 'I'm sorry. I'm sorry.' She was shaking her head from side to side. 'The snow . . . if only we could see where we're going . . . the way the flakes dance turned me dizzy for a moment and . . . oh, my poor legs!'

She pulled at her skirts, and I stooped to look at the damage. Both her calves were red from the rubbing and pinching of the leathers, and the left one was bleeding a little.

'You can't go on riding like that,' I said. 'Oh, dear heaven.'

'What are we to do?' asked Dale. Hunched in Bronze's saddle, she was shivering violently.

We were all shivering. We were benighted in a world where there was nothing but the snow and the cold and the silence. Then Brockley said decisively: 'I'll get back on to Mealy and take Mistress Jester up in front of me. He's a good weight-carrier. Madam, can you dismount and lead Rusty and Blaze and help Joseph to do the pathfinding?'

'All right. Thank you, Brockley.'

He remounted briskly, pushing his feet into the stirrups, and Sybil, bravely trying to pull herself together, put one of her feet on one of his and tried to heave herself up. Brockley got hold of her shoulders, Joseph and I pushed from below, and at last we got her on to Mealy's withers. Mealy, fortunately, stood still throughout. I took the bridles of Blaze and Rusty, and turned to go onward.

And couldn't find the path. Nor could Joseph. Picking Sybil up, rearranging ourselves, we had strayed aside from it. Neither of us, I realized in panic, even knew which way we were facing. I blundered forward, and then stopped short, having come face to face with the big outcrop. 'I think,' said Brockley's voice from behind me, 'that we're going the wrong way, madam. I can see our hoof prints.'

He was right. Though the snow had already begun to fill them, there were still traces of the prints to be seen, coming towards us from beyond the outcrop.

'We've been going backwards.' Joseph's calm voice was reassuring. 'Best turn around.'

We did this, and with the outcrop as a point of reference, it should have been easy enough to find the path again, but it wasn't. Joseph stopped short, obviously bewildered, and rubbed his forehead, while I was frankly too frightened to be efficient. I swept at the snow with a frantic right foot, while my skirt hems became soaked with the hateful stuff and I felt exhaustion and cold beginning to weaken me, legs, arms, and brain. I wasn't on the path. Where I had brushed the snow aside, there was nothing under it but heather. Where were we? Somewhere I had heard or read that if caught in such weather, to stop trying, to give in and rest, meant death, and that might mean the deaths of all of us. I found myself crying, and the tears froze on my face. I heard Dale moaning softly.

Then Sybil, her voice faint but resolute, called: 'There's a verge on our right. Mealy has just trodden on it and kicked the snow off. I can see it. I think it's the edge of the path.'

It was. Joseph went ahead now while I, secretly sending up prayers of gratitude, followed on his heels, with Mealy and Bronze close behind us. We plodded on.

And on. We were back on the path, but we still seemed to be getting nowhere. I don't like to remember it. In one brief glance back, I saw that Sybil was now leaning against Brockley with her head turned into his chest. Brockley had pulled his hood so far forward that I couldn't see his face at all. I felt as though we had indeed died, and this was eternity.

And then, for the second time, it was Sybil, rousing from her faint or her sleep or whichever it was, who re-awakened hope, by calling out: 'Stop and listen! I'm sure I heard a dog bark. Somewhere ahead!'

We halted. We were all silent. Then, faintly, far in the distance, we heard it. There was indeed a dog somewhere ahead. Brockley at once raised his voice in loud halloos and we all began, slowly and cautiously, to move forward again. A few moments later, a huge, hairy, tawny something bounded out of the blizzard and pranced round us. I had seen the menagerie at the Tower of London and for one wild moment I thought the creature was a lion, until it let out a volley of throaty barks and I realized that the dog, or rather the hound, that we had heard in the distance had arrived to inspect us.

But it looked so fierce and it was so bouncy that it upset the horses. I had to cling hard to the two sets of reins I was holding, and make soothing noises at Rusty and Blaze as they snorted and trampled. Rusty, normally so well mannered, was sidling and throwing his head about, while Blaze, his ears flattened back, was trying to stand on his hind legs. Joseph could not help me because Splash was also plunging. Fortunately, Bronze, really the least excitable horse I have ever known, just stood there, stolidly. Dale was patting him and telling him not to be alarmed, but where dear placid Bronze was concerned, she could have saved her breath.

The dog, however, was followed in another moment by a human shape, wrapped in cloak and hood, with great leather boots up to its knees, who snapped: 'Quiet! Down!' at the dog and sensibly added his weight to mine to steady my two horses.

'Where are we?' Brockley demanded, from on his perch on Mealy.

'Thorby village, and lucky tha be to get here in this,' said our rescuer. 'Coom on, then – *will* thee shut thy noise, Fangs! – not far now. Hoondred yards, no more. This way.'

Joseph and I got back into our saddles and Joseph took charge of leading Rusty. The dog, despite its alarming appearance, which indeed included a most impressive set of fangs, was fortunately willing to accept us as friends, presumably because its master had. It went ahead of us, panting and leaping through the snow and in its wake we made our way onwards, coming to a stop in front of a squat stone building. It had an oaken door, split in half, and the top half was open.

'This here's my alehouse,' said our guide. 'Silas Butterworth, that's my name. Thee'll have to bide here, I fancy, not that I takes folk in mostly, but no decent Yorkshireman'll leave fellow creatures out in a snowstorm, least of all lasses. Whatever brought three lasses travelling this road anyhow?' He looked up at Brockley. 'Get down, if thee will, man, and hand thy lass down to me. Thee'll find stabling round the back . . .'

'It wasn't snowing when we started out,' I said.

'Mebbe not, but where was thee bound for? Thee can't have business here, surely! There's nobbut a handful of cottages here and a bit of a church and the fields round about and this is a long way round to get to York, if that's where thee's bound. What brought thee by this track?'

Brockley, who had not attempted to dismount and was still holding Sybil in front of him, said: 'We're making for a place called Stonemoor House. Isn't that near here?'

The snow had eased a little. Silas Butterworth was now revealed as a stocky old fellow with white hair hanging round his ears, a weather-reddened skin, and round blue eyes. He stood with feet apart, taking us in, and for a long moment, he said nothing. Then he said: 'Stonemoor? Thee's bound *there*?'

'Yes.' His evident surprise was itself a surprise to me. 'We have business there,' I said. 'Is it far? Can you direct us?'

'Aye. Well, the ladies'll tak thee in, sure enough. They take guests. Say it's tradition, so they do. Don't happen often, though. They keep theirselves to theirselves mostly. They're odd folk and there's some in the village don't care for them. Queer goings on, so some folk say, and so does vicar, and they could be things that'll mebbe bring trouble on us one day.'

I remembered Cecil saying that some of the Thorby folk suspected the ladies of witchcraft. I wasn't sure how to reply to this broad hint and it was Brockley who said bluntly: 'What's wrong with the ladies of Stonemoor? We have to go there and if something is amiss with them, we would like to know what it is.'

'They're Catholic ladies,' said Butterworth. 'That's enough, ain't it? Though, mind you, there's plenty as are glad of work on t'farm that goes with the place, and they buy things from us – butcher's work and barrels o' my ale, and the like. They physic some on us too, when we get ill, though there's been trouble over that since Master Harry Henley died after Mistress Bella up at the house gave him some herbal brew or other when he was sick with terrible headaches and took to his bed. Doctor Rowbotham, that's our vicar, the next Sunday, he said it wasn't right for a woman to be acting the physician. If you ask me, Harry was dying any road and no brew of herbs would make nor mar him, but some aren't so sure. I've nowt against Mistress Bella myself. My guts have been giving me trouble on and off for this past year, near enough, and her remedies ease me and I'm grateful for it but there's some who mutter about witchery. So, what kind of business is it that folk like thee have with Stonemoor?'

Brockley scowled at that and Sybil drew her breath in sharply and I felt much as they did for it was an impertinent question. But there was no point in annoying the man. 'They have a valuable book for sale. We have come to pay for it and collect it,' I said.

'I see. Well, it's not my affair, I grant thee. Thee'll do better there than here, truth to tell – they've rooms for travellers, aye and provender. It's nobbut a short way if thee had wings, but for horse or man it's up a good long hill path. You want to get there now?'

'Yes, we do!' said Brockley.

Master Butterworth looked at the snow. 'Thee'll do best wi' a guide. Tracks'll be buried, like.' We all murmured heartfelt agreement. 'Well . . . I've customers inside, drinkin' my ale, but there's someone I can send with thee, 'less thee'd like to stop for a drink?'

I yearned for one and probably we all did, but Brockley said: 'We'd all like to, but we ought to get on before the snow thickens again.' He considered the sky. 'I'd say there's more up there waiting to come down. We'll pretend we've drunk in your alehouse, though. And pay for the drinks and the guide you send with us.'

Whereat Master Butterworth's weather-beaten face split into a wide and satisfied smile. He was as gap-toothed as the Thwaites or Gladys. Brockley pushed back his cloak, found the purse at his belt, and saw to the transaction.

'Will Grimes'll show thee the way,' Butterworth said. He raised his voice. '*Grimes! Get out here, Will! Move thy worthless legs!*'

The lower half of the door opened but I didn't see Will Grimes until he was out of it and almost up to us, because my eyes were looking for him at a level too high and there was still quite enough falling snow to be bemusing. He seemed to materialize just in front of me, so suddenly that I was startled. He was barely five feet high, a skinny little man with a brown wizened face like a goblin, and a pair of bright pale eyes on either side of a hooked nose. He was like the description one of Aunt Tabitha's maids had given me of Robin Goodfellow, the mischievous sprite for whom countrywomen so often put out bowls of milk at night. 'And they bowls of milk do get drunk, my ma says, for she puts them out, regular, every night!' she had told me, nodding emphatically, eyes wide with earnestness.

Aunt Tabitha had overheard her and boxed her ears, and both she and Uncle Herbert had explained to me that Robin Goodfellow was just a story believed in by the ignorant – 'And of course the bowls of milk get drunk!' said Aunt Tabitha. 'By farm cats!'

Aunt Tabitha's outrage hadn't damped the maid's enthusiasm for old-time stories. She had another one, about a Green Man. I had once seen a tavern called by that name, which puzzled me. It had an inn sign showing a man's bearded face peering out through a mass of thick green foliage. The man's face was green as well. It was that same maid who told me that he was a figure from the past, a god of the forest. My aunt never heard her tell that story, which was probably just as well for the maid. I liked her stories as I had liked the tales told by my cousin's tutor. I had never met anyone who resembled the Green Man but I now wondered if whoever began that legend of Robin Goodfellow had known someone who looked like Will Grimes.

'You called on me, maister?' he said, looking sidelong at Butterworth.

'Aye, I did. Now get thy pony, quick, and tek these folk up to Stonemoor,' said Butterworth. 'Then get back here, fast. Hurry, now!'

'Aye,' said the goblin, and turning, strolled off round the corner of the alehouse. The order to hurry had obviously not had much effect on him. Butterworth was still grinning and I noticed that Brockley looked amused. I reckoned that what we had just heard was a standing joke between man and master. However, it was only a few minutes before Will Grimes was back, leading a diminutive pony, as notably hairy as the dog, to the point that one wondered how it could see where it was going through the curtain of its forelock. It was bridled but not saddled. Grimes hopped astride it with casual ease, and waved a beckoning hand to us.

We said goodbye to Butterworth, and turned the horses' heads. They had sensed the nearness of stabling and were somewhat unwilling to leave the alehouse, but we kicked them determinedly on. 'We're nearly there,' said Brockley, into Mealy's ear.

Grimes led us back a little way along the track that had brought us, passing a turn to the left, the way that we had come, though now we were led straight on. We found ourselves going uphill and then realized that the path, which we couldn't see though Will and his pony (forelock notwithstanding) seemed sure of the way, was climbing the hill in a zigzag. It took a long time. The snow was falling lightly now but Brockley had been right, I felt sure, for the sky above was the colour of lead. There was more trouble to come.

At last, we saw ahead of us a crenelated gatehouse, built of grey stone, with a studded double door that didn't look inviting. Grimes, however, leant from his pony and pounded on it, shouting to someone within to open, and one leaf of it was pulled back, with a loud grating noise and a very obvious effort on the part of the woman who was pulling it. All we could see of her was a female shape cloaked and hooded in dark blue. We could hear her panting for breath as she pulled.

'Visitors for thee,' said Willy laconically. 'Say they've

business with thee and any road, they need shelter for the night. Two men and three lasses.' He swung the pony round and nodded to us. 'I'll be getting back, afore I *can't.*' He pointed up at the sky, kicked his mount, and was gone, so swiftly that it seemed as if he was anxious to get away, vanishing into the snow which was now thickening again. I could almost believe that Will Grimes had summoned the new blizzard by goblin magic.

'You'd best come in,' the woman said to us. Her voice was educated, a southerner's voice, I thought. We rode through, passing an open door into the gatehouse. A waft of warmth came from it; presumably the little gatekeeper had been inside, keeping snug, when we arrived. We emerged into a courtyard and found ourselves facing the main house. Through the snow, we made out a long frontage with an imposing air. A flight of several steps led up to its main entrance, though another doorway, some way to the right, had a more modest staircase.

Like the gatehouse, the place was built of grey stone and partly crenelated, with a sharply sloping roof visible behind the imitation battlements. Most of the windows were small and pointed at their tops in the fashion of the previous century, but the whole building had an oddly lopsided shape. It looked as though the smaller entrance led into a wing that had been built later and differently, since it wasn't crenelated and the roof did not slant so steeply. The windows were larger, too.

A man appeared from round the right-hand corner. 'I thought I heard someone hammering at the gate, and I heard a horse snort, too.' He was a big muscular fellow with a heavy-boned face. He went to help the woman to shut the gate again, and as he turned back to take Rusty's bridle from Joseph while he dismounted, I saw that the hand that took the rein was enormous. He was very much the type of man we had all seen at fairs, offering to fight all comers, but his accent, by contrast, was well bred and his manner was courteous.

'So we've guests! Welcome to Stonemoor House. Ladies, go in out of the snow. Gentlemen, I'll show you where to put the horses. They could do with a rub down and a bran mash, I fancy.'

'This is Walter Cogge, our steward and the bailiff for our

farm,' said the woman. 'He will take you to the stable and you can put your horses in with ours. Walter will see them warm and fed.'

Brockley and Sybil slid to the ground together. She was looking better, and took Mealy's bridle while I went to help Dale down. Then Joseph, Brockley, and Walter Cogge took charge of all the horses and prepared to lead them away. First, though, Brockley paused, looking at me. The wind was rising and blew a thick flurry of snowflakes across his face. He brushed them off his eyebrows.

'We're here, madam,' he said. 'Safe in sanctuary.'

'Safe from the snow, at least,' said Sybil.

She didn't enlarge on what she meant by that but I knew what she meant without being told and so did Brockley and Dale. Brockley shook his head but I saw Dale flinch. I looked at the snow, which was now falling heavily and already piling up round our feet, and then looked at the house in front of me and the closed gate, and had a horrid sense of being trapped. Whatever awaited us in Stonemoor, we had little chance of getting away from it very soon. We were going to be snowed in with it. Whatever it was.

NINE
Chanting in the Night

The men led the horses away and the small woman who had with such difficulty dragged the gate open turned to us.

'My name is Margaret Beale,' she said. 'Whatever brought you here and in such terrible weather? Did you miss your way somehow? You must be long miles out of your proper road. You're in luck as it chances for we're expecting a party of five guests soon, but I can't suppose they're likely to arrive now, not until the weather clears. Which means that our best guest rooms are free and we can make you properly comfortable. Please come with me and I will show you to our guest quarters.'

She glanced to where the men and the horses were just disappearing round the corner of the house. 'Are those your grooms? Master Cogge will find them somewhere to sleep and will see that they have a meal and . . .'

'The younger man is a groom,' I said, 'and can be accommodated with your own man, but the older one is Roger Brockley, my personal manservant. My tirewoman Frances Brockley—' I indicated Dale – 'is his wife. I wish them to have a chamber in the guest quarters, close to myself and my gentlewoman here. I am Mistress Ursula Stannard and this is Mistress Sybil Jester. We didn't miss our way. We intended to come here. We have an errand from the court of Queen Elizabeth, to a Mistress Philippa Gould, who lives here, I believe.'

'Really?' Mistress Beale was so diminutive that she had to turn her face upwards in order to look at me. It was a pleasant face, a little pink and a little wrinkled like a last season's apple, and her brown eyes were lively, like her chatty conversation. 'Well, come in and be welcome,' she said. 'I will send someone to fetch your Master Brockley, if that is your wish. This way.'

Head bowed against the snow, she led us, not towards the main entrance but towards the smaller one to the right, leading into the wing without the battlements. We followed her inside, to find ourselves standing in a flagstoned entrance vestibule. It had stone walls and a vaulted ceiling, high above us. We were out of the wind but otherwise the place was just as cold as the courtyard.

'Wait here,' said Margaret Beale, sounding flustered. 'I must find someone to look after you and then get back to my little room at the gatehouse.'

'Are you always the gatekeeper?' asked Sybil with concern. 'That gate was very heavy for you, surely.'

'We all take our turn,' said Mistress Beale. 'Excuse me for a moment.'

She scuttled off through a low door on the left. We stood there, shivering, colder even than when we had been on our horses, for horses are warmer-blooded than their riders, and one always gains heat from them. However, it was not long before someone came, in the shape of two more ladies. Both were dressed in sweeping dark-blue gowns, with small ruffs and no farthingales, and their hair was hidden under close-fitting dark-blue wimples. As a form of dress, it was not precisely the garb of nuns, but it was similar. Neither woman was young, but the one who was probably the elder was tall and held herself as straight as any guardsman at the Tower of London. She had a long, bony face with a grim, tight mouth. The other was shorter, plump and obsequious and half a pace behind her companion.

'This is most unexpected,' said the tall one disapprovingly. We dripped melted snow on to the flagstones and said nothing. 'Mistress Stannard and Mistress Jester, I think Margaret said? And a tirewoman – Brockley is the name, I think.'

'Yes,' said Sybil. I added: 'And you are?'

'I am Angelica Ames.' A misnomer, I thought, as no one could have looked less angelic but perhaps she had been pretty as a baby. 'And this is Mary Haxby, who will prepare your rooms. Your tirewoman and your manservant are man and wife and you wish them to be accommodated in the guest quarters, so I hear.'

'Most definitely,' I said.

'And you have business with Mistress Gould, our . . . Principal?'

'Indeed we have,' I said. 'Though tomorrow will do for talking about that.' My teeth would be chattering audibly before long, I thought.

Sybil voiced what I was thinking. 'For the moment, we are glad just to be in shelter. We are cold and very tired.'

'Quite. Mary will have the rooms ready very quickly. Meanwhile, come into the guest hall. Mary, make haste and fetch kindling and light fires in the hall and in rooms one and two. Then get bedlinen and covers and prepare the beds.'

We were shown through a door on the right, opposite to the one through which the two women had come, and found ourselves in a hall, stone-walled and flagstoned like the vestibule, and provided with a hearth. At the moment, it was a dark, unheated mouth with an empty fuel basket beside it. In the middle of the hall there was a table with benches along each side, and against one wall stood a wooden settle with no cushions. At the far end of the hall a flight of stone steps led up to a gallery running round two sides of the place, and up there we could see doors, all alike, solid oak by the look of them, with heavy iron hinges. The guest bedchambers, presumably, though the immediate impression was that they were a row of prison cells. Since there seemed to be nothing else to do, the three of us sat down on the settle. Angelica and Mary bustled off, leaving us for the moment alone.

'A real, homelike welcome,' said Sybil unenthusiastically. 'I'm not given to complaining, but just now . . .'

'I know,' I said. 'This doesn't feel too hospitable and if you're about to say, Dale, that you can't abide such a state of affairs, I'd agree with you! We're all tired out and longing to be warm, fed, and asleep. Ah. Something is happening.'

Mary Haxby had come back, carrying a big basket full of firewood. She set about lighting a fire in the dismal hearth, bringing it to life and somewhat mitigating the bleakness of the place. The unsmiling Angelica Ames reappeared a few moments later, followed by another woman, even smaller and more inclined to scuttle than Margaret Beale. Both were laden with sheets and fur bedcovers. They went up the stairs and into one of the guest chambers, and then Mary Haxby, having got the fire going and filled the fuel basket by the hearth, went up after them, carrying the big basket, in which there was still a good supply of firewood. Faintly, we could hear Mistress Ames' voice, supervising the making of a bed.

Presently, they returned to us. Mary and the little scuttling woman, whose name was apparently Annie, were sent away and Mistress Ames said that our rooms were ready. We accompanied her up to the gallery and she showed us into our quarters.

'We have put Mistress Stannard and Mistress Jester together,' she said, opening a door and motioning to me and Sybil to go in. 'Your tirewoman and her husband are next door, in accordance with your wishes. Our guest chambers are nothing special, but we hope they're adequate. They're not much used,' said Mistress Ames, standing with her hands folded at her waist and watching us as we took in our surroundings. 'To begin with, they weren't used at all! The house was chosen for us because it was reasonably priced, but at first it was much too big and this guest wing was just a nuisance that had to be kept dusted. At the start, there were just four of us though Mistress Gould already hoped that others would join us. We rattled around in the place until they did, I must say, though now that there are sixteen of us, we sometimes feel quite crowded. Now, of course, we use the guest wing for guests in the usual way, though we have only a few. This is a lonely place and benighted travellers would find only poor hospitality in the village.'

'And providing for guests was part of Benedictine life,' I said. 'We do know that you live more or less as Benedictines did. There is no secret about that, apparently.'

'Quite right. I see that you are well informed about us. Now, if you wish for anything, there is a bell on the table down in the guest hall. Ring it loudly – you had better go to the hall door and ring it there; the walls of this house are quite thick and it may not be heard otherwise. Warm water and towels will be brought up shortly and a meal will be served to you down in the guest hall in an hour or so. We ladies have our own refectory in the main part of the house, but we eat in silence, which wc would not inflict on our guests. I will leave you now. Mistress Haxby will bring your manservant up when he comes in.'

She nodded in farewell and left us. We stood looking round us. Sybil said: 'Well, I agree that it's much better than being out in a blizzard.'

'We can give thanks with due formality,' I said drily. 'There's a prie dieu over there in that corner. With candles, ready to be lit.'

'We may as well light them now,' said Sybil. 'It's nowhere near nightfall but it's so gloomy in here that we won't be able to see to unpack.' She took one of the candles to the fire to kindle it, and then used it to ignite the others. 'I see we have a graphic crucifix on the wall above the prie dieu,' she remarked. 'It's plain enough which faith our hostesses follow. They don't hide it.'

'I never thought to see that kind of thing in England,' said Dale, with a sniff.

I sent Dale to inspect her room next door while Sybil and I went to warm our hands by our hearth. The fuel basket beside it was now full but the fireplace was tiny and the fire didn't give off very much warmth, even though the room was far from spacious. Nor was it warmly furnished. The walls were of bare stone, with no hangings, and the crucifix was the only ornament. The bed had no hangings either, though it was a four-poster with the fittings for them. As it was, its uprights and crossbars stood starkly, skeletal and uncompromising. Still, the window was glazed and the bed was at least wide enough for two and had pillows and a fur coverlet. A utensil for calls of nature lay beside it.

There was a press for clothes and Sybil, having thawed out a little, crossed to the window and raised the wide window seat to reveal a further storage space beneath. I wandered to the window as well. It was leaded, with small panes, little upright oblongs, of the same thick, blue-green glass as in the Earl of Morton's anteroom. It let in a little light but there was no seeing out of it.

Wanting to know what was outside, I unlatched it and pushed it open. It was equipped with shutters, which at the moment had been latched back, out of the way. Our room overlooked the back of the house. Immediately below was a garden, now deep in snow, forlorn and empty, though a row of pea-sticks and some small, leafless bushes and what looked like the outlines of some raised flowerbeds suggested that in summer it might be a pleasant enough mixture of kitchen garden and place for recreation. The wall which we had passed through by way of the gatehouse apparently went all the way round the place, for the garden was bounded by what looked a continuation of the same wall. Beyond this, the hillside continued upwards and as the wind blew the curtains of falling snow this way and that, I caught a glimpse of a distant crest of moorland, remote and lonely.

Turning from the window, I heard a welcome sound. 'I think that's Brockley's voice,' I said.

He tapped on our door only a few moments later and we let him in. He was carrying our saddlebags, which he put down on the floor.

'This isn't the jolliest place I've ever seen in my life,' he remarked. He had shed his damp cloak and hat, and exchanged his boots for slippers. 'Our horses are settled. The stabling's good. The ladies have a couple of heavy horses and two riding horses and one of those is a really well-bred animal, a striking strawberry roan. I saw a couple of side saddles in the tackroom. I don't think our hostesses live quite the enclosed lives of the Benedictine nuns they're said to be imitating. And there are no red chalk signs anywhere in the stable or the tackroom. I made sure I looked and so did Joseph, though I think Walter Cogge was wondering why we kept peering into corners. It really would be tricky, you know, deciding where to put such marks. How *does* one find a place where someone who was looking for them could find them, but they wouldn't be noticed by the wrong people, who would say tut-tut and wipe them away with a sponge?'

'There are certainly no red chalk signs here,' I said, glancing round at the bare walls. 'Nor in your room, presumably. You have a fire there? I sent Dale in to see what kind of cheer the ladies had prepared for the two of you.'

'Yes, there's a fire. Fran has built it up and is thawing herself out – poor Fran, she was so cold! I'm thankful to have got her under cover. She'll come back in a moment and do your unpacking. Our room is exactly like this. I understand that we've been given the two biggest guest bedchambers. Joseph is all right, too. The man Cogge has two very comfortable rooms over the tackroom, and a spare pallet. He seems to be a friendly fellow.'

'They're going to send us washing water and food,' I said. 'We're to eat in the guest hall downstairs, so that we can talk to each other. The ladies dine in a religious silence, it seems.'

'I wonder when we can see the chief lady of this establishment,' said Brockley. 'Not that there's any real hurry. In weather like this, I should think we'll be here for days!'

'I fear we are,' I said, somewhat grimly.

We made ourselves at home as well as we could. The water and towels arrived, along with basins and soap. Sybil's calves were very sore where her stirrup leathers had rubbed, and even if the weather had been good, I didn't think we could have ridden back the next day. Sybil needed two days at least to get over this. Dale and I had managed our skirts a little better and our calves were no more than slightly reddened and should be all right after a night's rest. Dale helped to bathe Sybil's abraded skin in warm water and clean it with soap and then, resourcefully, sacrificed a spare petticoat to create makeshift leggings which we could all use when next we got into our saddles.

We all helped with the unpacking. The purse of money for John of Evesham's book, I placed carefully in a drawer at the bottom of the clothes press with some shawls and spare sleeves on top of it. My formal gown was regrettably crushed after travelling in a saddlebag, and so was the amber-coloured dress that Sybil had brought for best. Dale produced a smoothing iron, heated it on the fire, and got the worst of the creases out of the two gowns before tenderly stowing them in the chest under the window seat. We did not wish to wear them here. Stonemoor House didn't feel like the place for finery. Then we went down to await our dinner.

This, when it came, was quite good, though not exhilarating. There was a stew with dumplings afloat in it along with beans and pieces of meat – salted pork, by the taste of it – and we each had one small wedge of a game pie. This was actually excellent, but it only amounted to a few mouthfuls.

'They weren't expecting guests in this weather,' said Brockley acutely. 'They were having game pie themselves but they didn't have enough for extra mouths.'

The bread was rye bread, black and heavy though freshly baked, and to follow there was a dish of preserved plums and an egg custard. There was also a flagon of white wine. The wine was thin and sharp; it quenched one's thirst but not much else could be said for it.

Plump Mary Haxby and little scuttling Annie came to clear the dishes afterwards, arriving unexpectedly and silently. Margaret Beale had had ordinary outdoor shoes which clip-clopped as such shoes normally do, but the ladies we had met indoors all moved silently. Their shoes looked substantial but must have been soled with something that deadened sound.

When the clearing was finished, a lady we had not seen before came into the guest hall and stood for a moment, surveying us. Then, in a thick Yorkshire accent, she said: 'I'm Mistress Bella Yates, sister to our Principal, Mistress Philippa Gould. My sister's that busy just now but she'll see thee coom the morning. She says as thee've business here. She says I'm to ask what it's about as she wants to be prepared, like.'

I wondered if the unknown Philippa Gould would resemble her sister. If so, then surely we had little to fear in this house. Bella Yates didn't just speak with a strong local accent, she was also decidedly rustic, though she was not a typical Yorkshire woman, for the folk of Yorkshire tend to fairness and Bella did not. She was another example of someone whose parents had named her unwisely. The word *bella* is the Latin for *beautiful* but Bella Yates wasn't. She was short and thick-shouldered, with a face both soft of flesh and heavy of bone, a swarthy complexion and small dark eyes, like currants in dough, although they did not have the bloom of healthy currants, but were opaque, hiding the thoughts of their owner.

She stood with her hands folded at her waist, awaiting our reply.

I said: 'It is quite simple. Mistress Gould has been in correspondence with the royal court – in particular with one Doctor Dee – about a book that she wishes to sell and he wishes to buy. We have brought the money and have been asked to collect the book.'

The currant eyes snapped. '*That* book? That heathen thing? What are decent Christian folk wanting with that?'

'We're not buying it ourselves,' I said mildly. 'It is wanted by Doctor Dee, the queen's . . . adviser.' The word *magician* might not, I thought, be very pleasing to Bella Yates.

'Shameful, that's what it is. That book should be burnt. Full of heresy and numbers in the infidel fashion and a wicked blasphemous drawing, that's what it is.'

'Nevertheless, we are here to collect it. Surely your . . . your Principal has been expecting someone to call for it.'

'Ho! Yes, so she has, and for a long time now. Very well. I shall tell my sister. She can sell it to thee if so be she wants. No one else'll have any say. She's our Principal right enough.'

She turned away and went out, to be replaced a moment later by Angelica Ames, who announced that Mary Haxby would bring us more wood so that we could make up our fires before we slept.

'It is cold tonight,' she said. 'Would any of you care for a hot herbal posset? Mistress Yates, whom you have just seen, is skilled at such things.' A contemptuous expression crossed her face. 'Some of the villagers come to her for medicines, but others regard her gift as witchcraft and mutter about it. They are simple people and easily affrighted by things they can't understand.'

I thought about Gladys Morgan, back in Hawkswood. 'At home, I have a servant who was once, quite wrongly, accused of witchcraft because she is clever with herbal medicines. It's very unfair.'

'Quite. Well, would you? Like any hot possets, I mean.'

We all declined. I don't think any of us feared that Bella Yates would actually poison us, but she obviously didn't like us. As Brockley remarked after Mistress Ames had gone: 'Well,

I hope we don't have to stay here too long. I can't believe there's danger here, but I don't think we're all that welcome, either.'

In the night, I woke suddenly and found myself cocking my head, trying to catch the sound which had disturbed me. Beside me, Sybil also stirred and then sat up. 'Ursula! Surely I can hear chanting.'

We had closed the window shutters before we slept but there was some light from the embers of the fire. I slid from the bed and made my way, shivering, to the window, opening it and unfastening the shutters so that I could peer out. Snow was no longer falling. There were patches of starlight between the clouds and I could see the glimmer of the snow that covered everything outside.

To my left, I could make out the back of the main house and at the far end I could see that an extension jutted out. Its bulk was just visible. I couldn't actually see the outline of any windows, but there was at least one, for there was a faint vertical line of light, such as one often sees when a shutter doesn't fit perfectly. The room within must be lit with candles. On such a night, one would have expected the world to be full of the muffling silence of snow, but the sound of chanting was quite unmistakeable, and it came from that lit room.

Leaning out and straining my ears, I realized that I recognized the chant. I pulled my head in, closed shutters and window, and came back to the bed. 'They're chanting matins as Benedictine nuns would do. It must be midnight or close to it.'

'How do you know?' Sybil asked sleepily.

'When I was still living at Faldene with my uncle and aunt, the year before I ran off to marry Gerald, Queen Mary came to the throne and the state religion was changed to Catholic. On Christmas Eve that year – 1553, it was – Uncle Herbert made all the Faldene household attend a midnight mass in the Faldene church. An old-fashioned matins chant was sung – the one that used to be sung in abbeys before King Henry abolished them. The vicar was trying to revive the old chants, as far as his little choir of village singers could manage to learn them. It was to please Queen Mary, he told us. He had been an earnest Protestant and I expect he was afraid of losing his position. He was currying favour, in case the queen had any spies in the district. That's how I know what matins sounds like. My aunt and uncle approved. They still cling to the old faith, even now, and back then they were pleased to see Queen Mary on the throne, and I think the sound of matins made them feel quite nostalgic.'

'Well, we knew that the ladies here are living as unofficial nuns,' said Sybil.

'I know. But it's eerie – actually hearing it. It's like an echo from the past.'

'Let's just go back to sleep,' said Sybil.

TEN
The Beautiful Book

We rose early next morning, though someone was ahead of us, for when we descended to the guest hall, we were pleased to find an encouraging welcome. A fire was already lit and breakfast things were laid. Someone must have been aware that we were up, for Mary Haxby and Annie appeared almost at once, bringing the food. Breakfast consisted of porridge, with salt, in the northern fashion, black bread and honey and small ale, hardly luxurious but at least there was plenty of it, and we were thankful for the fire, for our bedchamber hearths by then held only grey ash and the morning was savagely cold. Outside, it was snowing again.

Mistress Haxby told us that we would be sent for presently, and asked us to wait in the hall until we were fetched. Mistress Ames did the fetching, at about ten o'clock.

'Your manservant is to attend you as well?' she enquired, realizing that Brockley had risen to his feet with the rest of us and made it plain that he meant to be one of the party. Mistress Ames eyed him with disapproval. Brockley, who had dressed in a very decent dark-brown doublet and hose, finished with a neat ruff and polished footwear, looked blandly back at her.

'It is my preference, whenever possible,' I said. 'Is it permitted?'

It seemed that it was, though grudgingly. Mistress Ames shrugged bony shoulders but said, 'As you wish,' and led the way. Once out of the guest hall, we crossed the vestibule and went through the low door we had noticed the previous day, which led into the main part of the house.

The chill hit us like a blow.

The door led into a short passage, which was icily cold.

There were a couple of doors on the right and some windows
on the left. The windows were like the ones in the guest
bedchambers, admitting little light, and as the world outside
was thick with falling snow under a grey, heavy sky, the
passage was very dim. It was also silent. It presently led out
into another vestibule, a much bigger one than the guest
entrance, with what was evidently the main front door to the
left. This had windows on either side of it. They were
mullioned, with bigger panes, but the glass was the same as
in the other windows we had seen and snow was piled up on
their outer sills, so that here, too, little light could get in.

There was little light anywhere. Above us was a ceiling
criss-crossed with heavy beams, but it was high up, and the
shadows there hung like dark mist. Indeed, shadows seemed
to cluster in every corner and just as in the guest quarters, all
the walls were stone, all the floors flagstoned, and there were
no hangings, rugs, or rushes and no furniture to soften the
bleakness. From the floor, the cold struck upwards through
the soles of our shoes. It was depressing. The guest quarters,
where we did at least have furniture and fires and beds with
fur coverlets, seemed like sybaritic luxury by comparison.

Unlike the passage, however, the vestibule wasn't silent. We
could hear raised voices coming from behind a door to our
right. Angelica Ames had turned towards it but stopped as the
voices crescendoed and then took a step backwards as the door
opened, spilling Bella Yates and another lady out into the
vestibule. I say *spilling* because it really was like that; they
seemed to topple out rather than step, close together and locked
in argument. They saw us at once, and Bella tugged at the
other's sleeve, only to be shaken impatiently aside.

'Yes, Bella, I can see them. Our visitors are here, and I repeat,
you had no business to come intruding on me when you knew
I was about to receive them. Now will you please . . .?'

'If only you would listen! Mother Philippa, I *implore*
you . . .'

'Yes, you may well implore me!' So the tall woman was
presumably Philippa Gould, the Principal and the sister of
Bella, though in Benedictine fashion, her subordinates called
her Mother and that evidently went for Bella as well. If they

really were sisters, they were not in the least alike. Then I remembered that Cecil had said Bella was actually Philippa's half-sister, a natural daughter. So they had had the same father but different mothers and different upbringings. *Very* different, it now seemed to me, for Philippa Gould had a thoroughly educated accent and an unmistakeable air of command. Her head was tilted back and her chin haughtily raised. 'I have had to put up with so much from you that I would be justified in casting you out of Stonemoor . . .'

'Tha wouldna do that to me, me that's your own sister!' Bella was pawing at Mistress Gould like an importunate puppy.

Mistress Gould, glancing towards us once more, pulled herself away and said fiercely: 'Mortification of the flesh may well be good for the soul but hunger and cold aren't good for the body and we shall all be ill if we are forced to endure too much of either. I insist . . .'

'What's the matter with thee? I'm telling thee we shouldna . . .!'

'Be quiet, Bella! I don't agree and the responsibility is mine. The supplies of salt, candles, and firewood that we need are to be ordered at once. Walter Cogge is to go into Thorby and see to it. Do as you are told. Now go about your daily tasks and let me attend to my guests.'

'Salt and candles! I tell thee, thee'll find out! Thee'll find out I'm right!'

'Bella! Go!'

Muttering, heavy shoulders bent, Bella went, departing through a further door. As she thrust it open, a faint, homely smell of baking bread and savoury stew wafted out and then faded as she shut the door behind her. Philippa Gould stared exasperatedly after her for a moment and then straightened her wimple, pushing a strand of dark hair out of sight. She was dressed like all the others we had seen, in a dark-blue gown with a wimple and a very small ruff. She came towards us, her right hand outstretched.

'Mistress Stannard, I believe? With Mistress Jester and your servants, the Brockleys. I trust I have your names correctly. Please come this way. Thank you for bringing them, Angelica.'

'My pleasure,' said Mistress Ames, though her voice didn't

suggest pleasure at all. She too departed, following Bella. We accompanied Philippa back into the room from which she and Bella had come. It turned out to be a study, blessedly warm because here there was a good fire. It was more normal than anywhere we had yet seen in Stonemoor, for there was a desk, strewn in businesslike fashion with papers and writing materials. There was a small silver bell too. There were also some padded stools with colourful embroidery, and a tapestry on one wall.

'You have slept well, I trust,' said Mistress Gould, indicating that we should sit down and taking a stool herself. 'And eaten? Our fare is plain but filling. I am sorry you had to witness that scene just now. I fear that my sister has over-strict attitudes and believes that to have sufficient to eat, and to be warm enough to work and sleep adequately, is a kind of sin. She covers this up by constantly pretending that we can't afford it. We can. Not that we are as well off as I would like, which is one reason why I am happy to sell John of Evesham's book of strange lore. I understand that you have come to buy it. I . . . I am quite surprised. After such a long time . . . such a long wait . . .'

She sounded almost confused, which surprised me, but then seemed to shake herself free. 'I am very glad to see you. I – well, all of us – have been waiting for an emissary from Doctor Dee to arrive but you are the first to do so although we have been given to understand that two others had been sent, before you, but for some reason failed to reach us.' She shook her head in puzzled fashion. 'They hadn't been here. We could make no sense of that.'

'Who was it who gave you to understand?' I asked.

'Two officers from York, from the High Sheriff's office,' said Philippa Gould. 'A new High Sheriff has just taken office, a Sir William Fairfax – very anxious, I fancy, to make his mark by finding the lost men. They came twice, the same two officers, once asking about . . . Master Hardwicke I think was the name. Then again, enquiring after a Master Spelton. But we could tell them nothing. I believe the sheriff's officers also tried to question the shepherd who lives on his own about two miles from here, but all they got from him' – she gave us an austere smile – 'was rude answers. He'd never harm anyone, though. Walter Cogge has met him in York at wool-selling time. The man is just a natural solitary who prefers sheep to people. One of the sheriff's officers did say something about the two missing men having some other errand, in Scotland, and that it might have brought them into danger. He was rather excited about it. He said it was an unusual case.'

She sounded indulgent, as though the man concerned were a small boy who had been shown a popinjay or been offered some exotic treat, such as an orange. 'He was quite young and I really think that being ordered to ask after men who had gone missing when on some kind of official errand for the queen was a thrill for him. The other man was a little older and more serious and I think felt uncomfortable, questioning ladies. He kept apologizing for troubling us. Though, the second time, he did insist on searching the house.'

Indulgence turned to indignation. 'I was polite, and personally escorted them through the various rooms, even the row of little rooms where we all sleep! We have separate rooms, not a dormitory. There were already several bedchambers upstairs when we moved in, and when our numbers began to increase, I had further partitions and doors put in to give each of us some privacy. I couldn't believe that the sheriff's officers really imagined we might be hiding the lost men on the premises! Well, I don't think they did imagine it – one of them at least was apologetic, as I said. However, you seem to have found your way to us and you are very welcome. You have the money with you?'

'It is in my bedchamber,' I said. 'Can we see the book first?'

'Yes, of course. It is in our library. We will go there in a moment.' Mistress Gould scanned our faces thoughtfully. Her own was a patrician face, I thought, her nose thin and high-bridged, her arched eyebrows also thin, her mouth well cut and firm. Her eyes were dark, like Bella's, though beautifully set, with a far more open expression.

'I take it,' she said, 'that you realize that all the ladies here are of the Catholic persuasion and that in this house we live more or less as nuns. This is known to the authorities and is permitted. I say this so that you will not go scurrying home, full of an eager desire to report us. Such things have happened, when guests have come our way.'

'Yes, we did know,' I said. 'I have said so, to Mistress Ames.'

'Our way of life will not impinge on you,' said Mistress Gould. 'You will live separately, in the guest quarters, until such time as the snow melts and you can go on your way. You can't go yet, of course. It is two or three feet deep outside and still coming down.' She stood up. 'I will take you to the library now.'

We trooped after her across the shadowy vestibule and out through the door which Bella and Angelica had taken. Once more, a smell of cooking greeted us, bringing friendliness into a gloomy gallery. The windows to our left were as inadequate as all the rest. There were doors on the right-hand side, and Mistress Gould, producing a set of keys from her girdle, unlocked one of them. She led us into a room with bookshelves on one wall, laden with a considerable number of books, as well as piles of documents and a number of matching boxes in a brown, glossy wood, probably walnut, with brass clasps. There was a desk and some stools so that anyone wishing to consult a volume could do so at leisure, and a triple-branched candlestick was there to cast light on the print. Here again, the windows were not much use, least of all when snow was piled against them.

Mistress Gould went straight to the shelves and lifted down one of the boxes, which she placed on the desk. 'We have a number of valuable volumes here,' she said, 'and we take good care of them. I had a set of boxes made, in three different sizes. They protect their contents from damp, and insects – even from mice. Mice did once get at a book of some value and nibbled it badly.'

She unlatched the box lid and put it back. Then, surprisingly, there was a hiatus, during which she stood quite still, looking down into the box, and I heard her draw in a sharp breath. But at length, very gently, she lifted a book out of the box and set it down on the table. She saw our expressions and smiled.

'It is so beautiful,' she said. 'We do take great care of it, and I don't open its box very often. So, every time I do look at it, I am startled anew and catch my breath. It is such a privilege to have such a book here. It makes me feel reverent. Always, I am wary of touching it, for fear of doing it harm. I suppose its purchaser will want to study it, so he will have to handle it! I hope he will take care. Now.'

We crowded round to see the book properly. It was bound in pale leather, which had perhaps been white originally though age had evidently discoloured it, muting it into a dull cream. On the front, was a crescent moon and seven stylized stars in gold leaf, and a title, also in gold leaf, although I could recognize only a few letters of the archaic script.

'We believe it was made in the twelfth century,' said Mistress Gould. 'Though it is not known where it was made. It was brought here by one of our ladies, Mistress Eleanor Overton, from Gloucester. Her family had owned it for centuries. Poor Eleanor, she has no family now. She is the only surviving child of her parents, neither of whom had any living relatives left by the time she was grown up. They never found a husband for her, and when they died, she was much alone. She had heard of us through a friend – Katherine Trayne, who joined us not so very long ago. Eleanor decided to come as well and bring this book as a kind of dowry.'

She turned a few pages for us. As we expected, it was not a printed book but an illustrated manuscript, hand-written and painted. Capital letters were entangled with brightly coloured and minuscule pictures of birds and animals, sun, moon and stars. The birds and animals included some legendary creatures, such as a unicorn and a camelopard. They were a curious choice to illustrate a book that was essentially about astronomy, I thought. The Latin script stood out as clear and black as though it had been penned yesterday, though I still could not read it for although I knew a good deal of Latin, the lettering inside was as archaic as that on the cover. There were charts as well as text, which seemed to show the sun and the movements of planets, though in what seemed a very complex way. I could make little of any of this and nor, I knew, could my companions. The colours were all fresh and bright. Sybil, wide-eyed, cautiously fingered a square in which the capital letter A, in gold, was set in a cerise background, with two tiny birds, cerulean blue and shaped like swifts, one above and one below the crosspiece of the A.

'It's exquisite,' I said sincerely. Sybil and Brockley murmured in agreement.

'It pleases you? I am at heart unwilling to let it go,' said Mistress Gould. She was staring at the book as fixedly as though she were trying to memorize it. 'I can barely endure it to be touched and to think that it will actually be studied – may be handled carelessly – truly horrifies me. Only, the money would be welcome. There are improvements I would like to make to this house.'

I could well understand *that*. I said, 'We will be glad to buy this on behalf of Doctor Dee.'

Philippa Gould closed the book and placed it reverently back in its box. 'I will keep it here in its place until you are ready to leave. Then you can pay for it and take it away. It is so precious that I would rather it stayed on its usual shelf until the last moment, instead of being kept in a bedchamber, where things are being moved all the time and cleaning is done. As you saw, the door to the library is kept locked. Only I and Angelica Ames and Margaret Beale, who was the doorkeeper when you arrived, have keys. We three are all thoroughly literate and educated in Latin, and we were among the four who were the founding members of our little community. My sister Bella was the fourth, but although she is literate – my doing, since she could neither read nor write when first she came here – she does not often consult books. I have tried to instruct her in several branches of learning, in fact, but she is not responsive.'

'This is clearly a valuable collection,' Sybil observed. 'Where did you come by so many volumes?'

'I brought some of them with me from my father's house,' said Philippa. 'Father is something of a scholar, as was his father before him. Between them, they assembled a considerable library. My grandfather came from Italy, as I believe John of Evesham himself did originally, and had studied there. He spoke several languages,' she added proudly.

Here was the likely reason why Philippa and Bella were both dark. An Italian grandfather would account for it.

Philippa was saying: 'My father picked out a number of

books and let me bring them here. He is a man of business and doesn't have as much time to read as he would like. Other volumes were brought by Angelica and Margaret. Except for Eleanor Overton's donation, that is! We take good care of this room.'

'Quite,' I said.

And suddenly, the audience with Philippa Gould was over. We left the library, to find Mistress Ames waiting for us in the gallery. Mistress Gould nodded to us and went away, while Angelica requested us to come with her, and led us back to the guest quarters. Left alone in the guest hall, we looked at each other.

'Breathtaking,' said Sybil. 'Quite beautiful.'

I nodded, but distractedly. Mistress Gould had puzzled me. She gave the impression of being highly educated and very dignified, and that she should be so very sensitive as to pause in wonder every time she set eyes on a book which must surely be familiar to her seemed surprising.

Brockley said: 'I wonder why she didn't ask for payment at once, and hand the book over. She can't really suppose it would come to harm in your room, madam. Why should it? I thought there was something strange in her manner. Did you?'

'Yes,' I said. 'I did. It was as though our presence here confused her, somehow. But why?'

ELEVEN
Light and Shadow

For the next few days, the bitter weather continued, and there was no question of leaving Stonemoor. Each morning, we looked hopefully from our windows, but the world remained bound and hushed in deep snow, white and unfriendly under leaden skies. Some people managed to get about, though. In between the snowstorms, to our surprise, we saw a rider, well wrapped up in a heavy cloak but riding side saddle and therefore, presumably, one of the ladies, out on horseback in the snow. She was walking her steed – it was the striking strawberry roan that Brockley had mentioned – up the hill behind the house.

Walter Cogge came to ask if he could have Brockley's and Joseph's help in clearing some of the track down to the village. I agreed, of course, and we saw them all toiling with spades, working their way down towards a couple of small figures who were struggling to get the track clear from the village end. The next morning, we watched a cartload of something, pulled by a couple of straining oxen, struggle up from the village and in at the gate, to be unloaded in the courtyard. We recognized Silas Butterworth and the goblin-like Will Grimes as the men in charge of the wagon.

'Provisions of some sort,' Brockley said, as we stood in a row and stared from a window in the guest hall. 'That's a side of beef – the ladies have had an ox slaughtered, I fancy. That's probably a keg of ale or wine and that's a sack of flour, for sure. There are supposed to be sixteen women under this roof, not that we ever see much of them. They must take some feeding.'

He was right in saying that we saw few of the ladies. We were waited on exclusively by Angelica Ames and Margaret Beale, with Mary Haxby helping them, clearly as a subordinate, and occasionally, the scuttling Annie. We saw no one else, though we did learn some of the customs of the place. The ladies addressed Philippa Gould as Mother and each other as Sister, but that was among themselves. To us, they were Mistress so and so. We were already comfortable with that, and accepted the rules.

We remained in the guest quarters, although to mitigate the tedium, Angelica brought us chess and backgammon sets and at Sybil's request provided embroidery frames, some silks, and two cushion covers, with half-completed embroidery, which gave some occupation to me, Sybil, and Dale. We ladies never went outside, though Brockley did, since as well as lending a hand with clearing snow from the track he also spent a good deal of time in the stables, helping Joseph to care for our horses and developing a friendship of sorts with Walter Cogge.

'Who isn't what he seems, madam,' he said, as he came in for supper on the second day. 'He wasn't there to start with this morning and I filled the mangers on my own, and then he did come, but there was something – different – about him and after a minute or two, I knew what it was. He smelt of incense.'

'This is a Catholic household,' I said mildly. 'Cecil knows that the man who acts as groom and bailiff for the women here is probably their priest as well. I expect he'd been saying Mass.'

'Here in England, I *never* thought to find myself in a house where Mass is said and no one does anything about it,' grumbled Dale.

'I doubt if he's doing much harm,' I said. 'Anyway, as we know, the authorities are already aware of him. I think we'd better close our eyes and ears to his activities. And our noses.'

'We can't very well close our ears,' said Sybil. 'We've heard matins being sung.'

'Yes, I know,' I said, somewhat tartly. 'Mistress Gould said openly that they live as much like Benedictine nuns as they can and Cecil thinks that Walsingham wants them left alone for some subtle purpose of his own. We must mind our own business.'

Chess, backgammon, and embroidery barely filled those three days, though. Time dragged. The feeling of being trapped grew on me steadily and I felt nervous in a formless yet very real way. I wanted to get away from Stonemoor. I slept badly at night and once had a confused and alarming nightmare, in which I was searching for John of Evesham's book and thought I had found it, except that when I tried to pick it up, it turned into a demon which leered at me from an evil face and bared hideous, yellowed fangs at me. I woke suddenly and sat up. My heart pounded and I was sweating. The dark of the night seemed terrifying and only the solid presence of Sybil, breathing peacefully beside me, kept panic at bay. In my mind, something connected with the dream – an idea, a memory, I didn't know what – nagged irritatingly and then faded. Whatever it was, had gone. I tried to breathe calmly, like Sybil, and gradually the incipient panic receded.

Dimly, in the distance, right on the edge of sound, I once more heard chanting. It couldn't be matins this time; I knew I had been asleep for many hours, far past midnight. This was probably one of the early services – lauds or prime. Because Uncle Herbert and Aunt Tabitha had preferred the old faith (they had deplored King Henry's destruction of the monasteries), I knew the names of the Benedictine chants.

I knew I should not be alarmed because I could hear chanting now. We sometimes heard it during the day as well, and were growing accustomed to it. It was natural enough if the ladies really were following the Benedictine order of services. I lay down again and tried once more to sleep but couldn't. I stayed uneasily awake until dawn. I was thankful when daybreak edged through a crack in our shutters and I could get up and open them to the light, such as it was, since the day outside was iron-grey as usual and it was much too cold to leave the window open as well as the shutters. Light still had to filter through those thick panes of glass. Even so, normal daylight helped to smooth ugly images away.

The sense of imprisonment bore heavily on all our spirits. Most of the time, apart from the occasional chanting, Stonemoor House was not only shadowy but very quiet and the silence was oppressive, as though our, ears were stuffed with wool.

The slightest sound from the outside would have us hurrying to the window, to relieve our boredom by watching such thrilling spectacles as Walter Cogge briskly shovelling more snow, creating paths between the gate, the doorways and the stable or, once, a couple of cats fighting. Our longing for life and movement was as great as that.

'This house needs people in it,' Sybil said once, sitting with needle upraised over her embroidery frame, and cocking her head as if to listen for sounds that were not there.

'It does have sixteen ladies,' I said mildly.

'No, I mean *real* people.'

'But aren't the ladies real?' said Dale, genuinely confused.

Sybil snorted. 'You know what I mean! It's a house that ought to be full of movement and voices. It needs a family – husband, wife, servants bustling about, children running and playing, somebody's old mother or aunt always wanting errands run, somebody practising a spinet, visitors coming to dine . . . *life.*'

'I know,' I agreed. 'It feels like a house of the dead. If only the sun would shine!'

On the fourth day, we awoke to the sound of rain, and the air felt noticeably warmer. The rain fell all day, washing the snow away and blowing against the windows, and the sound of running gutters was everywhere to be heard. The cheerless stone walls around us were suddenly kinder to the eye, even showing glints of flint and crystal here and there. We retired that night feeling heartened, and on the fifth morning there was the longed-for sunshine, in a clear, washed sky.

Looking out of our window, we saw for the first time the outcrops that had given the house its name. Now that the snow was gone, we could see that they littered the hillside as though a giant wagon, laden with stones, had at some time overturned.

'I think,' said Sybil, when we had breakfasted and Mary Haxby had cleared the table, 'that we might put a few things into our saddlebags. I fancy we'll be able to get away soon – today, even! Tomorrow, anyway.'

'Tomorrow, most likely,' Brockley said. 'I understand from Cogge that there's been some flooding along the road we'd have to take, going back to the Thwaites' farm. We might do best to wait a little. Still, the horses can be exercised properly now; they've been cooped up too long. Walter and Joseph and I have done what we can with them, leading them round and round the stable yard, and the heavy horses are quite stolid, but ours'll be mighty fresh if they don't stretch their legs before we start our journey.'

'I'll make a start on the packing,' said Dale, and rising from the table hurried up the stairs. 'I'll help,' said Sybil, and followed her. Brockley, showing no immediate signs of leaving for the stable, leant back with a sigh. 'I'm thankful to feel we'll soon be away from here, madam,' he remarked. 'Fran will be glad, too. She doesn't like this place at all.'

'Nor do I,' I said. 'I shall pray, tonight, that we can pay for that wretched book, collect it, and be off in the morning.'

We smiled at each other, easy in each other's company. We had never been lovers in the physical sense but we really had come very close to it once, and we had found a substitute intimacy in a link between our minds. It was strong, strong enough on occasion to arouse Fran Dale's jealousy. I sometimes thought that Queen Elizabeth, who was, after all, my half-sister, had a similar relationship with her favourite, Robert Dudley, the Earl of Leicester. Many people thought she was, or had been, his mistress but I knew it wasn't so. Their bond, too, was one of the mind.

At length, however, I said: 'Well, Sybil and Dale are already preparing for our journey back to the Thwaites. I had better go upstairs and . . .'

'Ursula!'

'Ma'am!'

Up on the gallery, Sybil and Dale had burst out of our room and were calling to me together as they rushed down the stairs. Both were wide-eyed, as if with shock. 'Please come!' Sybil gasped as she reached us.

'And Roger too. We've found something!' cried Dale.

Brockley and I both sprang up. 'Whatever is it?' I demanded.

Dale started to answer but Sybil gave her a silencing push and in a lowered voice, as though she feared eaves-droppers, she hissed: 'Upstairs, in the window chest! Come quickly!'

We sped up the stairs in a body. Either Sybil or Dale had opened the window and our room, because for once it was full of bright sunshine, looked completely different from the bleak place it had been hitherto. Sybil's and my saddlebags were on the bed and the lid of the chest below the window seat was thrown up.

'I went to the chest to take out the dresses I put there,' Dale said, pointing, 'and Mistress Jester came to help and . . . see there! Mistress Jester and I both looked into the chest when we first got here, but there was hardly any light then, the whole room was so gloomy, and neither of us saw. Even now, I didn't understand at once but then Mistress Jester said . . .!'

'This time, I realized straight away,' said Sybil. '*Look!*'

Brockley and I gathered round, and saw.

It was a red chalk circle, quartered by a cross.

I looked at it, and the unease which I had felt about this house, even before I set out for it, quietly congealed into genuine fear.

'It was in shadow the first time I opened the chest,' Sybil said. 'Deep shadow – I just didn't see it! But this is just the kind of place where Master Spelton might have put it. Not too obvious, but where it might be found by someone who was on the watch for it!'

I took a grip on myself. 'So Christopher did come here!' I said. 'He *was* here. He must have slept in this very room! That woman – Mistress Gould – has lied to me, lied to all of us. All the ladies have lied, in a way. They must know why we are here, and if so, they must have recalled Christopher's visit. They must all have seen him or at least known he was here. What in God's name has been going on in this house?'

'Something has, that's for sure,' Brockley said. 'I was so certain at first,' he added ruefully, 'that there could be no danger here, but doubts about that have been creeping in, bit by bit. Well, here's the proof.' He frowned. 'I suppose no one actually looked for signs in this house. Mistress Gould said the men from York made a search but she didn't say that they opened cupboards and chests. They probably didn't. Would they have known about Master Spelton's signs, I wonder?'

'I expect Cecil gave full information to various county

sheriffs,' I said. 'Local constables would have been alerted and various private contacts that Cecil has in the north. Landowners and merchants and the like – he said as much to me. Most would have passed the work on to underlings – well, that's understandable; think of the area they had to cover! Details like secret signs might not have been passed down and even if they were, the sheriff's men might have hesitated to pry overmuch when they were going through a house full of women. Didn't Mistress Gould say that one of them was young, which probably means inexperienced, and that the other one kept apologizing? They might well have thought of Stonemoor as a great house, full of dignified ladies, and been a little awed by it and unwilling to poke about too thoroughly. Besides, they probably had instructions already, issued by Walsingham, not to harass the ladies of Stonemoor. The idea of searching this house might have embarrassed them.'

Sybil, reasonably, said: 'Well, now what do we do?'

'What I would like to do,' said Brockley grimly, 'is to seek a private interview with Mistress Gould, hold my dagger to her throat, and recommend her to explain herself.'

'Only you would never be able to make yourself cut her throat,' I said, 'nor would it be legal! You would find yourself on the gallows for it and she would know that perfectly well. No. I think we should simply get our hands on that book, get out of here as fast as possible, and report what we have found to the High Sheriff in York. His name is Sir William Fairfax, I believe. Let him take the responsibility after that.'

'Are we to go straight there, or keep to our plan of collecting the coach?' asked Brockley. 'If we go back to the Thwaites first, we would have to go in the opposite direction from York, and waste time.'

I thought about that for a moment. 'I think you should ride for York, and that Joseph should escort the rest of us to the Thwaites to collect the coach. Then we'll make for the main road and join you in York.'

'But just what is the report to say?' asked Sybil querulously. 'It's all such a muddle. Master Spelton must have been here since he left his sign, and that probably meant that he felt he was in danger here – but why should he? I don't understand.

I know none of us feels happy here but it's not reasonable. Why *should* there be danger in this house? Master Spelton didn't collect the book, obviously, because that's still in its place in the library. Does this sign mean that something happened to him *here*? And that he expected it to? But that Principal or Mother or whatever she calls herself, she exchanged letters with Doctor Dee, didn't she? She *wants* someone to buy the book. What's it all about?'

'We don't know,' I said. 'An enquiry needs to be made but not by us. I agree that it all sounds quite crazy but there must *be* an explanation!'

'I feel, madam,' said Brockley, 'that you should be the one to make the report.'

'I can write it, perhaps,' I said.

We all stood silent, thinking about it, and then, breaking into our silence, came mundane noises from somewhere outside. A horse whinnied and someone was shouting, apparently for attention. Whoever it was kept on shouting; presumably the attention wasn't forthcoming. Brockley made an impatient noise and then strode out of the room, to run down the stairs and cross the guest hall to look out of the windows on the far side. He turned to call up to us. 'It's Will Grimes! With a horse and cart this time and he's on his own. There doesn't seem to be anyone on duty at the gatehouse. I'm going out to see what's the matter.'

The rest of us trooped downstairs after him and made our way out into the courtyard in his wake, tramping through snow to reach him. We found a depressed-looking horse in the shafts of a cart loaded with two large bags of something and a crate, and Will Grimes, who greeted us with irritated demands to know where everyone had got to.

'Last time I was here, Mistress Bella Yates, she said as salt and candles was wanted and would Master Butterworth see to it. He arranges to supply the ladies with things like that. Well, we had plenty to hand – we allus lay things o' that sort in for the winter. We've sent to order more for us, so here's some for the ladies – two big bags of salt and a crate of candles. And here I am and the gate was open but who's in charge of it? No one that I can see! So who do I give this here to, and who's a-going to pay me?'

'Where's Walter Cogge?' said Brockley, looking round.

'Oh, him. Out on the farm – I seed him go through the village. Happen he'll be looking to see how many acres are under water. But meanwhile, what do I do with this?' Grimes gestured at the contents of the cart. 'And I was to ask for medicine for Master Butterworth – his guts are giving him trouble again. Bad trouble; looks right cheap, he does. Where *is* everyone? How can I go and look for someone? Ladies that's almost nuns don't like men wandering round their house.'

I said: 'We women will go and find someone. Meanwhile, you'd better come into the guest wing for the moment, Master Grimes. You'll be out of the wind there.'

Grumblingly, Will produced a cloth from the cart to fling over the back of the horse, and then came indoors with us. He and Brockley went into the guest hall, while Sybil, Dale, and I plunged through the door into the main house and into the chilly passage, searching for signs of life.

We reached the big main vestibule without finding any, but having got that far, realized that we could now hear something. There were raised voices, not that far off. 'I think it's this way,' said Sybil, making for the entrance to the gallery.

We went on, along the gallery and past the library. The voices, which by now were clearly those of women arguing, grew louder. At the end of the gallery, there was a staircase and beside it, a door, and the voices, a welter of indignant exclamations and protest, some of it hysterical, came from the other side of it. We stopped.

'What do we do?' Dale whispered. 'We can't just walk in on . . . dear heaven!' One voice, which sounded like that of Philippa Gould, had burst out so loudly that it overwhelmed all the rest.

'Why,' Philippa was demanding, in tones of the utmost exasperation, '*why* must I be burdened with such an ignorant and obstinate fool of a sister and why do so many of you listen to her? Tell me that!'

'Oh dear,' said Sybil. 'Surely there must be *someone*, in the kitchen, maybe. If only we could find them.'

'I think they're *all* in there,' I said.

'But we can't . . .'

I also felt that it would be highly ill-mannered and tactless
to intrude on what was obviously a major quarrel among the
ladies, but there was Will Grimes waiting in the guest room
until someone could be found to receive what he had brought
and pay him for it, and there was his horse, standing out in
the courtyard in the cold, even if it did have a cloth over its
back. And down in the village, Master Butterworth was ill and
in need of medicine. I took a deep breath and then, stepping
forward, I rapped on the door.

There was no result. A surge of exclamations had followed
Mistress Gould's outburst and my courteous knock hadn't
been heard. I tried again, louder. There was still no result. I
lifted the latch and edged the door open, just a little, so that
I could peer round it.

The ladies of Stonemoor were embattled. There is no other
word for it. They were, virtually, in two camps, facing each
other. Each had, so to speak, a spearhead in the form of one
lady standing forward of her supporters. One was Mistress
Philippa Gould and the other was Mistress Bella Yates. They
were both red in the face and trembling with fury and they were
confronting each other across a space of only a few feet. Crowded
behind each of them, was a group of ladies, presumably adding
up to the rest of Stonemoor's occupants. All were angry and
mulish and some of them were shouting. All were dressed alike,
in the dark-blue gowns and wimples and little ruffs, and it was
hard to recognize faces but I did see Mary Haxby and Annie
among Bella's supporters. Philippa's, who were slightly greater
in number, included Margaret Beale, whose bright brown eyes
were flashing fire, and Angelica Ames, who was actually shaking
her fist.

I had been very stealthy, but when the door opened, the
movement caught Mistress Gould's eye. Suddenly, she swung
round and stared at me. Then she pointed, and numerous pairs
of startled eyes followed her finger.

'*Quiet!*' She shouted it like a word of command from an
officer to a band of soldiers and quiet actually fell. 'Mistress
Stannard? What are you doing here? This is a private
meeting!'

'Will Grimes is here,' I said. 'He has brought salt and

candles and wants to buy medicine for Master Butterworth. We said we would try to find someone to attend to him.'

Mistress Gould flung up her hands. 'As though I hadn't enough to deal with. Very well.' She swung round again, glaring furiously at Bella Yates and her entourage. '*Very well.* It seems that although I am the senior lady here, your abbess in all but name, I am not to be allowed to discipline someone whose behaviour, frankly, has been not only disobedient but stupid, the action of someone who knows nothing about anything but still takes it upon herself to inflict her ignorant ideas on the rest of the world. *So be it!* Bella! Go and see this man Grimes and supply him with the medicine he requires. Go now!'

We got quickly out of the way as Bella went.

TWELVE
Dangerous Questions

'It's raining again,' said Brockley.

It was hardly necessary to say so, for we could all hear it. We were gathered in Sybil's and my room, and could hear the wind flinging it against the windows. We had returned from that uncomfortable discovery of the Stonemoor ladies in conflict to find that our rooms were once more as dismal as when we first saw them. The skies had now become so heavily overcast that we had lit candles. I knew, though, why Brockley had stated the obvious.

'We need to get away from here as soon as we can,' I said. 'If the weather keeps us here tomorrow . . .'

'If it does, we had better go on doing what we've been doing for most of our time here,' said Sybil. 'I think we'd do best to keep to the guest quarters, play games, sew, talk only of harmless subjects, make no attempt to enquire into anyone or anything, and pray for the skies to clear.'

'You are right. But the sooner we are on our way, the better,' said Brockley grimly. 'None of us knows what is wrong here but something is and we'd rather not be here when whatever it is comes to a head.'

Dale, her protuberant eyes bulging, said: 'Do you think *we're* in any danger?'

'I hope not,' I said. 'I don't see why we should be, but . . .' I did think so, of course, but I could not have pointed to the source of it.

'I suppose,' said Sybil, 'that that red chalk mark really is Master Spelton's mark? There couldn't be a mistake of some sort?'

I picked up a candle and all four of us made for the window seat. I threw up the lid. The red chalk sign was there, on the underside. It was a little bigger than the one that Cecil had shown me, but it was cut cleanly into four equal segments by the red chalk cross inside. There was no question about it.

'I don't think we can doubt this,' Brockley said. 'And it's in the sort of position where Master Spelton very probably *would* place it. It most likely wouldn't be noticed by a woman just opening the lid to put something in or take something out.'

'If one of the ladies did notice it, she might not pay much heed,' said Sybil. 'The ladies . . . they're not . . . not . . .'

'Keenly alert?' suggested Brockley.

'Mistress Gould is,' I said. 'And Angelica Ames. But they don't go in much for doing menial work. They wouldn't often open storage chests. The rest . . . I know what you mean. I think Mary Haxby would just say to herself, "Oh, a red chalk pattern, how odd," and then shut the lid down. So would Annie.' I closed it myself and went to sit down on the bed. I was trying to think.

'What have we got now?' I said. 'We know that Christopher was here, and we know that Philippa Gould and her ladies have denied it, to the men from York, and to us. We have also seen the ladies quarrelling violently about something. Might it be about the lies they have told concerning Christopher? And possibly – Hardwicke as well?'

We all considered this for a moment. Dale sank on to a stool, looking petrified. Then Sybil said: 'The book *is* still here. And if Christopher Spelton came here to fetch it, he either left without it or . . . And did Bernard Hardwicke also come here? And if so, why didn't *he* collect the book? It doesn't make any sense at all.'

'Are we wondering,' enquired Brockley, 'whether neither Master Hardwicke nor Master Spelton actually left Stonemoor House? That they are prisoners here still – or . . .'

'Dead? Could the ladies possibly have . . . but whatever *for*?' I cried out. It was a cry of anguish because it was Christopher we were talking about and I did not want Christopher to be dead. 'Philippa Gould offered the book for sale; invited Doctor Dee to buy it! Why should she want to harm whoever came to collect it?'

'She's quarrelling with her sister,' Sybil said. 'And the rest of the ladies are split between them. They could be quarrelling because of the lies that have been told, but could it be about the book instead? That Yates woman doesn't approve of the book; she said so.'

I was trying to think. 'Since Christopher felt the need to leave that mark, it means he did sense danger here. I think that's definite. Oh, dear God, I wish we could leave at once! Or yesterday! If only we could understand what kind of danger it can possibly have been, here in a house full of middle-aged, devout ladies! I've been afraid of this place all along but I can't see *why*. I wish I could even begin to work out a theory . . .'

I stopped. An extraordinary thought had come to me, had surfaced in my mind like a leviathan emerging from incalculable depths.

'What is it?' asked Brockley, watching me.

'When we were all looking at the book,' I said, 'didn't we all feel that Mistress Gould's manner was, somehow, odd; confused, surprised . . . didn't we even comment on it? Well, when Philippa Gould was showing it to us, I noticed things . . . only at the time, I only noticed them in passing. They didn't seem important then. Look, Cecil described the book to me. He got that description from Doctor Dee who in turn got it from his friend, the executor of the will left by the father of a woman here, called Eleanor Overton. Well, a description passed from one person to another – from the executor to Doctor Dee to Cecil, possibly via the queen! – could easily get garbled. I fancy that that's why I discounted the things I noticed. I dismissed them too easily, I think.'

Sybil looked bewildered. Brockley said: 'Madam, what are you talking about?'

'Perhaps,' I said, 'either Hardwicke or Christopher *did* collect the book after all. I can't see beyond that. I can't make out what happened next, but I can't help wondering because . . .'

'But the book's still here! We've seen it!' Sybil expostulated.

'Have we?' I said.

'I don't understand,' said Sybil. 'We *did* see it. Mistress Gould showed it to us.'

'Did she?' I asked.

'Madam, what is all this?' Brockley was impatient.

'I had a dream,' I said. 'I dreamt I was looking for the book and I found it but it turned into a demon with yellow fangs. Well, yellow-ish. The same colour as the cover on that book. That's one of the things I noticed. It's suddenly begun to niggle at me.'

Once more, I could hear Cecil's voice in my head. 'Cecil said that according to the description he had – which he got from Doctor Dee who got it from the Overton executor – the book was bound in white leather, with the title and the name of the author on the front in gold leaf. The book we saw was a dirty cream – a yellowish cream. *That's* why the demon in my dream had yellowish fangs. The dream was telling me that the book wasn't the one it was supposed to be.'

'But the book's cover could have been white to start with,' Sybil broke in. 'Perhaps the executor just said that to Doctor Dee – that it was white originally, and Doctor Dee didn't pick up the hint it had darkened with age.'

'That could be so,' I agreed. 'But that's not all. I couldn't make out much of the gold-leaf lettering on the cover, but I did recognize at least some of the letters. Cecil said that there was a gold leaf pattern on the cover. I don't call a crescent moon and some stars a *pattern*, and even though, as I said, I couldn't make much sense of the lettering, now that I really think about it, I'm becoming more and more certain that it didn't say *Observations of the Heavens by John of Evesham*. The lettering bothered me even then but I didn't know why. It's just come to me. I don't think that the letters I could make out fitted in with that title and I don't think the words were the right length! And besides, do you remember how Mistress Gould paused in that odd way when she set eyes on the book. Suppose she was surprised because it wasn't the book she expected to see?'

'But she pretended that it was,' said Brockley.

Sybil said: 'If she expected to see the real book, she would have been startled. She didn't have time to think. She might have pretended, just to gain time.'

'In that case,' said Brockley, 'what does she propose to do now? Try to cheat us by sending the wrong book away with us, and hope that it will be taken for the right one? Surely not!'

'She might,' said Dale. 'One book about stars and moons and things, with numbers in it and things like that, might be very like another. Perhaps even Doctor Dee doesn't know exactly what to expect.'

'I think he does,' I said. 'He's seen a copy of the book, belonging to someone else. He probably remembers.'

'Can't we just ask Mistress Gould about it?' said Sybil. 'Wouldn't it be simpler? We could even ask her why she didn't tell us that Master Spelton was here.'

Brockley and I looked at each other and between us there occurred one of our curious moments of mental rapport. I hoped that Dale wasn't aware of it. Then we both looked at Sybil, with pitying regret.

'Mistress Jester,' Brockley said, 'we know that Master Spelton was here. We also know that he has disappeared. The man Bernard Hardwicke has also disappeared and although we have no proof that he came here, he did intend to and he seems to have vanished after he left York, bound for Stonemoor. That happened to him *and* to Master Spelton. It seems possible, even probable, that whatever happened to them, it was the same in both cases. Which in turn suggests that Hardwicke came here too. It looks as though their disappearances really are connected to Stonemoor. I see it now.'

'It could be,' I said, 'that in both cases, they found something here, something that the ladies didn't want anyone to find.'

'What sort of thing?' Dale wanted to know.

'It could be anything,' I said. 'Something to do with a Catholic plot, perhaps. That's more likely than anything else. Though where, in that case, the book comes in . . .' I shook a puzzled head. 'John of Evesham's book may even have nothing to do with it. But whatever it was, the ladies might have realized that suspicions had been aroused. Perhaps both men asked questions. In that case, this could be a very dangerous place for nosy people who ask questions. The more innocent and gullible we seem to be, the better! We are certainly not going to ask Mistress Philippa Gould anything whatsoever.'

No, we weren't! Most certainly we weren't! Spelton's red chalk sign was a warning and I had taken it to heart. If there were plots under this roof, I didn't want to enquire into them.

But the oddity about the book troubled me. There was a mystery surrounding it, and there was certainly a mystery surrounding Christopher's red chalk sign. Two mysteries under one roof? Could they possibly be separate? They were far more likely to be facets of one central mystery.

I said: 'I really think that what was in that box, wasn't the book we have come for, and somehow I can't quite believe that it has nothing to do with . . . whatever made Christopher Spelton put his mark here. I would like to see that book again, examine it at leisure, taking time over it, and not with Mistress Philippa Gould looking over my shoulder.'

Brockley said: 'We know what that means, madam.'

'I know,' I said. 'Secret wanderings after dark and work for my picklocks. But I think it may be necessary.'

THIRTEEN
Menacing Whispers

'You don't like doing that sort of thing,' said Sybil, and Dale looked worried.

'I hate doing that sort of thing,' I said.

I quailed at the thought. I had had to do such things so many times. I had in my time opened quite a few document boxes belonging to other people; once, I had entered a bedchamber to examine a corpse, and once opened a strongbox in the captain's cabin on a ship. I had always, every time, been in dread of being caught so that although I was skilled with the picklocks, my hands invariably shook when I used them. I had been caught, too, on one very memorable occasion. One never got used to it. The fear was the same every time, and this place, Stonemoor House, was frightening me quite enough already. But . . .

It would have to be done. I couldn't *not* do it. 'It's the only way. Brockley is right. Yes it will have to be at night. This night, I suppose,' I said. 'I don't want to waste time. We should leave here tomorrow.'

Brockley said: 'If you are serious, madam, then I suggest that we wait until we can hear what you say is matins being chanted, or sung, or whatever the proper word is. I imagine all the ladies attend. That would be the safest moment.'

'I am glad you said *we*,' Sybil observed. 'I don't think either Dale or I would want to be left to wait and wonder.'

'No. Though . . .' Dale bit her lip, and fell silent.

Poor Dale. Life with me so often meant being frightened, and with good reason. Just now, I heartily sympathized with her.

'I agree,' I said, 'that you should come with me. We must warn Joseph – just in case. He must know what is happening. I must give him a letter to take to York, if he can get away and we cannot.' I took heart. 'But even if we are caught, what can Mistress Gould do to us? She surely can't make all of us disappear! Or imprison us all, either. It's the sort of thing that might become noticeable!'

'That would apply if we just asked openly for another look, ma'am,' said Dale, but I shook my head at her.

'I know. But I don't want to make them – or even just Philippa Gould – aware that we . . . that we have suspicions about this house, or any kind. Just in case something is seriously wrong here. If we let the ladies know that we are, well, wondering about this household, that will give them a chance to . . . to hide traces or prepare lies. I can't put it more plainly than that. It sounds very vague,' I added lamely. 'But that's what I feel.'

'But what *could* be going on here?' asked Sybil. 'I can't even begin to imagine.'

'Nor can I,' I said. 'But I think there's something. In fact, I feel sure of it, and I don't want us to fall foul of it.'

We could do nothing until nightfall. Time dragged. I wrote the letter for Joseph and Brockley took it to him. Cogge was back from the farm and with his help, they set about exercising the horses, and I, left behind in the guest quarters with Dale and Sybil, found myself intolerably restless, staring from windows, pacing up and down the hall. The rain stopped, which was a relief, for no one fancied riding out into a downpour next morning and we were all agreed that we would go tomorrow unless conditions made it totally impossible.

At last, unable to settle, I said: 'The path down the hill is usable. Brockley and Joseph and Cogge have been riding up and down it, taking all the horses out to stretch their legs. Let us go into the village and call at the tavern to find out how Master Butterworth is faring. Grimes said he was poorly.'

We put on cloaks and hats and set out. The air was cold and damp, but fresh, and the deathly silence which had prevailed while the snow was on the ground had lifted. We could even, somewhere, hear birdsong. The downward path was certainly muddy but we went slowly and from the foot of the hill it was only a short distance to the tavern. It was

closed when we got there, but there was a volley of barks
from the tavern dog and then Will Grimes darted out to meet
us. *Darted* is a better word than any other; there really was
something unearthly about the way he appeared in front of us
so suddenly. He stood in our path, gripping the dog's collar
with one hand. 'Comin' to call, are thee?'

'We've come to see Master Butterworth,' I said. 'Is he
better?'

'You can come in and see him and welcome,' said Will
sourly. 'But better, no, he ain't. Mistress Bella's done him no
good this time, though I don't doubt she's tried. It's a bad day
and a sad day, that it is.'

We followed Will into the tavern. It was dark inside, since
all the windows were shuttered, presumably as a signal that
the tavern wasn't functioning today, and the usual tavern smell
of ale and sawdust was mingled with something else, which
after a moment, I recognized. Someone, recently, had been
sick.

Will led the way through a door to the back regions and
took us into a further shadowy room. Here, the smell of vomit
was stronger still. There was a curtained space at the far end
and he pulled the curtain back. Within, was a tumbled bed,
and on it, Butterworth was lying. A horrible bucket, the source
of the stench, was beside the bed. Butterworth himself lay on
his back, his face gaunt and stiff with pain.

'Visitors from Stonemoor House, Maister,' said Will.

Butterworth turned his head. There was no heat in the room
but his white hair was soaked with sweat. The blue eyes were
sunken and beneath the weathering on his skin, he was deathly
pale. 'Sorry, can't get up,' he said. 'Fever . . . pain. Oh God,
so much pain.'

'Where is the pain?' Sybil asked briskly, and Butterworth
laid a wasted hand over the right-hand side of his stomach.
'Started all over my belly; now it's settled here. S'awful. Can't
keep any food down. Nothing helps.'

'It will before long, I expect,' said Sybil cheerfully. 'You
have the remedy that Mistress Yates sent?'

'Yes, course. It did me good before. Not now.'

We stayed for a while. I got Will to put a small brazier in

the room, while Sybil and I plied the sick man with Bella's medicine and gave him a long drink of water. Dale helped me to tidy the bed. Butterworth thanked us but his hollowed eyes and obvious anguish told a grim story. As we were settling him back against his pillows, his fingers, hot and dry, closed round my wrist.

'Tell Will . . . get vicar.'

'The vicar?'

'I'm done for. Best make my peace,' said Butterworth.

We said all the right things, 'you will be better soon' and 'keep your heart up', but he was insistent and so I called to Will, and asked him, in Butterworth's hearing, to fetch the vicar.

'Dear Christ,' said Will, distressed, but he went. We followed him out of the room, though we thought we should remain in the tavern until they came back.

'He's going to die,' Sybil said in a low voice. 'I've seen that malady before. Saw it in a maidservant when I was in Cambridge.'

'What is it?' I asked.

'No one knows, but the physician I called, he said he'd seen it several times in the past and he'd never known anyone recover. It's always fatal.'

We waited until Will returned with the vicar, who turned out to be a small, pink-faced man who stared at us hard and I noticed that despite his round, almost cherubic face, his eyes were like chips of flint. He said: 'You're the ladies who are staying in Stonemoor House? Not a good place for honest Christians, in my opinion,' and then, with Will, went into the tavern.

'I don't take to that man,' said Dale.

'Well, it's Butterworth who wants him. We need not stay now that the poor fellow has someone with him again,' I said.

We turned away and then, unexpectedly, came face to face with a group of villagers, both men and women, who barred our way. We looked at them enquiringly.

'We've seen our Doctor Rowbotham go to our tavern-keeper,' one of the men said. 'Saw that Will Grimes brought him. Seems Butterworth thinks he's not got long to live. Now, why would that be?'

His voice was accusing. 'We came to see how he did,' I said carefully. 'We felt concerned. He was kind to us when we first arrived, in a snowstorm, and we are upset to see him so ill.'

'As you may well be!' said one of the women. 'Wonder how upset that Mistress Yates would be, though.'

'I don't understand what you mean by that,' I said sharply. 'I am sure that if her remedies fail, she will be very sorry.'

'Aye. If her remedies fail, sorry'll be the word,' said another of the men.

'Please let us pass,' I said, and they did so, though with an air of reluctance.

The day was wearing on, and the cold was making itself felt. We made haste up the zigzag hill and were almost glad to find ourselves once more within the walls of Stonemoor. We saw the men reappear soon after, bringing back the final batch of horses, and presently, Brockley came to the guest quarters to join us. It was close to sunset when Will Grimes suddenly arrived in the courtyard, slithering off his scruffy pony and loudly demanding to see Mistress Gould.

We had seen him ride in and gone out to meet him and were startled to see how distraught he looked. The lady who was acting as porteress went in haste to tell Philippa Gould that he was asking for her, and I said: 'Will! What is it?'

'Master Butterworth's dead, that's what! Died just after vicar'd been with him. I'd thought he were better; he said t'pain was easier, but he didn't look better, no he didn't, and then . . . then . . . he just passed out and lay there breathing harsh, like, and then t'breathing stopped!' We saw that Will Grimes was crying. 'And God alone knows what t'village is going to say to this! They're saying that Mistress Yates's potions killed him! *Witchcraft*, they're saying. I got to warn her and Mistress Gould! Dear God, here's the porteress to take me to Mistress Gould. How'll I find words . . .!'

The porteress took him away. Walter Cogge came into the courtyard and took charge of the pony. The rest of us trooped back indoors.

'I knew it,' said Sybil. 'I could see it was going to happen. Dead! And now this talk of witchcraft!' She added, with feeling: 'The sooner we are *miles* away from here, the happier I'll be!'

'Tomorrow morning,' I said. 'If we aren't caught tonight.'

FOURTEEN
After Dark

When night fell, we retired, though not to our beds. We all remained fully dressed and sat up together in the room that Sybil and I shared. Except for the firelight, we sat in the dark. Brockley advised it.

'Best not light any candles, madam. Everything ought to look as ordinary as possible. I don't trust this place.' He gave me a grim smile. 'First of all I couldn't believe there was anything here to fear; now I have my sword at my side even indoors and put my hand on the hilt if a shadow stirs! We shouldn't show any lights at unusual times. Somebody might be on the prowl, just might catch a glimpse of candlelight through a chink in a shutter and wonder about it. We'll do best to wait in the dark until we hear the chanting begin. We shouldn't talk too much, either, and only in low voices if we do. Oh, and I suggest that we should all wear slippers.'

None of us knew exactly when matins would take place. Midnight was the most likely hour but it wasn't certain. Dale made up the fire but Brockley closed the shutters. I regretted this, for the sky had cleared and there was light from a waxing moon. As our windows faced north and north-west, the moon itself wasn't visible but I felt that any extra light would be comforting.

Then we sat by the hearth and waited. Maintaining complete silence was scarcely possible, and the dark hours, somehow, create an atmosphere of intimacy. Eventually, I found myself saying: 'I keep trying to think out what could have happened to Christopher Spelton. He came here, we know that. He was supposed to buy the book. He may have done so – we should know soon whether the book we've seen is the real one or not. If it isn't, then perhaps he did buy it. But then what happened to him, and why?'

'You are very worried about Master Spelton, are you not?' Sybil said. 'You like him, I know. Ursula, did you never actually consider accepting his proposal?'

'No,' I said. 'It was kind of him but I don't want to marry again. I don't think I can ever again find the depths I found with Hugh, and marriage without them isn't worth much, or not to me. I don't think it went very deep with him, you know. I think he was just sorry for me. He was offering me a kindness, a way to share my burdens. In all the years you've been with me, why have *you* never thought of re-marrying, Sybil? I'm sure you could have done.'

'I'm past the age for such things,' said Sybil, 'and besides . . .' she paused and then resumed in a voice that was still muted yet shook with the strength of her feelings '. . . even if I were not, I would never, never, never enter into another marriage, considering what my first one was like. Roland Jester was a brute. He ill-used me to the point that I feared for my life. That's why I ran away from him. And even at that, there were people, respectable people, who thought I'd done wrong, that a wife should never leave a husband, even if she fears he might murder her. Once the vicar pronounces the words *I declare that they be man and wife together* the woman is in the man's power. After I once got away, I promised myself that I would never allow myself to be in any man's power again!'

'I can understand that,' I said, and thought of Queen Elizabeth, my sister, who, I knew, also feared the power of a husband. Her mother and her young stepmother Catherine Howard had both been helpless in King Henry's power and died for it. I sometimes wondered what, if anything, I felt about King Henry, since he was my father. I had never known him. He was just a name, and my relationship to him was simply a fact, with no emotions attached to it. Yet I knew that my strange way of life might well owe something to abilities inherited from him. Thinking about him had stiffened my courage, more than once.

I hoped it would stiffen my courage now. I said: 'I can hear chanting.'

'I have a lantern here,' Brockley said. 'I had it in my luggage;

one never knows when a light will come in useful. It's risky to use it for this business but we may not be able to find our way without it. Those passages are probably as black as witches' cats are supposed to be.'

He stooped to light his lantern from the fire, and then we were ready.

'Here we go,' I said. 'We had better pray for good luck!'

On our noiseless, slippered feet, we made our way out of the bedchamber and down the stairs. The guest-hall windows faced the moon, so the stairs were lit by it, and the windows cast white images of themselves across the floor and the table. We slipped out into the guest-wing vestibule, and then through the door to the main building. The moon was helpful all the way, for here too, the windows were on the southern, moonlit side. Brockley had been wrong to expect Stygian blackness. The big main vestibule was eerie, though, for here, the angle of the moonbeams and the tall, narrow windows made the white shapes across the flagstones resemble the ghosts of elongated people, motionless, stretching out underfoot, while the shadows clustering in the corners were utterly dark and impenetrable. There was a heavy feeling in the air, as though it were full of hidden menace.

From here, the sound of the chanting was not audible, but the silence thrummed in our ears. We stole on, into gallery with the doors upon the right.

'Which one?' Sybil breathed.

This was a difficulty that I hadn't foreseen. Here again, there was moonlight, but the poor windows distorted it, and it is a strange, unreal kind of illumination anyway. It makes familiar things look strange. I had been perfectly sure when we set out that I knew which door was the right one, but now I found myself confused and uncertain. My companions couldn't decide, either. After we had wasted a few moments muttering about it, none of us able to be definite, I said, 'Well, we must just guess,' and with that, I got out my pick-locks and made a first attempt. The door I chose, however, wasn't locked at all and as it opened, the beam of Brockley's lantern revealed racks of piled sheets. We had found a linen store.

'Try the next one,' whispered Sybil.

The next door, also unlocked, was full of spare furniture. The lantern light played over piles of stools, stacked upside down and nesting into each other, half a dozen long benches standing on end and leaning against the wall in a tidy row; a small table standing on a bigger table; an assortment of candlesticks among the small table's legs.

I closed the door quietly and tried the next one. This was certainly locked. I set to work with the picklocks.

The lock was resistant and as ever on these occasions, I was shaky. It took, I suppose, three or four minutes to get in, although it felt more like three or four hours and beside me, I could hear Sybil's breath coming short, and was aware that Brockley, playing the lantern beam on the lock to help me, was vibrating with tension. I knew that because the beam wasn't altogether steady, any more than my hands.

Once the door was open, we all pushed hastily through it and Brockley closed the door behind us. To my alarm, the sound of the chant was no longer to be heard, though the window was not shuttered and the built-out chamber where the service was almost certainly being held was quite close. I stopped short, holding up a hand to keep the others still. Then, to my relief, the chant began again, sounding quite loud. All was well.

All the same: 'Take care with that lantern, Brockley!' I breathed and he hurriedly lowered it. I turned back to the door and spent a few moments in locking it from the inside, praying that when it was time to leave, I wouldn't find it difficult to undo. 'Where's the box?' I said as I put my picklocks away.

'It was over here, surely.' Brockley played the lantern along a laden shelf. 'I think this is it.'

Sybil lifted the box down and put it on the table. I clicked the brass latch back, lifted the lid and took the book out. 'Here we are. Now. I've been doing my best to remember just what Cecil told me, about what the book looks like. He said – I'm sure I've got this right – that it was bound in white leather, with the title and the author's name on the front in gold leaf. And there was a gold-leaf pattern on the front as well, apparently. Hold the lantern nearer, please, Brockley.'

'Dingy, I call this,' said Brockley. 'Even in this light – dingy.'

'I think you're right,' Sybil said, peering. 'And so were you, Ursula, when you said you didn't call moon and stars a pattern, either. They're pictures, not a design. And . . .' She wetted a finger and rubbed at the leather cover, staring critically at the result. All three of us did.

'How can one tell?' Brockley was fretful. 'We need daylight for this!'

I looked round and then took the lantern from Brockley. 'I thought I saw . . . yes, look. A pile of paper over there, at the end of that lower shelf. White paper, I think. Let's compare.'

I brought a sheet of the paper over and set it beside the book. And now, even in the difficult lantern light, we could see. The paper was unquestionably white. The leather of the book's cover was not. Even where Sybil had rubbed it clean, it had hardly changed colour at all. It was yellowish-cream, genuinely, and not just because it was dirty.

'And,' I said, pointing, 'although I can't make out more than a little of the title, I don't see how it can say *Observations of the Heavens by John of Evesham!*' I ran my finger along the two lines of gold-leaf lettering. 'I can make out some of the initial letters, they're big and much clearer than the rest, and there just don't seem to be any words beginning with O. Or with E. Or H.'

I turned the pages. 'And from what Cecil said, there ought to be tables of some sort . . . I can't find any. There are some diagrams showing planetary movements but no tables with numerals. Cecil also said that where numbers were mentioned, they were in Arabic numerals. There are numbers in the text in places but they're Roman, not Arabic. And I can't find anything that looks like a chart of the planets going round the sun. The charts that are here, have all the planets tracing complicated paths. That's quite different. Planets going round the sun is supposed to be one of the important things in John of Evesham's book.'

I paused again, turning more pages. 'I can't find any disrespectful drawings, either,' I said. 'The only drawings are the charts of the planets and the little pictures wrapped round capital letters or in the margins here and there. They're all quite harmless – mythical birds and beasts, nothing more. This is *not* the right book. It can't be. Surely, even if the description did become altered, because of being passed from one person to another, that couldn't account for *all* these discrepancies.'

'It will be interesting,' said Brockley thoughtfully, 'to see what Mistress Gould says when we take leave of her tomorrow and offer her a purse of money and wait expectantly for her to hand over John of Evesham's *Observations*.'

Sybil said nervously: 'The chanting has stopped again. We don't want to get caught.'

'Let's go!' Dale pleaded.

I put the book into its box and returned the box to its shelf. I was replacing the sheet of paper on its pile when Sybil pulled at my sleeve and when I turned to her, she put a finger to her lips. Holding up the lantern, I saw Brockley standing rigidly, staring towards the door, while Dale's eyes were wide with fright. Then I heard the approaching footsteps, and the sound of voices.

Quickly, I put the lantern out. We all stood unmoving, hardly breathing. The footsteps had stopped outside the door. Someone – I thought it sounded like Angelica Ames – said, in an argumentative tone: 'I tell you, I was *sure* that I heard voices. I said, it was when the chant was interrupted because Sister Annie felt faint – again; I really think she isn't strong enough for our regime and ought to be excused from attending the night offices. I threw a window open to give her air. My hearing is good and I don't imagine things. I *know* I heard voices. And I was half sure I saw a glint of light from the library.'

Another voice, surely that of Mistress Philippa Gould, said: 'Well, let us see,' and we heard a key being pushed into the lock from outside.

Brockley moved, grabbed Dale with one hand and me with the other, and elbowed Sybil. We crowded where he dragged us, to a position behind the door, which fortunately opened inwards. Philippa Gould's voice said: 'The door is locked as it should be.'

Angelica said something, and Philippa answered: 'Oh, very

well, we'll make sure that nothing's amiss,' and the door opened, pressing us all back into the angle between it and the wall. Jammed together, we held our breath and tried not to stand on each other's feet. Mistress Gould took just two steps into the room, holding up a candle, and then remarked that the library looked as usual.

Blessedly, it did not occur to either Philippa or Angelica to walk round the door and look behind it, nor did they attempt to push it fully open. When we first found Christopher's sign, Sybil had implied that the ladies of Stonemoor were, in some ways, naive. I had been inclined to exclude Philippa Gould and Angelica Ames from that, but now I saw that it applied to them too. One glance round the room by the light of a single candle had shown them nothing out of place, nothing disturbed, and that was enough for them.

'You imagine things, Sister Angelica,' said Philippa. 'I thought so from the start. I didn't hear any voices or see any lights.'

'I was the one who opened the window and put my head out, Mother,' said Angelica protestingly. 'It seems I was wrong, but I could have sworn I saw and heard something. I don't trust Mistress Stannard or her people. They are too sharp for my taste, too much creatures of the world.'

'But they are not here now. However, you were right to insist that we made sure,' said Mistress Gould soothingly. 'I approve and I am not annoyed with you. Now, however, let us go to our beds.'

They withdrew. We heard the door being locked again. Footsteps and voices receded. Angelica sounded as though she were grumbling; Philippa's tones were soothing. They were gone. We stayed where we were for several long moments, but nothing more happened. Finally, we moved away from the door. 'That was close,' Brockley remarked grimly.

'Too close,' I muttered. So far, throughout all our adventures, I had had no need of the potion that Gladys had given me, to deal with any migraine attacks. Now, I felt the first hammer blow strike, as it always did, above my left eyebrow. 'Let's get back to bed,' I whispered.

'Wait just a little,' Brockley said warningly.

We did wait but the silence of the house endured and became oppressive, and the pain in my head grew and grew. 'I'd better let us out now,' I said at last. I managed it, but I was shaky now not only with nerves but with pain and it took several long minutes. We were all quivering like guitar strings by the time I had finished. At last, we tiptoed out. I locked the door after us and we made our stealthy way back to the guest wing, where I asked Sybil to find the phial containing the potion, and took a dose before lying down.

The potion had little effect. The morning found me unable to lift my head. The pain nailed me to the bed and an increasing sense of nausea made me hesitate even to move.

'I'm sorry,' I said wanly to my companions. 'Believe me, I'm sorry. I want to get away from here. We have to leave this place as fast as we can, with or without John of Evesham's book. Oh, dear God. My head!'

FIFTEEN
Salt and Lemon

I t was Dale, dear Dale, so often resourceful in a crisis, who dealt with this one. After gazing concernedly down at my no doubt greenish countenance, and brushing a lock of sweat-soaked hair out of my eyes, she said: 'That Mistress Yates is supposed to be clever with potions. Let's see what she can suggest for this,' and set off forthwith, seizing the bell from the guest hall table, marching out to the vestibule with it and ringing it as though the building were on fire. It went through my head like a skewer and made me retch, though nothing came up, but meanwhile Dale was getting results. Ten minutes later she came back with a jug.

'Mistress Yates gave me this, ma'am. She said it might help.'

'What is it?' Brockley demanded suspiciously.

'Nothing to worry about,' said Dale. 'I watched her make it. She's got lemons in store. Never seen one before, but I've heard of them. Seems the merchant who's the father of her and Mistress Gould knows other merchants and gets luxury goods from them sometimes, and being half Italian, he had Italian books in the house, handed down, some from the women in his ancestry, with recipes and advice about medicines. He passed them on to her. This is fresh lemon juice with a drop of well water to dilute it and a little salt to take the edge off the taste and she says it could help. No harm in trying, anyway.'

'It sounds quite useless to me,' said Sybil.

I said: 'I feel so ill, I'll try anything. Even if it tastes awful and makes me sick, that might do me good in itself.'

The lemon juice potion didn't taste particularly bad, and presently, to my surprise, the nausea in my stomach began to subside. The headache began to ease as well. Gingerly, I sat up and then, as neither my head nor my guts felt any the worse for the effort, I smiled at Sybil, who gasped with relief, said, 'You'll need something to eat after a while,' and rushed away.

She told me presently that she had found her way to the kitchens, discovered that a little white bread had been made that day, as well as the usual black rye bread, and insisted on bringing some to me, with butter and a little pot of honey. Half an hour later, I found that I was sufficiently restored to eat just a little.

Dale and Sybil, however, discouraged me from getting up at once. I was sure that I was ready but they begged me to rest, so I stayed where I was and thought wistfully of Hawkswood, and wished with all my heart that I could be safely back at home. What was I doing here? My constant adventures were not suitable for a woman. Brockley thought that, and he was perfectly right. Why was it that though I longed for the life of a dignified lady, I never seemed able to achieve it?

At home, I had a life that was busy, varied, and infinitely satisfying. I wanted to be back there, living it. I wanted to play with Harry and attend to his upbringing; make plans about the stud of trotting horses I was developing so that one day it could be part of his inheritance. I wanted to look after the people of my household, maintain my linen store and my still room, amuse myself with embroidery, at which I was quite skilled, tend my garden, argue with John Hawthorn about what he should prepare for dinner, exercise my mind now and then with a little reading in Latin and Greek.

Instead, I was having migraine in a house where a discredited religion was being practised, where books did not contain what they ought to contain, where visitors left signs to prove that they had been there, and then vanished.

It was not to be borne. We must, must, must, get *out* of this place. I could *not* linger in bed. I threw back the covers and went to the door to call Dale to help me get dressed.

The morning was wearing away by then. 'Do we leave today, or wait till tomorrow?' Brockley asked, considering me with anxiety as I joined my friends round the fire in the guest hall.

'Today,' I said. 'I'll be all right now.' I knew that I would be. The extraordinary thing with migraine is that once it has passed, it has passed. With me, it sometimes left weakness and exhaustion behind it, but only when it had been prolonged. This attack had been short. I was already myself again.

'We shall have to seek an audience with our hostess,' said Brockley. 'It ought to be interesting. Just what is that charming lady going to say when we ask her to hand over the precious book we're here to buy and she can't produce it? In a way,' he added thoughtfully, 'it's a pity she didn't catch us last night. She couldn't have done anything to us. Not *all* of us. And it might have brought matters to a head.'

'I'm thankful she didn't catch us,' said Dale candidly. 'I'm afraid of her. You never know what people like her might do.'

'I agree,' I said, in heartfelt tones. 'Why do you think I've just had migraine?'

'She may well have much to lose, if Master Hardwicke and Master Spelton really did come to harm here,' Sybil agreed. 'Panic can make people go to extremes sometimes. No, I feel we were lucky to get safely away last night.'

'Yesterday,' I said, 'both you and Dale thought she might offer us the book that she showed us, the one we saw last night. What if she does? It's possible. She may not realize how much is known about the real book, contents or appearance.'

'So, what *do* we do if she offers us the false book?' asked Sybil.

'We hand over the money, take the substitute volume, and leave,' said Brockley. 'What else? We *leave*. We get away from here and put all that we know in the hands of authority. It's common sense.'

I nodded in agreement. Brockley said: 'I can see to getting the horses saddled at once and by God's good grace, it's a bright morning. How long will it take to get everything packed?'

'It's nearly all done,' said Dale.

It was settled. We would leave at once. It would be a long ride and Sybil wondered aloud if we would be offered any food to take with us. 'We'll ask,' said Brockley, 'and if the answer is no, we might be able to get something in the village. There's probably a bakery.'

'Let's get our outdoor things on, and bring the saddlebags down,' I said. 'I'll fetch the purse of money for the book. Brockley, will you see to the horses straightaway? Then we'll find out if Mistress Gould will see us.'

There was no difficulty about that. When, after the horses had been saddled and all the baggage was downstairs, we set off to seek an audience with her, we at once met Margaret Beale, on her way to look for us. Her nice wrinkled face looked surprised to see us already cloaked and hatted for our journey.

'Mistress Stannard! You are recovered? Mistress Gould has been so very worried.'

'A headache, nothing more,' I said. 'I have them sometimes. I am quite well again now. Mistress Yates knew what to advise.'

'Oh yes, she is clever in that way. She medicines us all when we fall ill!' said Mistress Beale happily. 'Please come with me; Mistress Gould wants to see you.'

We found our hostess in her office, seated behind her desk. She rose at once when we came in, and once more I explained that I had only had a headache, and was quite recovered now, with the help of Mistress Yates. She smiled at that and repeated what Margaret Beale had said about Bella Yates' services to the ladies when they ailed.

'The villagers have been talking foolishly of late. Someone died that Bella was trying to help, but she cannot do miracles, any more than any physician can. In fact, she is skilled and compassionate. I am so glad that you are better, Mistress Stannard. However . . .'

A walnut box, presumably the one with the questionable book in it, was ready on her desk. She looked at it but did not touch it. 'I see you are all prepared to set off and you no doubt wish to take John of Evesham's book with you.'

'Yes.' And now, I must bring matters to a head. I held out the purse I was carrying. 'Yes, of course. Here is the price of it. There are three hundred pounds in this purse, which I think was the agreed amount. You may wish to count it.'

Mistress Gould shook her head, making no move to take the purse from me. 'Will you all be seated, please.' With a wave of a slender white hand, she indicated that there were sufficient stools for us all. 'I have something to tell you.'

We sat down as requested. I caught Brockley's eye and we exchanged a wordless message. *This is the moment. What will she say?*

'I have to inform you,' said Mistress Gould steadily, 'that the book I showed you is not the one you have come to buy. I did not realize that when I brought it out for you to look at. I expected to find the real book here in this box—' she touched the box with a forefinger – 'and it was a shock to me when I saw that another had been put in its place. Oh, there is no mystery about what has happened! I am sorry to say that among my ladies, there are some who disapprove strongly of John of Evesham's book. They consider that it contains pagan lore, unsuitable for Christians to read, and that anything it says about the movements of stars and planets, and any conclusions it draws, must be false, the teaching of the Devil. In particular, they regard the theory that the earth circles the sun as heretical, being contrary to the teaching of the Church. There is also a drawing that is disrespectful towards the Holy Father. I myself consider it amusing but some of my ladies, I fear, lack humour. Also, some are illiterate and others, though literate, are opposed to modern thinking. I myself am not, for my father taught me to respect the world of scientific discovery, but I have never been able to influence the diehards in my household. The most vociferous of those who disapprove, I regret to say, is my sister Bella. She is their leader, as it were. She is a good woman, a kind woman, who helps the sick, but in matters of religion she is as stubborn as any mule ever was. She says that the book must not be sold; that to do so would be to spread the Devil's teaching beyond these walls, and that money made from such a sale would be tainted with evil and bring catastrophe upon us! Such nonsense!'

None of us spoke, mainly, I think, because none of us was sure what to say.

'You have heard me disagreeing with my sister. The first time we met, when you heard the two of us arguing, we were not in fact discussing salt and candles. I pretended that we were, so as to keep you from knowing that John of Evesham's book was a cause of contention. Later, you walked in on the more serious dispute, when the ladies were divided into factions, one supporting me and the other upholding my sister's regrettable views.'

'But what has happened to the real book?' I asked.

'Bella has hidden it. When I saw what was really in this box, I suspected her and challenged her. She admitted it freely.'

'Hidden it?' asked Brockley. 'Or destroyed it?'

'Oh, she wouldn't destroy it,' said Mistress Gould. 'There is a curse on anyone who does that. The curse is said to have been laid on it many years ago – centuries, perhaps – but recently, I reinforced it by laying a curse of my own. Mummery!' she snorted. 'A performance, such as the dramas that strolling players create, but though I say it myself, it was an effective performance. Bella may be embalmed in superstition but that can work two ways. If she is afraid of John of Evesham's theories, she is also afraid of my curse and has encouraged her followers to fear it too. But she will not tell me where she has hidden the book and . . .'

She stopped for a moment and I realized that beneath her dignified air, she was actually furious. Her face, framed by its dark-blue wimple, was suddenly white with temper and her eyes were bright with anger. When she resumed, it sounded as though the words were being forced out between her teeth.

'I wanted to make her tell me! I wanted to get the book back quickly, so that I could pass it to you! Of course I did! And I could make her tell me, if I had the chance,' she said. 'It would grieve me, for yes, she is my sister, and yes, she is a good woman and many of us have had cause to be grateful to her, but this . . . this is the other side of her and it isn't to be borne! If I could, I would do what is needful. A few days locked up on bread and water, a little use of a birch, and she would talk, oh yes. But her followers won't let me! You saw them for yourselves! There are enough of them to be formidable. Bella's supporters say that if I . . . if I *do* anything to Bella, they will do the same to me. My own supporters would try to stop them, of course . . . but I don't want my ladies to . . . Dear God, they might – they *would* – take to fighting! Like wildcats. Like heathen maenads! Like savages! That really is what would happen! And the threat against me might well be carried out! I dare not proceed against Bella. I have ordered a search. Those who agree with me are doing that now, although they are being hindered by Bella's faction.

'We are having an epidemic of mislaid keys!' said Mistress Gould in a ferocious parody of humour. 'But there are a million hiding places in this house and the book may not even *be* in this house. My ladies do go out on occasion. In twos and threes, we attend the church on the Sabbath; sometimes one or two will go to the village or walk or ride on the moors. We have our two horses and some of my ladies come from homes where they were accustomed to ride. My sister Bella is one of them – she grew up riding the workhorses on the smallholding where she lived as a child. I don't enforce too strict a Rule. We may live very much as Benedictine nuns would, but not entirely.'

Sybil and I both nodded, having seen one of the ladies riding in the snow. As if she had picked up the pictures in our minds, Mistress Gould said: 'Bella rode out, despite the weather, the day after I found that the book had vanished. She could well have hidden it somewhere in the house at first, but then taken it out with her and concealed it somewhere outside. I'm sorry. You will have to take your money back with you. If I do find the book, I will send word, but for the moment – I haven't got it to sell to you.'

'We understand,' I said.

That seemed to be that. Philippa Gould was at least honest. None of us felt inclined to pursue the matter. We all longed to be away. We expressed our regrets. I took back the purse. Mistress Gould picked up a bell from her desk and rang it, and one of the ladies, who must have been hovering nearby, came in carrying two leather bags which she handed to me.

'There's some food there,' said Mistress Gould. 'In one bag, fresh bread, some ham, sliced ready to eat, and some dried fruit; in the other, three flasks of water. You have a long way to go and at the moment, I would not recommend stopping in Thorby to buy anything. According to Will Grimes, who is friendly towards us, some of the villagers are now very suspicious indeed of this house, because of Master Butterworth's death. There have been renewed whispers of witchcraft, it seems. It is worrying, as we expect further guests soon; a party of five gentlemen, in fact. It would be upsetting if they found a bad atmosphere here.'

'We knew that further guests were coming soon,' I said. 'When we arrived, the porteress – Mistress Beale I think it was – mentioned it. You will be glad to say goodbye to us!'

'In a way, though you have been exemplary guests and we all like you.' Mistress Gould, blissfully unaware of our midnight activities, smiled at us again.

'If you expect other guests, you *will* want us out of the way,' remarked Brockley in cheerful tones. 'We will depart at once.'

'Quite,' I said. 'We thank you for the hospitality of your house.'

It was over. We withdrew, to collect our saddlebags and go out to mount our horses. Joseph had brought them out into the stable yard and when we were mounted, he scurried round us, checking our girths, before mounting Splash. The damage done by Sybil's stirrup leathers had healed and both she and Dale now had the makeshift leggings that Dale had made. We were all prepared for the ride.

I was so very thankful to set off. To the last moment, I had had an irrational feeling that something might intervene to stop us. Christopher Spelton had been here and in the deep places of my mind, I was wondering if he still was, in which case – oh, poor Christopher! – he was probably dead. But if he had got away, where was he now? I hated and feared Stonemoor House and I was sure that Sybil and Dale felt the same. So, obviously, did Brockley. He was sitting very upright on Mealy's back, with an air of looking sharply around him, as though he were searching for some source of danger.

But no one hindered us. We rode unmolested out of the

gateway and started down the hill towards Thorby. At the foot of the hill, the zigzag path straightened out and then divided just short of the tavern. One arm went straight on, becoming the village street, though it remained an earthen track. Cobblestones had not reached Thorby. The other fork veered right and shortly after that joined the track that would take us back towards the Thwaites. Just before the fork, we realized that our descent had been noticed. A small crowd had gathered outside the tavern. They were watching us. No one moved towards us and they were silent but they didn't exude friendliness.

In a low voice, Brockley said: 'Pretend we've noticed nothing. Just ride on to the turn.' I saw that his hand was on his sword hilt.

We went forward, but just as we turned on to the right-hand path, away from Thorby and those staring eyes, one voice in the crowd did speak.

'What sort of folk come visiting witches?' it said.

Out of the tail of my eye, I caught a sharp movement and something hit me in the small of the back. I twisted sharply and saw a crumbling clod of earth fall to the ground. Then the goblin figure of Will Grimes suddenly shot out of the tavern door, shouting: 'Doan be fools, the lot of you! They're folk from the queen's own court!'

He was answered by a chorus of angry voices, though no one actually attacked him, and Will, far from seeming intimidated, confronted them with his hands on his hips and shouted something back which sounded like a threat to close the tavern if they gave him any trouble, and where would they get their ale of an evening then? The enormous tavern dog also came bounding out of the building and planted itself beside him, where it stood angrily barking, head lowered, hackles raised and a fine array of fangs bared in a snarl.

'Nothing like threatening to cut off a man's supplies of drink,' muttered Brockley. 'Or having a hound the size of a small pony beside you. Let's get out of this. Go ahead of me!'

The path here was good enough for speed. I faced forwards again and Sybil and I stirred our mounts into a canter. I heard Mealy's hoof beats following us. In moments, we were clear of Thorby and the sound of the noisy altercation outside the tavern was fading behind us.

We were away. *We were away.* Whatever had happened to Christopher Spelton and presumably to Bernard Hardwicke too, had not happened to us.

Well, not yet, anyway.

SIXTEEN
In Spate

I n sunshine, and without the covering of snow, the moorland looked different, though I wouldn't say it looked more friendly. The heather distances were as dark and threatening as storm clouds and the frosty wind hissed across them. The pale stone outcrops were like bared teeth and the path, soaked by the recent snow and rain, was deep in mud. But every furlong increased the distance between us and Stonemoor. When possible, we put the horses into a canter, to increase it faster. We really were getting away. Nothing had happened to us. We were free.

To do what?

'What exactly are our plans now, madam?' Brockley asked as we slowed to a walk after a particularly long canter.

'I thought at first that I might send you straight to York,' I said. 'There's the note that I got ready for Joseph, in case something went amiss last night – you could have taken that. But now I think it's best that we should all ride back to the Thwaites to collect the coach. *Then* you can ride ahead of us to York. We shan't lose more than a day, and I can't see that that will matter. It's a long while since the two Messengers disappeared, anyway. That means that you won't have to find the way to York through moorland tracks! We'll all be using the main road.'

'As you will, madam. I think you are right.'

We pressed on. We came to a little dip in the land, which I vaguely recalled from our earlier journey, where a few trees offered some shelter from the wind. Here, we dismounted, loosened the horses' girths, and ate some food. Brockley said he thought he could hear water flowing somewhere and after reconnoitring, he found a stream where the horses could drink. It was a lively little river, which had obviously overflowed its banks as a result of the thaw and the recent downpours, and Brockley was careful, saying that its real banks were under the surface and he didn't want the horses stumbling into it.

We tightened the girths again and rode on. I could not remember clearly how far we would have to go to reach the next landmark that I could recall, which was the ford where the horses had drunk when we crossed it, coming the other way, and we came to it sooner than I expected, rounding the corner of a hillside and then reining in, in consternation.

The lively little river where the horses had drunk, wasn't the only watercourse that had broken its bounds because of the rain and the thaw.

The ford was gone. In its place, a fierce torrent, running as swiftly as a horse could gallop, leapt and hurtled where the shallow crossing had once been. On its angry brown surface swirled broken branches and clumps of twigs, torn from trees and bushes on the overwhelmed banks upstream, while downstream, the flood plunged into its shadowed ravine, thundering on with its surface only a foot or so below its confining sides. The sound of the racing current all but deafened us.

'We'll never get across that!' Brockley said, or rather, shouted, to make himself heard.

'We've got to find a place where we *can* cross,' I said fiercely. 'We're not going back!'

'Rivers are usually narrower near their source,' Brockley said, 'and this must rise somewhere on the moors to the east. Let's take a cast upstream.'

Following the river upstream was difficult, for the top of the slope on our side was a mass of outcrops and loose stones and we could not ride close to the water. However, there was little chance of losing it for when we couldn't see it, we could hear it. We persevered for something like a mile, and then, startlingly, even above the surge of the river, we heard something else. It was a shrill whistle, and was followed by a shout or rather, a call. It sounded like a command. We pulled up, looking about us. Then, rising up, as it were, out of a dip in the moorland, came a flock of sheep, bleating loudly and driven by a black and white dog, which was following them in a semi-crouch, its belly near the ground. Behind the dog, came the shepherd, crook in hand. The sheep veered when they saw us and the shepherd shouted another command to the dog, which at once began to herd them away from us. The shepherd strode over to us.

He was an odd-looking man, dressed very roughly in cross-gartered hose and a heavy cloak. It fell open in the front, revealing a long, thick tunic, and on his head he wore a leather cap. The hair that showed beneath it was yellowish-white and as curly as the fleece of a sheep, and his eyes, disconcertingly, were also like those of a sheep, for they were almost amber in colour. They were not friendly

'So, what would the likes of thee be doing, wandering on my moors, disturbing my flock?' he demanded. 'I doan't like people,' he added.

I was too taken aback to answer, but Brockley was not. 'Do you own this land?'

'I live here. Same thing.'

'I wouldn't agree there,' said Brockley sharply. I caught his eye and sent him a pleading look. *Don't offend the man. Ask directions!*

As so often, Brockley read my mind with ease and moderated his tone. 'We have no wish to stay in this district. We wish to go to the Thwaites' farm, on the other side of this river. Do you know it? We're looking for a crossing place. The ford is flooded.'

'Aye, it would be, seeing we've had the thaw and the rain.'

'Do you know of a crossing place?' Brockley was keeping his temper with visible difficulty. 'Do you know the Thwaites?'

'Riding upstream, aren't thee? Wrong way. Go downstream. Three miles or thereabouts. There's a bridge. Thee'll find a track t'other side, and it branches and one branch goes east to the Thwaites. Aye, I know of them.'

Abruptly, after giving us all another unfriendly look, he turned away and whistled to his dog. A moment later, shepherd, dog and sheep were on the move again, going away from us, heading south-west across the moor. A fold of the land soon hid them from us.

'What a rude man!' said Dale indignantly.

'I think he must be the shepherd Cecil mentioned to me,' I said. 'He told me there was such a man hereabouts and said that he didn't like his fellow men. Well, he did at least give us directions. We had better turn round!'

'I hope they're the right directions,' said Brockley. 'That fellow looked capable of giving us the wrong ones just for the sake of it!'

It took a long time to retrace our steps. We passed the flooded ford and then continued on for so long, riding between the bleak moors and the torrential river, that Brockley began to mutter that he was sure we really had been given the wrong instructions. But he was mistaken about that, for a few moments later we arrived at a place where the hills gave way to a valley, allowing the river to spread out again. Here, the current, no longer so constricted, ran less violently, though it was still swift and had topped its banks on both sides so that it was wider than normal. It still looked deep. It curved round a spur of land, and then, wonder of wonders, there was a wooden bridge.

'Thank God,' said Brockley devoutly.

We clattered across. 'But where are we?' said Brockley, when we had reached the other side. 'Where is this bridge? It seems to be in the middle of nowhere!'

'There's a track leading on from here,' I said. 'It looks well used.'

'And I can see chimney smoke over there,' said Dale, pointing. 'It could be a village. I expect there's a landowner who maintains the bridge.'

'It's in the wrong direction,' said Brockley. 'It's west of here, and the Thwaites must be well to the east. Well, that man said the track branched.'

I had the maps in one of my saddlebags, and now got one of them out, which I should, of course, have done before. If I had, we wouldn't have wasted time riding upstream and wouldn't have encountered the disagreeable shepherd, either. The bridge was marked and so was the village, which was called Hickley. Also marked was the track we were on, and another which did indeed branch off not very far ahead.

'That's where we must go,' I said. 'Well, at least we're across that river. I really was beginning to wonder . . .'

Dale interrupted me. '*What's that?*' she said, and in such a tone that we all turned towards her. 'What is it?' I asked.

'*That!*' said Dale, pointing.

Her forefinger was jabbing towards the river; to be precise to the bank on our side, and only a few yards away. Just there, a drowned bush stood in the flood water, and I saw that something seemed to be caught up in it. 'It's just an old boot,' I said.

'But there's something sticking out of it!' said Dale.

Brockley and Joseph dismounted together. Sybil and I held their horses while the two of them went to the water and waded in towards the bush.

'Careful!' Brockley said. 'We don't want anyone falling in. It's too cold to risk a wetting.'

They disentangled the boot eventually, with little more harm to themselves than wet sleeves. The water, just there, wasn't that deep. They laid their trophy on the ground. We all stared at it, registering varying degrees of horror. Dale clapped her hand over her mouth and Sybil gasped. I swallowed hard. There was indeed something sticking out of the boot. It looked remarkably like a bone. The top of a shinbone, I thought. A human shinbone? Only human beings wore boots.

'Some poor soul fell in and drowned, I fancy,' said Brockley. He had stood up and was now staring at the water. He gazed upstream towards the bend in the river, where it rounded the shoulder of moorland. 'The current, coming round that curve, would have swept this poor relic into the bank.'

I handed the reins of Brockley's horse to Dale, to free my hands, and began to study the map again. 'Where does this river come from and go to? It does seem to rise in the moorland to the east.'

Brockley came to look, and I handed the map down to him. 'Downstream it goes westward and ends up in a distant lake, according to this. Very likely the rest of him will never come

to light. He'll be all in pieces and the fish will get them.'
Dale squeaked. 'We could ask, when we get to the Thwaites,
if they know of anyone who has disappeared from this or
any neighbouring district, but . . .'

'We know of two,' I said.

SEVENTEEN
Turning Back

There was a fraught silence.

'So,' said Brockley at last, 'you think, madam, that this could be one of them?'

'And whoever did it just pushed the body into the river?' Sybil frowned. 'But it might easily have been found, in that case. Would a killer want that? It would have been better to bury it, surely?'

'How?' asked Brockley. 'Look round you. Scrape at the ground. It's muddy, but it's sure to be frozen just under the surface, and around here, stones stick out of it every few yards!'

'But who says he was killed?' said Dale, her voice shaking. 'Couldn't he have had an accident?'

'I doubt it,' said Brockley. 'Madam is right. Two men have vanished, not just one.' He stooped and picked up the boot, peering into it. 'There's something stuck inside this. Other than part of a leg.'

'*Brockley!*' Sybil protested. 'That was . . . almost flippant!'

'I'm an old soldier, Mistress Jester. It's the way we sometimes talk. It doesn't mean any disrespect. Let me just try . . .'

Carefully, he pushed his fingers into the top of the boot. 'It's stuck very tightly . . . ugh! There's still some flesh in there . . . ah. I've got it.' He stood up, holding his discovery.

'It looks like a wallet,' I said.

'It's made of some kind of thin, oiled leather,' Brockley said, feeling it with his fingertips. 'And it was jammed fast. It's survived the river very well. It's mucky, though, and so are my fingers.'

He crouched to dabble fingers and wallet in the water. I stood watching him. Cecil's voice spoke in my memory.

I handed it to him myself. And he winked at me, put it in a wallet, and thrust the wallet down inside one of his riding boots. That was where he always put confidential documents when he was asked to carry them.

'Is there anything in that wallet?' I asked.

Brockley got to his feet and stood fumbling with his discovery. Finally, between a finger and thumb, he extracted a small scroll of paper, flattened by being inside the wallet and the boot. With it came a piece of vellum, not rolled but folded. He unrolled the scroll, cautiously. 'It's damp,' he said, 'and the ink's run a bit but some of it is still legible.'

He studied it for a moment and then handed it to me. I looked at it and at once made out enough to tell me what it was. 'It's the letter to James Douglas,' I said. 'It has to be. I can make out the greeting, and there's something in the middle about precautions being taken to keep Mary Stuart well guarded. What is that piece of vellum?'

Brockley gave it to me and I unfolded it carefully. It cracked along the folds but I was gentle and it held together. The black ink lettering inside had survived surprisingly well. 'This is legible, too, just about,' I said.

It was a receipt, for three hundred pounds, made out to Bernard Hardwicke, for the sale of a book entitled *Observations of the Heavens by John of Evesham.*

It was Dale, once more, who noticed that the current, surging round the curve, had swept something else into the bank besides Hardwicke's boot. This object wasn't tangled in brambles, but had hooked itself over a bit of projecting rock. Joseph fetched it. It was a bridle, a plain one except for some metal trimming on the browband. The reins, by which it had been caught on the rock, were not scalloped in the fashionable style but plaited, to give a comfortable grip. It was a practical bridle, for long journeys. The bit had rusted, as though it had been in the water for some time.

'It could belong to one of the missing horses, either Hardwicke's, or the mare that the Thwaites have taken in,' I said. 'I wonder where Hardwicke's horse is. Wandering on the moor, I suppose, poor thing. All these things will have to be carried to York, as evidence that Bernard Hardwicke met his death here.'

'We're not at Stonemoor,' said Sybil thoughtfully. 'We're miles from there. There's no evidence that the Stonemoor ladies had anything to do with this.'

'Except that Christopher Spelton was there,' I said.

'It's difficult to imagine any of the ladies murdering someone,' said Brockley. 'But Walter Cogge probably could. He's their bailiff and groom and is said to be their priest. He clearly undertakes all kinds of things! Maybe murder as well.'

'Yes. I see.' Sybil frowned. 'I *do* see. Stonemoor probably does come into it somewhere.' She frowned even more, her brows drawing together, and then took us all by surprise. 'We ought to go back to Stonemoor and confront them.'

'Do *what*?' said Brockley disbelievingly.

I said: 'What do you mean?'

'I mean,' said Sybil, 'that if we leave it to the York sheriff, well, yes, he'll send men to question the ladies but they'll surely have some story ready for him, about footpads in lonely places, and God knows I've never seen anywhere as lonely and benighted as these moors. Dozens of outlaws could hide among these hills. Or perhaps the ladies will tell some tale of murderous farmers who prey on wayfarers . . .'

'They could tell the same story to us!' I protested. The idea of returning to Stonemoor appalled me. I had been so thankful to get away from the place. It had frightened me, and all the more because the reasons for being afraid of it were so tenuous. The trace that Christopher had left, the enmity towards the idea of selling the book, the . . . the *atmosphere*. I had been through many dangerous adventures and I shouldn't be such an easy prey to panic, but I was.

While Sybil, usually so calm and reasonable, was not. 'Oh, don't you *see*?' Suddenly, she was as animated as I had rarely known her to be, though in exceptional circumstances she could be astoundingly forceful. She had once flown at me in a rage, with fingers clawed.

'*Why* can't you see?' she demanded. 'For one thing, if we leave it to the sheriff's men, we'll have to carry all these things to York and that would include that horrible boot! But will the sheriff's men take it with them when they go to Stonemoor, so as to thrust it under Mistress Gould's nose and shock her into speaking the truth? We can't insist that they do that and they might not. Ursula, didn't you tell us that Lord Burghley hinted to you that the Stonemoor ladies might be getting gentle treatment for some unknown purpose of Walsingham's?'

'Yes, he did, but . . .'

'I don't think we can rely on the sheriff's men to question those ladies as hard as they ought to be questioned. They may not feel they have the authority to do that. *But we can do it ourselves!* Even if Walter Cogge did the actual deed, I would wager that it was at that Gould woman's orders. We can take her unawares, while . . . while in her mind it's all still . . . raw. If she ordered this, I can't believe she didn't know that she was committing an enormity. She must have a conscience! I should think that what she's done is giving her bad dreams! We can thrust these poor remains at the so devout Principal of Stonemoor and take her by surprise. We might jolt her into telling the truth that way.'

'We *can't* go back!' wailed Dale. 'We're not really turning back, are we, ma'am? I don't want to go back to that Stonemoor place! I can't abide the thought of it!'

Neither could I, though I didn't want to reveal the depths of a dread for which I couldn't reasonably account. 'I don't think we'd be very popular if we reappeared,' I said. 'According to the ladies, they expect a party of five to arrive at any moment!'

'Really?' said Sybil. 'Do travellers visit them so often, then? In this wild district?'

'Apparently,' I said. 'That's what they told us, anyway. You heard that yourself, Sybil. So I don't think . . .'

'Never mind the convenience of the Stonemoor ladies!' Sybil was excited and determined. 'After what they've maybe done to Bernard Hardwicke and Christopher Spelton! Why should we worry about their extra guests? Let them do the worrying! We could get back to Stonemoor today!' She was alight with eagerness. 'What we want to do is wake up Mistress Gould's conscience – or maybe the consciences of some of the other ladies. If Mistress Gould ordered this, some of the others probably know. Perhaps they're having bad dreams too! But with every day that passes, they'll go further into pretending that it was footpads or something like that. They'll almost convince themselves! You know what I mean.'

'That's my sensible Sybil,' I remarked. I didn't really mean it to come out in such a mocking tone, but it did, and Sybil flushed. I blurted out my real feelings after all. 'It isn't safe!' I said. 'Stonemoor is a dangerous place! I know it is, and so do you, Sybil. I don't want to put any of us in danger. It's time to let the sheriff at York take over.'

'No, wait.' Brockley spoke sharply. 'Now that I've heard what Mistress Jester has to say – well, I can see her point. I can indeed. And as for the danger, well, after all, there are five of us. From the start, we've reassured ourselves by thinking that being a sizeable party means safety.'

'That's right.' The taciturn Joseph put in a word. He was grinning. 'They can't murder us all. Even Master Cogge couldn't manage it. Besides, I don't think he's like that. Not a murderer, anyway. I've been staying with him, got to know him. That don't make sense to me.'

We didn't decide at once. In fact, we stood about beside that river and argued for a good half-hour. But at the end of it, little as any of us liked the idea, we settled that we would return.

'Who carries the boot?' Sybil enquired.

'I'll take it,' said Joseph. He opened his saddlebags and hauled out a spare cloak. 'I'll wrap it in this. I need something to tie round it, though.'

I fished in my own saddlebags and found a girdle. 'This will do,' I said. I added ruefully that I didn't think I would ever want to use that girdle again.

'Nor I my cloak,' said Joseph. 'But it does make the thing less horrible to handle.'

'Have you got the wallet and receipt safely, madam?' Brockley asked.

'Yes,' I said. They were now in my hidden pouch, along with my picklocks, dagger, and spare money. The purchase money for the book was too heavy for the pouch and travelled in my saddlebag.

We started back across the bridge and thereafter made what speed we could. We made just one stop, when we finished the food and water, but didn't linger. We were all tired and wanted to get the journey over. Even so, it was late in the day before we got back to Thorby.

EIGHTEEN
Face to Face

When we reached Thorby, we became cautious, looking sharply round us in case another unfriendly crowd should appear. The street stretched away to our right, though not very far, for Thorby really was a small place. One side of it had some small businesses, such as the tavern, a carpenter's, a smithy, and, as I had surmised, a bakery. The opposite side of the track consisted only of cottages, with smoke rising from their chimneys. At the far end, we could see the church, which was a small timber affair, only recognizable as a church because of the tall wooden cross on its front gable.

There were few people about and the tavern appeared to be closed. Then we caught sight of a black-cloaked figure emerging from the church and hurrying towards us, waving. We drew rein.

The figure, which was short and plump, came up to us, breathless, and I recognized him as the vicar, Doctor Rowbotham. He looked worried and was clutching at his black hat, which didn't seem to be on quite straight. He was in so much haste that he was in danger of tripping himself up on his cloak, which was a little long for him. He started to talk the moment he was within earshot.

'I thought it was you . . . even from a distance I recognized some of the horses . . . I saw them when they came through the village, being exercised a few days ago . . . what are you *doing* back here? You shouldn't have come, no indeed you shouldn't! *Why* have you come back?' He sounded angry as well as worried.

'We have returned for good reasons,' said Brockley. 'We can assure you . . .'

'There's going to be trouble! Did I not say to you before

that I did not recommend Stonemoor as a place for any honest Christian to frequent? I have complained to the authorities in vain. I have the souls of my parishioners to consider, after all. That Will Grimes laughs at me openly sometimes . . .'

He wasn't a Yorkshireman; his speech was that of the south. It was educated, too, but not well controlled for he was plainly over-excited. His voice was high-pitched, full of what sounded like an unhealthy degree of emotion.

'There have been deaths associated with those ladies! Especially with one of them. It is not proper for women to pretend to be physicians! Ever since the original sin of Eve, women have been doors through which the Devil can gain entrance to this world, unless those doors are kept shut. We must be always on our guard. In some families, the women cultivate secret knowledge that is handed down from mother to daughter and that knowledge gives them power, and once a woman has power, then her door is wide open.'

I saw, with a sharp twinge of alarm, that there was spittle at the corners of his prim little mouth, and the flinty eyes were sparking as though someone had struck the flint.

'What deaths do you mean?' I asked, seizing my chance to speak when Doctor Rowbotham stopped to catch his breath.

'A man called Harry Henley died and now it's Master Butterworth. Two deaths, after one of those accursed ladies came offering sympathy to the sick man, and making potions for him. It is my duty to resist evil but some of the villagers are so simple that they mistake it for kindness. Sometimes I feel like King Canute, who couldn't order the tide to stop rising. This is no place for any of you! I beg you, turn away and go back to wherever you came from and . . .'

Doctor Rowbotham seemed to be a talkative man. Once again we had to wait until sheer shortness of breath forced him to pause before anyone could say anything more. Then Brockley said: 'We can't turn away. We have been brought back by something too grave to ignore. And yes, there is certainly going to be trouble for the ladies of Stonemoor.'

Then, taking the lead, he spurred on and the rest of us found ourselves following, willy-nilly, leaving the vicar to stand in the road, staring indignantly after us. As we rode up the zigzag track up to the house, I looked ahead at the crenelated walls. To me, it seemed impregnable enough to repel any number of impassioned witch-hunters.

It also looked threatening.

Walter Cogge was in charge of the gatehouse and pulled the gate open to let us through, though he was visibly surprised to see us. 'What brings you back here? You only left this morning.'

'Something urgent has arisen,' I told him. I slid to the ground. 'We must see Mistress Gould at the first possible moment, and you should be present, Master Cogge.'

'Quite right.' Brockley and Dale were also dismounting. 'Quickly, now. We have no time to waste.' Brockley's tone was deliberately commanding.

'The ladies are at their devotions,' said Cogge. 'I am not permitted to interrupt them.'

'Chanting the office, I take it,' said Brockley. 'Well, we have to stall the horses. Perhaps by the time that's done, the chanting will be over. If not, we can wait – where should we wait, Mistress Stannard?'

I had run up my stirrups and was unfastening Blaze's girth. 'In Mistress Gould's study,' I said. 'That would be best.'

'I can't take you there without first consulting with Mistress Gould,' said Cogge.

'We'll see about that,' Brockley told him, and for a moment, the two of them stood face to face like rival hounds, bristling.

Then Cogge seemed to collect himself. 'I am sure something can be arranged. Perhaps in the meantime, the ladies would care to wait in the guest hall.'

Dale at once stepped close to Brockley, a silent signal which declared that in her opinion we should all keep together. I agreed with her. It was instinctive, but strong. 'The ladies will help in the stable,' I said, and started to undo Blaze's girth.

With so many pairs of hands, the work didn't take long. We deposited our saddlebags, packs, and Joseph's cloak-wrapped burden beside the steps to the main entrance, and then saw to our mounts. We soon had them stalled, with water and fodder.

We didn't rub them down but Cogge produced some rugs to throw over their backs. 'And now,' he said as we all went outside again, 'just what is all this about?'

I decided to take charge. 'Show us,' I said, 'to Mistress Gould's study and wait there with us. There is no question of seeking her permission to enter the study. We must see her, and that is the proper place, and you will find out why soon enough, because you need to be there. The matter we are here about may concern you.'

'Me?' Cogge's heavy eyebrows rose. All he said, however, was: 'If it is a serious matter, and by your manner, it must be, I ought to be there in any case to protect Mistress Gould's interests. I have a responsibility towards all the ladies of this house, especially when such a crowd of people are demanding to speak to Mistress Gould, and have such grave faces. Do you all need to be present?'

'Yes. All of us,' I said firmly.

'Even him?' He glanced at Joseph.

'Even me,' Joseph agreed equably.

We went in by way of the main door, picking up our baggage and Joseph's unlovely bundle on the way. There was no sound of chanting when Cogge, if reluctantly, led us into the Principal's study; presumably the office was finished. We dumped our packs and saddlebags on the floor.

'Where does Mistress Gould usually go after completing her . . . devotions?' Brockley asked. 'Do you need to fetch her, Master Cogge?'

'She is likely to come to her study,' Cogge said. 'She usually does. Let us give her a few moments.'

In fact, it was only a few seconds later that the study door, which Brockley had closed, opened again. Philippa Gould came in and then stopped short, raising her thin eyebrows. 'What is this? You have returned, Mistress Stannard? Surely I remember telling you that we expect other guests shortly, five of them, in fact. They will probably be here tomorrow!' She walked round her desk and took her seat behind it. 'What is the reason for this . . . invasion? Please state your business.'

'Sheriff's men have been here,' I said, 'seeking to know if

two men, Master Bernard Hardwicke and Master Christopher Spelton, had visited you. You said you had not seen them.'

'Of course. And we hadn't.'

I took Joseph's bundle from him, laid it down on Philippa's desk, and unwrapped it. It lay there, an ugly sight, with its protruding bone. It gave off a foul smell of decay. Philippa jerked backwards. 'What is this?'

'The remnant of a dead man, found in the river a few miles north of here. We had to cross it to come here.'

'So? People do fall into rivers and drown, now and then,' said Philippa. 'Why do you bring this . . . this horror . . . to me?'

I put back my cloak and reached inside my divided overskirt for the wallet. Drawing it out, I took from it Bernard Hardwicke's receipt and spread it on the desk, turning it so that Philippa Gould could read what it said.

'This,' I said, 'was found in the wallet I have here, and *that* was found thrust down inside that boot. What have you to say to that, Mistress Gould?'

NINETEEN
Mea Culpa

Philippa Gould looked at the receipt and went white. She sat quite still, as if she had been turned to stone. We waited. Eventually, she said: 'I see. That is proof that the man Bernard Hardwicke did come here and did buy the book you seek. I can't deny it.'

'The other man, Christopher Spelton, was also here,' I said. She began to shake her head but I raised my voice, speaking strongly. Now that I was here and face to face with her, my fear had retreated, to be replaced by a simple loathing of this place and its mystery. 'We know he was here, Mistress Gould. Master Spelton habitually undertook secret tasks for the queen and her council, and sometimes he went into danger. If he felt himself to be at risk, he would place a mark so that if anything happened to him, anyone who came in search of him would know that he had been – wherever it was. Anyone seeking him would know how to look for the mark and how to recognize it. We found it, a sign in red chalk, on the underside of the window chest in the guest chamber that I and Mistress Jester shared. Christopher Spelton has been in this house. And like Bernard Hardwicke, he failed to continue his journey, which should have taken him on to Scotland. What have you to say?'

'Neither Master Hardwicke nor Master Spelton ever came to harm under this roof!'

I said: 'This morning, you admitted to us that the book we had come to buy was not available, that another book had been put in its box in its stead. As a matter of fact, we already knew that, because something about the book you showed us aroused our suspicions. It didn't match the description that I was given. Therefore, last night, we entered your library to examine it more closely . . .'

'So you *were* in the library? Mistress Ames . . .' Philippa stopped.

'Mistress Ames was right,' said Brockley. 'She did hear voices; she did glimpse my lantern. We were in the library when the two of you came to investigate and we heard what you said, outside the door.'

'But the door was locked! And no one was in the library!'

'I have ways of unlocking doors,' I told her, 'and we were certainly in the library. We were behind the door, as a matter of fact. You opened it but you didn't come right into the room, nor did you thrust the door right back. We were on the other side of it, within a foot or so of you and Mistress Ames.'

'What? You were hiding from me and Mistress Ames? You were *afraid* of us?' Mistress Gould began to laugh. 'You were *afraid* of us? But why, if you wanted to examine the book again, didn't you just ask me?'

'After finding Christopher Spelton's mark, we would naturally be wary,' I said, so dampingly that Philippa's laughter subsided. 'He left that mark because he felt that there was danger here. Tell me,' I said, 'if you had found us, what *would* you have done?'

'Whatever do you suppose I would have done?' Amusement was now changed to outrage. 'I would have asked you what you were doing there and when you told me, I would have confirmed – as I did this morning – that the book you had come to purchase was not the one I showed you. You had no need to go creeping about in the middle of the night, forcing locks and hiding behind doors. Do you seriously suppose that if I had come face to face with you last night, I would have injured you in some way? And are you saying that I *did* injure Master Hardwicke and Master Spelton? They left this place in good order and good health. Yes, they were here. I can't explain what happened to them after they left.' She wiped a hand across her lips as though to clean them. 'I didn't want anyone to know they had been here. You see, there was my foolish sister . . .'

Her words trailed miserably away. 'Your sister?' I said. 'Mistress Yates?'

'A good woman, though I fear she made some poor

confessions to me,' remarked Cogge. I glanced at him, surprised all over again at the contrast between his crude features and physique, and the well-bred calm of his voice.

'Yes, Bella is a good woman,' said Philippa. 'But ignorant. She is my natural sister. My father acknowledged her but he did not take her from her mother, which is why she grew up on a farm, living the life of a farmer's daughter, and unlettered. She never learned to read and write until she came here and I taught her. But from her mother, she did get some religious teaching, and her mother held by the old faith. Her beliefs were rigid, and shot through with superstition, too. My sister still holds by those beliefs. Her mother taught her to fear heresy, taught her to think new ideas were wicked and that laughter of any kind was suspect. Bella thinks all laughter is irreverent. I have tried to widen her mind but she has never broken free of her childhood training.'

'You think differently?' Sybil said.

'I have told you, have I not? My father was interested in modern thought. I was educated at home, by a most enlightened tutor,' said Philippa. 'I am still Catholic but like my father, I understand that some old beliefs may have been just that, just beliefs, and that new discoveries can't be ignored. Bella does not agree. She refuses even to listen to me. She was scandalized when Eleanor Overton brought John of Evesham's *Observations* here!'

'Yes,' I said. 'She told us herself that she disapproved of the book and didn't think anyone ought to be interested in it.'

'Quite. She looked at it, and she was able to read quite a lot of it, although the lettering is so old-fashioned, because I have myself taught her to understand such lettering. Bella does not care greatly for books but I have tried to interest her in the many old and beautiful works we have in our library. To show her the *Observations*, though, was a mistake. It shocked her. To her, the *Observations* is full of lore from infidel countries, which in itself makes it unfit to be studied by Christians; and it also recommends the theory that the earth goes round the sun, which in the eyes of the Catholic Church is most definitely heresy. And there is an irreverent picture, too. She wanted me to destroy the book and was angry when I proposed to sell it, because she said – her own words – that that would be to spread its poison beyond these walls. She would have destroyed it herself, except that as I told you only this morning, there is a curse on anyone who does so. Those of my ladies who share her prejudices are afraid of the curse too.'

She came to a halt. I said: 'Please go on.'

'I have lost the thread,' said Philippa blankly.

'Your sister Bella was angered by the idea of selling the book,' said Sybil helpfully.

'Yes. Oh, yes. Well, the man Hardwicke came to buy it and he paid for it and rode off with it, but Bella was violently upset. She had come to me and begged me not to let him take it. But I did . . . and then Bella, as she sometimes does, took a horse and went out. I thought she was just going to ride in the open air, to calm her mind, but she didn't. She came back, bringing the book with her. She said she had gone after Master Hardwicke. She caught him up near the river ford a few miles north of here, and stopped him and bought it back from him, paying him as much as he had paid me. Or so she told me.'

'Where did she get the money?' asked Cogge suddenly.

'She has money,' Philippa explained. 'When her mother died, which was not long after my husband also died, her stepfather didn't want her on the farm any more. He'd married her mother after Bella was born; and had children by her; he wanted them to have his farm and his goods after him, not Bella, who was only a stepchild. It wasn't a happy state of affairs for Bella. I was back with our father by then, but he'd married again and I could *not* get on with his new wife.'

For a moment, bitter memories seemed to distract her from the matter in hand. 'She swept into the house and started to behave as though she was the lady of a manor and I was one of the servants! *Do this, do that, go here, go there, fetch my embroidery frame, would you, Philippa? Oh, and I don't think we need so many kitchen staff, Philippa, so I've dismissed two of them. It will save money and that will please your father. You can help out in the kitchen when necessary.*'

'As a result,' said Mistress Gould trenchantly, 'my father had the idea of buying a house where I could live with women friends. So he bought this house, Stonemoor, and fetched Bella from the farm to join me. He gave us both some money. But maintaining this community is costly and we are now short – though we would be better off if Bella hadn't held on so tightly to her portion. She has never contributed more than she can help to our expenses. She keeps her money here, and yes, she had enough to buy the *Observations* back. And then,' said Philippa, 'Master Spelton arrived.'

'Did you tell him what your sister had done?' I asked.

'Yes, I did. And I showed him the money I had taken for it. I said I didn't want any further payment. That wouldn't have been honest. We agreed on that, and he took the book, in its box, and put it in his luggage. Next day, when he was leaving, Bella went to help him prepare for his journey and she carried his saddlebags downstairs, ahead of him. She seized a moment to exchange the book in his luggage for another, which was in an identical box. I told you, I think, that I had had boxes made for the more precious books in our collection. They all look alike. She used one of the same size. Afterwards, she told me what she had done. I was furious! For the second time, the book had come back, bounced, like a flat pebble on water! And this time, the messenger had gone off with the wrong volume.'

'But it would be found out,' I said. 'When Doctor Dee received it, he would look at it and know!'

'Bella,' said her sister bitterly, 'is not unduly intelligent. She thought that perhaps he wouldn't realize, that he might simply think that the description he had had of the book was wrong. The one she put in was another copy of the one you've seen. It has star charts and some text that includes figures. I was sure it would not deceive Doctor Dee. Oh, sometimes, Bella maddens me!'

'And now she has hidden the book,' I said. 'And won't say where it is. But this is beside the point. The fact remains that Bernard Hardwicke somehow met his death shortly after leaving here, and that Christopher Spelton has also vanished.'

'I can't explain that. Truly, I can't,' said Philippa wanly.

'Did your sister take a horse and go for a ride on the moors shortly after Master Spelton rode away from here, as she did when Master Hardwicke left?' asked Brockley sharply.

'No! I mean . . . I don't remember. Perhaps she did. She often does, if something has upset her. Are you accusing her of something? But of what? I am sure that Bella wouldn't . . . couldn't . . .'

Brockley said: 'You or she could have given orders to Walter Cogge here.'

'I received no such orders,' said Cogge. 'And if I had, I would not have obeyed them. I obeyed an order to conceal the fact that Master Hardwicke and Master Spelton had been here, because Mistress Gould did not wish her sister's foolish behaviour to be known. But that was all. Do you really think I would have accepted an order to commit . . . well, is it murder we are discussing?'

'None of us knows what to think,' said Sybil.

I said: 'We had better talk to Bella. By the sound of it, she was the last person to see Bernard Hardwicke and possibly the same applies to Master Spelton. Would you be good enough to send for her, Mistress Gould?'

In a mechanical way, as though she were a puppet, worked by strings in someone else's hands, Philippa picked up the bell on her desk, and rang it. 'When I am in my study, someone is always near enough to hear my bell,' she said, and sure enough, another moment brought a tap on the door and when Philippa called 'Come in', Mary Haxby appeared.

'Please find my sister Mistress Yates, and ask her to come to my study,' said Philippa. Her voice had no expression.

We waited in an uncomfortable silence. I sat down on a stool and nodded to Dale to do the same. Sybil also took a stool. Brockley stood where he was, his right hand resting lightly on his sword hilt. Walter Cogge had from the start been standing politely two steps behind the rest of us and he stayed there. Joseph just stared at the window, though there was nothing to see out there except the dark moorland.

Another tap on the door heralded Bella's arrival. Philippa said: 'Come . . .' but Bella was in before the invitation was finished. She said: '*Benedicite*, my sister,' and waited, though her currant-like eyes glanced rapidly at us, taking us all in.

'When you went after Bernard Hardwicke to buy back the

Observations of John of Evesham, how did you leave him? Did he just ride away?' asked Philippa.

'No one called Hardwicke has been here!'

'Nonsense, Bella. I know we have pretended to the guests who are in this room now that Hardwicke never came here, but of course he did. They now know that he did.' Philippa pointed to the boot and its protruding bone, which were still lying on the desk. 'That was found in the river. It is all that is left of Master Hardwicke. The receipt he gave me when he paid for the book was found inside that boot. He seems to have been killed close to the river, where you say you last saw him.'

Bella stared at her sister. Her mouth worked. She moved to look more closely at the boot and then recoiled from the sight of the bone that was sticking out of it. Philippa pushed the receipt towards her so that she could read it for herself. 'There is no doubt,' said Philippa, 'that that boot belonged to Master Hardwicke.'

'How did you leave Master Hardwicke? In good health?' Brockley enquired. 'And did you also ride after Master Spelton when he in turn took his leave of Stonemoor? Carrying the wrong book, which you must have known would be recognized as such when its purchaser looked at it? Did you also catch him up by the river?'

Brockley sounded as though he was using his voice and his words as hammers. I would not have liked to be questioned in such a way. Bella's eyes were darting from us to her sister and back again. They were bright, with malice, I thought, but also with fear.

'Master Hardwicke rode off over the ford and I didn't see him again!' Bella's voice was high and angry. 'I never went after Master Spelton. Who says I did?'

'I do.' Walter Cogge stepped forward. 'Just after Master Spelton left, you took a horse out.'

We had not expected an intervention from Cogge, least of all in support of us. We all turned to him in surprise. Bella was glaring at him. 'You weren't in the stables that day! You were out on the farm!' she snapped.

'I came back for the midday meal and I was there when

you came in, and I'd already seen that Roan Thorby was missing,' said Cogge imperturbably. 'You brought him in with sweat on his hide. You'd ridden him hard. You didn't see me; I was in my room in the loft above the stalls. I let you rub Roan Thorby down yourself. Serve you right, after getting him in that state.'

Bella had begun to shake. The currant eyes were bright now with something more than fear or fury; they were full of tears. Philippa saw them. 'What is it, Bella? What are you crying for? Why are you trembling like that? What do you know that you shouldn't? Bella?'

'Oh, dear Mother of God!' Bella's tears began to stream. Her mouth worked. No one spoke or offered a kind word. The air quivered with blame, with accusation. It broke her. Suddenly, she ran round the desk and threw herself on her knees beside Philippa. '*Mea culpa! Mea culpa!*'

'You've clearly learnt *some* Latin,' remarked Philippa. 'Though teaching you has been hard going.' Bella pawed at her sister's skirts and Philippa, half-rising, pushed her chair back, to get away from the clutching hands. 'What are you guilty of, Bella? What have you done?'

'It started with an accident! It were just an accident! Oh, God have mercy on me; sweet saints preserve me; I never meant . . . never meant . . .!'

'Never meant *what*? Get up, Bella, get up!'

'I can't get up . . . sister, doan't you push me off, doan't you abandon me, I'm your sister, blood of your blood . . .!'

'*Bella!*'

'That Master Hardwicke, he didn't want to sell me back the book; he said no to me, he said *no*! We'd got off our hosses and hobbled them and we'd sat down by the river; when I caught him up, he was nearly at the ford and I said I wanted to talk to him, so he said, let's get down and sit on that rock there and to tell him all about it, whatever it was. Only when I told him and showed him my money, he got angry. He said no and got up and went to his horse and he leant down to undo the hobbles and I was angry too, so very very angry . . .'

She actually sounded angry now, as though the memory had awakened the fury that must have possessed her at the time.

She stopped, I think because her rage had actually choked her. Philippa said: 'Go on!'

'That book mustna go out into the world, no it mustna! It's a wicked book, all heathen learning, not fit for Christian eyes, and saying things the Church says aren't true . . . and making fun of the Pope – let that go out into the world and it'll spread like a disease; it'll make folk sicken in their minds . . .'

'*Get on with it!*'

'I'd tried to say all that to him but he took no heed, he laughed at me. He went to his horse and turned his back on me. He wouldn't listen, and he'd laughed, yes, *laughed*!' Bella was gabbling, almost incoherent with fury. 'I had my little belt knife with me like always. I thought: I'll show him, I'll show him. My faith's not to be laughed at, no, it's not, and I ran after him and hit him in the back with the knife. I wasn't thinking to kill him, just wound him, make him turn round, make him *attend* to me! I didn't think that little blade could kill a grown man! It had to go through his cloak and all as well! But it's a good sharp blade; it went in like it was hot and he and what he had on were just butter. He didn't die at once, any road. He stood up and turned round and stared at me and I stared at him and I started to say summat . . . to tell him he'd got to listen, got to . . . and then there was blood coming from his mouth and he fell over and made funny noises and then he was dead!'

There was a frightful silence, until Philippa broke it with: 'And then?'

'I were that scared!' Bella was trembling violently. Tears poured down her face. 'I couldn't get the knife out. Any road, I took the saddle and bridle off his horse and threw them in the river, and his saddlebags too and then I got hold of him and dragged him – oh, God's teeth! He were such a weight! But I pushed him in the river too, the knife still in his back, and chased the horse away. But I got the book out of his saddlebag first, and I came home with it and said I'd bought it back!'

'And Master Spelton?' I said.

A shocking expression crossed Bella's face, made all the worse by the fact that she was still on her knees and that above the desk top, only her head was visible. It was as though she had been beheaded and it was her dead mouth that was talking. Despite her tears, her face, her little dark eyes, had become sly.

'I couldna just let him go. I'd given him a different book, but this Doctor Dee that wants to buy it – a wicked magician, he must be, tries to raise demons, so folk say, and reads the stars for that heretic queen we're all supposed to half worship . . . Doctor Dee would realize. I didn't think that at first, but after Master Spelton had gone, I thought about it again and then I realized. I'm not the silly fool you think I am!' Her look at Philippa was horribly triumphant. 'I take time to think things through but I get there. I get there. Happen it takes time but get there, I do. I'm nobbut a bit slower than you. I'm not *stupid.*'

Philippa made a disgusted sound. Bella's gaze came back to the rest of us, more sly than ever, hideously self-satisfied, 'It were easier t'second time,' she said. 'I knew what to do. I took Roan Thorby and I rode fast and caught Master Spelton up. I come up alongside him, leant over and drove t' knife in. I'd lost my belt knife but I'd got another from our stores and no one noticed, only I didn't use that one for Master Spelton. Wanted to be sure, so I got a second knife as well, a bigger one, from the kitchen. Just to be certain. He turned round and gawped at me and said, *What in hell's name do you think you're doing, woman?* And then he looked horror-struck, like, and his eyes rolled upwards and he fell off the horse.'

'I can't believe this,' said Philippa faintly. 'I *can't believe it!*'

Bella didn't seem to hear her. She was lost in her terrifying story. 'I grabbed the horse's reins,' she said, 'and got down and hitched it to a bush and went back and dragged the knife out. I got it out that time. Only he weren't dead; he tried to get hold of me, but I fought and somehow he rolled over and I hit him on the head with a lump of stone. There was plenty about. Then I . . . well, it was the same story. Everything in the river, t'book as well. I were sorry for that for it weren't the wicked Evesham book but what else to do? I thought it best, get rid of everything and know nothing.'

'So that's it,' said Philippa, in a voice of despair. 'That's the whole story. Oh, how horrible.' She stared at her sister and we watched the horror take hold of her, as she absorbed its meaning. She thrust her chair still further back and away from her sister, visibly shrinking from her. 'How *horrible!*'

'Yes,' said Bella. And then reality seemed to crowd in on her and the furtive, *aren't I clever* expression in her eyes changed to terror. 'But you'll not throw me to the law, sister; doan't do that to me; we're the same blood; and this is an abbey now; it's under Church law; I can't be taken by the sheriff's men; I can't be arrested for defending honest Christians from heresy, from wicked creeds; I can't . . . I can't . . .'

Her fit of rage had passed and now our stony faces, Philippa's recoil, were frightening her, more every moment. Behind my still countenance, I was actually in turmoil. Christopher Spelton was dead. I had feared it but now I knew for certain and grief was sweeping through me. I had never realized until now, as I heard his death confirmed, just how much I had valued his friendship . . . even his love, the love I had rejected. I wanted to get away, to be by myself, to cry my sorrow out. But I remained seated where I was, silent, stiff-faced. Walter Cogge, his voice genuinely appalled, said: 'I told you I thought her confessions had been poor. They are a great deal worse than I could have dreamed. These are monstrous things that she has done.'

'It's amazing to me,' said Brockley, sounding bewildered, 'that a woman *could* do it! Is it sure, even now – I mean, could she be shielding someone?'

'Me, you mean?' said Cogge. 'You are still thinking in that way? No, she is not!'

'Indeed not!' said Philippa. 'She is telling the truth, God help her. I believe her. It would have taken strength, but she is as strong as a man.'

Bella had moved, part of the way round the desk, and I could see her better now. I could see the muscle in those thick, bent shoulders, and in the meaty forearms that were reaching so that she could clutch her sister's skirts. Yes, Bella had the strength.

And Bella, recognizing her doom in her sister's words and in the faces of the rest of us, began to weep and beg and then to scream.

'Master Cogge,' said Philippa, ignoring her sister and raising her voice above Bella's cries, 'be good enough to take my sister down to the cellars and lock her in. The far cellar, the small one that isn't being used, will do. You had better provide a bucket and a pallet and blanket for the night. She deserves no comforts but she is still my sister. I will order soup and bread and water to be taken to her. Master Brockley, perhaps you would help him.'

The two of them bore Bella away, half-dragging her. The screams faded as they went.

And then, my own tears would not be controlled any longer. I began to cry. Dale came to put her arms round me; Sybil knelt beside me, murmuring words of comfort.

'I think,' Sybil said, 'that you should go to bed, Ursula. You don't want to have another sick headache. It has been a long day,' she added drily.

It was such a trite comment that through my grief, I almost burst out laughing. Then I checked myself, quelling both laughter and tears, before I became hysterical. We had seen enough of hysterics with Bella.

TWENTY
The Unexpected Ally

Philippa's face as she watched her sister go was full of misery. But when Bella was out of sight and hearing, she rang her bell again, and when Mary Haxby appeared, told her to show us to our guest rooms. 'You will obviously have to stay here tonight,' Philippa said. 'You can have the bedchambers you had before. Your groom can lodge with Master Cogge once again. My other guests have not yet come. If they arrive late today, they will have to share the rooms that are still free. Those rooms are smaller than yours and it will not be convenient but . . .' She let the sentence trail away as though she had lost interest.

We found that our bedchambers had been made ready, though presumably not originally for us. Joseph was still with us, hesitating a little because he didn't like to go to Cogge's quarters until Cogge had returned. He didn't like to enter our bedchambers either, however, and so, when Mary Haxby left us, we all hovered round the door of Sybil's and my room, until Brockley and Cogge suddenly arrived in the guest hall below and came up the stairs to rejoin us. They looked surprisingly cheerful, considering the unpleasant errand they had just performed.

'Is Bella safely shut away?' I asked.

'Yes. It was a disagreeable business,' Brockley said. 'But, madam, I have news.' He glanced at Cogge, who was grinning. 'Walter here is one of us.'

'One of . . .?'

Brockley made a gesture which said, *Let's all go right into your room, madam.* We were bewildered, but we did as he wanted. He gave Joseph a push, to bring him in as well. 'No point in standing out there,' he said as he shut the door. 'Someone could be skulking just behind the door to the vestibule, with their big ears flapping. Go on, Walter.'

'I thought it was time I spoke up,' Cogge said. 'These new revelations are so very serious. I had no more idea of them than Mistress Gould had. It's true that I knew that the two missing men had been here and I also knew that Mistress Gould didn't want to tell the tale of how her sister had bought the book back once and then stolen it from Master Spelton and subsequently hidden it so that you can't get at it. None of that concerned me. Mistress Gould bade me keep all that to myself and so I did. I am here on quite another matter, with orders to maintain my pretence of being in the service of the ladies until my task is done.'

'Pretence?' I asked. 'And who gave you the orders?' I sat down on the bed, and Sylvia and Dale joined me, seating themselves one on either side of me while all three of us gazed in astonishment at this unexpected ally. Joseph was staring, too. Things were moving too fast for comfort. I was tired and hungry, and wished that I could simply have something to eat, and then just get into bed and go to sleep. But no. It seemed that a whole new batch of revelations was about to be unloosed on us.

'My orders came from Sir Francis Walsingham,' said Cogge. 'Are you aware that he has been worried of late because of a suspected agent, at court, working secretly for Mary Stuart and the Catholic cause?'

'Yes,' I told him. 'I did know that. I believe he has some idea of who it is, but needs to prove it.'

'Exactly. He has laid a trap. He has agents on the Continent and through them it is known that the Jesuits are planning a kind of . . . invasion of England by Jesuit priests, whose task will be to raise money for Mary's cause and also to make converts if they can.'

'We knew that too,' Brockley said.

'One of those agents reported that this invasion is now beginning, in a small way. Five priests are due to arrive in England about now, travelling separately, apparently as respectable individuals here on business or to visit relatives, but intending to meet at the house of a family called Brownlow, who live between here and the east coast . . .'

'Is all this certain? The agent seems to have found out an amazing amount,' I said.

'Walsingham has also placed someone in the Brownlows' household. They've been suspect for a long time, but so far Walsingham has left them alone because he thought he might have a use for them, if priests started coming into northern ports, which was probable because there is a good deal of support for Catholics here in the north. We know that the Brownlows have been collecting details of routes and sympathetic families and so forth; in other words, the priests would get their final instructions from them. The priests will be coming in through Whitby and Scarborough, and the first plan was that they should gather at the Brownlows' house and spend a couple of days there, while they settled who precisely was to go where. Have I made myself clear so far?'

Several of us said, 'Yes,' in unison. Brockley said: 'What about this trap?'

'I'm coming to that.' Cogge was brisk and businesslike, displaying a cool, well-informed mind that negated his hulking build and massive facial bones so completely that I suddenly found it strange that I had ever noticed them. 'Sir Francis Walsingham arranged for the man that he suspects of being the spy at court to be approached by someone he didn't know well, but who declared himself to be a Catholic and one of Mary's supporters. This man told the suspect about the priests and said that they would be picked up at the Brownlows' house; that someone was on watch and the authorities would descend on them probably the day after they were all assembled, when they might well be caught in the midst of discussing their maps and lists. This obliging informant said he himself could not send a warning, for he was a very humble court employee who couldn't afford to hire a courier and couldn't take the time to go himself, either. Indeed, he didn't know where the Brownlows lived and doubted if he could ever find his way there, anyhow. But he did know about the ladies of Stonemoor, as he was related to one of them. He said that since he believed the suspect to be a sympathizer like himself, and knew him to be better able to communicate with people in the north, he was wondering – could the suspect get a warning to the Brownlows? He suggested that as soon as the priests had all arrived, they should be sent on to Stonemoor without delay. There, they would be welcomed.'

'I see,' I said. 'Or I think I do. You are here to warn the authorities if and when the priests arrive here?'

'Yes. They'll bring their maps, lists, and so on with them, to study them here. Nice, useful evidence! The helpful informant who talked to the suspect pointed out that the priests would need such things, and in any case, they had better not be found in the Brownlows' possession. The authorities would probably swoop on their house anyway and search it. The point is,' said Cogge, 'that if the priests *don't* arrive here, then the suspect probably didn't pass the warning on and may, after all, be innocent. But if they do – then it is as certain as it can be that Sir Francis suspects the right man. By the way, it isn't certain that Philippa Gould realizes that her prospective flood of guests are priests. When she told me to expect them, she said they were travellers on private business, journeying together as travellers often do, for safety in strange places. The Brownlows may have deceived her; it's quite possible. The ladies of Stonemoor are not very worldly, any of them. Not even Mistress Gould.'

'But we know that Mistress Gould does expect a group of five,' I said. 'So the trap has worked.'

Cogge smiled. 'I think so. But it must still be sprung. The quintet must arrive here before they can be seized. It will be my business to get to York and alert William Fairfax. He will be pleased with the news, I think.'

'Who is this suspect you keep talking about?' asked Sybil.

'I know his name,' said Cogge. 'But I mustn't risk pointing a finger at the wrong man. Even now, we don't *know* definitely that the expected guests are the priests. That's why I said that I only *think* the trap has worked. When the High Sheriff's men pounce, they'll search the quintet's luggage for evidence – the lists and maps, I mean.'

'What is going to happen to Bella?' I asked.

Brockley said: 'Her sister has withdrawn to her room to consider. But she has no choice, of course. Bella admitted her guilt in front of witnesses. Word about that will also have to be sent to York and that's that. We left Bella down on her knees in a cellar, weeping and praying.'

'And much good may it do her!' The words snapped out of me before I could stop them. Bella had murdered Christopher. It was coming home to me, more every moment, that I had liked Christopher Spelton more than I had ever dreamed of liking any man again. That when I refused to marry him, I had thrown away a golden opportunity. He would not have stopped me from continuing to care for Hawkswood and Withysham, or going on with my plans to create a good inheritance for my son. I had been too determined to keep my life unchanged, I thought. I had also been afraid of having further children, I recalled, but women did have babies successfully when they were in their forties, and why shouldn't I? Harry's birth had been easy.

They were all looking at me in startled fashion. I wasn't usually vindictive. 'She has killed a friend of mine,' I said shortly and added: 'Isn't it time we had something to eat and went to our beds? I wonder if anyone is going to provide us with supper?'

'I think I can find the kitchen,' Sylvia said. 'Didn't we smell cooking from the gallery where the library is? Perhaps Dale would come with me. We can ask for some supper or get it ourselves, if necessary. We'll bring it back with us.'

However, before she and Dale could depart on this mission, a tap at the door announced the arrival of Mistress Angelica Ames, tall, gaunt and unsmiling as ever, to tell us that supper was being put on the table in the guest hall. 'Mistress Gould has ordered it. Dear God, the revelations of today . . .!' She stared inimically at us as though it were somehow all our fault. 'If only you had stayed away – if only you had not found that accursed boot – none of this need have happened!'

'None of it would have been found out, you mean,' said Brockley. 'The worst *had* happened. Two men have died.'

'So Mistress Gould has told me. Bella Yates is a fool, an ignorant fool, and always has been, and there are others here who are not much better, and because of that, yes, two men have perished. But can today's trouble and the horrors that will follow bring them back to life?' enquired Angelica pungently, before whirling round and sweeping off down the stairs and out of the guest wing in what looked like high dudgeon.

'There have been rulers in the world who used to kill

messengers who had brought bad news,' remarked Brockley. 'Mistress Ames would agree with them, I think. Why ever did her parents name her for the angels?'

We laughed, and the laughter did us good, as did the supper that was indeed awaiting us downstairs. We ate fried chicken and this time there was good white bread to go with it. Afterwards, came a pie filled with preserved plums, and there was a reasonable wine as well. We were being well treated. Perhaps Philippa Gould was afraid of us. Well, that was a pleasant change, I thought, from us being afraid of her!

While we were eating, Brockley said: 'There's one more thing we have to do before we can retire to sleep.'

'Is there? Must we?' asked Dale wearily. I sympathized. 'What is it?' I asked, also wearily.

'Joseph and I will make everything ready,' said Cogge, standing up. 'One of us will fetch the rest of you when we've finished.'

'What . . .?' I began again.

'We have to dig a grave in the garden,' said Cogge. 'Just a little one, but those are Mistress Gould's instructions and I think she is right.'

Some time later, by lantern light, we witnessed the burial of the boot with Bernard Hardwicke's leg inside it. 'It's all we have of him,' said Philippa, when we joined her in the garden. 'But we must do what we can.'

So, wrapped in thick cloaks, we stood beside the tiny grave that the men had prepared – it could have been a place made ready for some departed pet – and there the pathetic remnant, wrapped in a white cloth and still inside the boot, was placed, with reverence. Walter Cogge, mindful of Philippa's presence and therefore maintaining his role as priest to the Stonemoor ladies, recited a Latin prayer and then asked God, in English, to receive the soul of Bernard Hardwicke, even though he died unshriven and did not subscribe to the true faith. Then the three men filled the grave in, and with that done, we all trooped away.

I wept during the night, though mostly, it was for Christopher's sake. That, for me, was a private thing and I did it silently. Even Sybil, lying beside me, did not know.

*   *   *

In the morning, which was cold and clear, we were all awake early and as soon as we were downstairs, I rang the guest hall bell, to ask for breakfast to be served.

We had just finished our porridge and were embarking on more white bread, with butter and cheese, when a disturbance out in the courtyard brought us all to our feet. We hurried to the outer door of the vestibule, where we stopped, not certain whether to go further. Joseph and Cogge were out in the courtyard. Joseph was standing aside, looking worried, while Cogge seemed to have joined an agitated conference which was going on between the porteress of the moment, whom he was loudly addressing as Mistress Greene, and the goblin-like Will Grimes, who had just slid down from his shaggy pony and was making frantic gestures and exclaiming in a voice high-pitched with alarm, though from where we were we couldn't make out his words.

Angelica Ames appeared, hastening down the main steps and marching on across the courtyard to find out what was happening. She listened to Will for a moment and then began to protest and shake her head. Will grew even more agitated. Cogge waved a signal to us to come. We went forward.

'. . . what dost tha mean, no, they can't be?' Will was shouting now. 'Who says no they can't be? I tell thee, they are, and they mean it and they'll be here afore tha knows it! Vicar's leading 'em! Go to t'gate and look down t'hill if tha doan't believe me! They're coming!'

I looked at the others and while Angelica continued to shake her head and make disbelieving noises, we all, including Joseph, did what Will had recommended and made for the gate. There we stopped. Walter Cogge, who had got there first, planted himself in the archway, hands on hips and feet apart, while Mistress Greene, who was round of face and figure, with plump arms and fat little hands, stopped at his side, visibly aghast. We were all aghast. Will was right. They were coming.

By *they*, he had meant a whole crowd of people, who were now making their way up the zigzag path from Thorby. They seemed to be coming slowly, but even from a distance, they had a curiously purposeful look, and in the forefront was a short dumpy figure who might very well be Doctor Rowbotham though I couldn't at this distance see his face. I stared in bewilderment.

'What's it all about? Who are they?' I demanded.

'It looks to me like about three-quarters of Thorby,' said Cogge. 'With Rowbotham in the lead. Will says they're coming for Mistress Bella Yates. And they mean business.'

TWENTY-ONE
The Deputation

'What do you mean, they mean business?' I demanded. 'They want Mistress Bella.' Will Grimes and Angelica Ames had joined us. 'Keep trying to tell thee, so I do!' Grimes said. 'They says she's a witch, that she did kill Master Butterworth with a magic potion; that this here's most likely a house of witches but it's her they're sure of, her they want, and they mean to have her. Village has been muttering for a while now and that there Rowbotham; he's egged them on.'

'Then why aren't we barring the door?' Brockley and I said it together and Brockley strode forward to seize one of the open leaves.

'Don't bother yourselves,' said Cogge, not moving.

'What do you mean?' I demanded.

'There's still the occasional cattle raid from across the Scottish border,' said Cogge, 'but here we're a long way from the border and this house wasn't built to withstand siege. These gates look impressive but one good bang from a battering ram and they'd fall straight off their hinges, and the villagers know it. Haven't you noticed that that crowd down there aren't in a hurry? Can't you see why? They've got a ram and they're bringing it with them. It's slow work, getting it up the zigzag.'

He was right. Rowbotham, who was now recognizable, was leading the crowd and turning round every now and then apparently to issue instructions and behind him, the slow-moving crowd had a hefty something in their midst that they were dragging along. 'Where did they get a battering ram from, for God's sake?' said Brockley.

'Probably cut a tree down during the night,' said Cogge

indifferently. 'Barring the gate's no use. It's sweet talk and common sense and a bit of diplomacy that we need now.'

Angelica said: 'I must tell Mistress Gould! Thank God Mistress Yates is safe in the cellar!'

She swung round and was gone. Cogge said: 'There are people in the village who know all about those cellars. Bella isn't safe anywhere. Let that leaf be, Master Brockley. We'll have the gate wide open. Better not to suggest guilt. Or fear.'

Rowbotham was coming up the final stretch of the zigzag. We could now make out that immediately behind him was a gang of roughly dressed men with unfriendly faces, some bearded, some stubbly as though their owners had had no chance to scrape their jaws clean this morning. They were pushing and pulling at a trolley with a stout tree trunk on it. The trolley had wheels but they weren't very good ones and seemed to be trying to roll in different directions, as though they had been assembled in too much of a hurry. The men who were doing the dragging were having a hard job. Behind them again came a further crowd, which included women and even some children.

We stood there helplessly and watched as the trolley was finally hauled on to the patch of flat ground in front of the gates. There it was set down. I stared at the villagers, noticing for the first time how many of them were alike. Nearly all the men were burly and most of the women were also heavy of build, and nearly everyone had light hair, round blue eyes and skin that had been reddened rather than tanned by wind and sun. They looked as if they were all related. Well, Thorby was small and isolated. Probably Doctor Rowbotham hadn't kept the kin-book up to date, or perhaps he had just given up on it.

With a chilly feeling in my guts, I also noticed that this was a long way from being a hysterical mob (though that would have been bad enough). It had a purposeful leader in Rowbotham, and he had organized them. Behind this deputation there had been consultation and planning. And it certainly did mean business.

Rowbotham stepped forward and opened the proceedings.

'You know who I am. I'm Doctor Rowbotham, vicar of

St Mary's in Thorby, and today I'm spokesman for these folk who are here with me. We want to speak with Mistress Philippa Gould, the principal lady of this house.'

'I am here!' I hadn't seen Philippa arrive but there she was, just behind me, a little breathless, with Angelica at her side. She pushed her way to the fore and addressed Rowbotham. 'What is your business?'

'First, we thank you for not forcing us to use our ram. That shows good sense.'

'Huh! Good sense! That's a joke, that is. There's no sense here, just wickedness. We've long had bad feelings 'bout this house!' A loud voice spoke from the ranks. 'Catholic ladies, that's how we saw them at first, not according to the law but harmless, but time and again we've heard chanting and that makes t'hair rise on the back of a man's neck, and the woman called Bella, she's been handing out potions with the Lord only knows what in them, and there's been rumours too of a curse being laid at midnight, on some book or other . . .'

'Bella certainly has no sense,' muttered Angelica. 'She's been gossiping; I'll take my oath on it.'

'This is Hal Drury, our blacksmith,' said Rowbotham, introducing his supporter.

'Aye, that's who I am and I tell thee, even the few papists among us feel the same as the rest of us, that the Devil's work is going forward in this here house!' bawled Master Drury, raising his voice to overcome an outburst of shouts from the other villagers. 'Chanting, there's been, like I said! And . . .'

'Incantations, that's what!' Another man joined in.

A dissenting voice from somewhere in the rear spoke up. 'There's no call to mind the chanting. That's nobbut the worship of God in the way of the old faith!'

The voice tried to say more, but was shouted down by its neighbours. 'Worshipping God or raising t'Devil?' somebody bellowed and was loudly cheered.

There was a new disturbance then, as other Stonemoor ladies now spilled out of the main door and ran across the courtyard towards us, exclaiming. Philippa looked round. 'Oh, no! I don't want them out here now. Angelica, take them all back inside. Go on! Get them all safely indoors! Now!'

Angelica did as she was bid, arms held wide, herding her fellow ladies back as though they were sheep and she a sheepdog. Her terse explanations and their cries of protest and distress receded towards the house. Doctor Rowbotham stepped forward to confront Philippa Gould, who turned back to face him, chin high. 'We are reasonable and moderate folk . . .' he began.

'What does he think unreasonable and immoderate folk are like?' muttered Brockley.

'. . . and we are here only to deal with the one against whom there is evidence, in the form of two deaths, those of Master Henley and Master Butterworth. You will observe that we have not brought any weapons other than the ram. There were those who wished to carry billhooks and carving knives . . .' here there was a united growl from some of the villagers, who obviously deplored this decision '. . . but I forbade it. Bring out the woman Bella Yates and hand her over to us, and we will withdraw peacefully.'

'I say burn the bloody house down and the whores of Satan in it!' bawled the blacksmith.

Rowbotham glanced at him over his shoulder. 'It's mostly solid stone and it won't burn very well,' he said. 'And that's not what we agreed at our meeting at dawn and I must ask you to restrain yourself, Master Drury. We are here to arrest Bella Yates on the charge of causing deaths through witchcraft. I ask you all to conduct yourselves with the dignity becoming good Christian folk.'

His eyes were more like flint than ever, I thought. And he was using the villagers as tinder. Cecil had told me that the vicar of Thorby didn't like the ladies of Stonemoor. I suspected that Rowbotham had been waiting for an opportunity to strike.

'We shall certainly not throw our sister – *my* sister – Bella to such a pack of wolves!' Philippa declared, in her most commanding voice.

'Really?' said Rowbotham. He turned to the villagers. 'Hal Drury, step forward. Also Jem Henley and Matt Butterworth, since you've both lost brothers.' The blacksmith shouldered his way to the front, followed by a man who was virtually the double of the Butterworth we had met, and was presumably his brother, and then by a third who said, 'Here we are, Reverend,' and whom I recognized as one of those who had accosted us when we left Butterworth's tavern after our visit to his sickbed. His voice was that of the man who had shouted about incantations.

'You know what to do,' said Rowbotham.

Brockley had his sword out at once but Philippa was well to the fore of any of us and it was Philippa who was their target. They laid hold of her, two gripping her arms and the blacksmith putting an arm round her throat.

'Where is Bella Yates?' Rowbotham said to her. 'You had better tell us.'

'Certainly not!' Considering Bella's confession the day before, Philippa had every reason to betray her but she chose instead to defend her sister and I could only admire her for it.

'Stop this!' Brockley shouted. He started forward, but half a dozen of the crowd at once thrust themselves in the way and Philippa let out a strangled cry as the arm round her throat tightened. It was in any case against Brockley's nature to strike down unarmed men. He lowered his weapon.

'If the woman Bella Yates is not surrendered to us,' said Rowbotham in measured tones, 'then her sister, the Principal of this house, will go to the gibbet in her stead, charged with wilfully obstructing the arrest of a witch and a murderess. Now, where is Bella? Mistress Gould, will you or will you not tell us? Ease your grip, Master Drury. Let the lady speak.'

'I will not tell you!' Philippa was pale and rigid with terror but she was resolute too. The woman inside the dark-blue headdress that was the uniform of Stonemoor might have been a white marble statue and her voice too resembled marble, in its hardness and its chill. I wondered if in her place, I would be as brave.

'Sheathe that sword.' Walter Cogge spoke in tones of authority. 'Brockley, do as I say.' Brockley, glowering, slowly obeyed. Cogge addressed Rowbotham. 'The woman Bella Yates is imprisoned in the cellars of the house. Go and take her if you wish.'

'Cogge! How dare you?' Philippa's voice this time was a shriek.

'Why has she been imprisoned?' enquired Rowbotham with interest.

'She has committed a . . . a misdemeanour,' said Philippa, glaring at Cogge and daring him to contradict her. 'It was to do with a valuable book that I wished to sell. My sister believes it to be a heretical book, saying things that are contrary to the teaching of the true faith, and also containing lore taken from infidel learning, which is unfit for Christian people to read. She didn't want it sold because that would spread its . . . its questionable ideas more widely. Just the way a witch would think, of course!' Philippa added, sarcastically.

Rowbotham looked at the men who had rushed forward to keep Brockley and Eric from attempting a rescue. There were six of them. 'Go and find her,' he said shortly.

'I will never forgive you for this, Cogge!' Philippa shouted.

I found myself trying to get in the way as the six surged forward but Cogge caught hold of me and jerked me back. The men plunged through the gate and across the courtyard and vanished through the main door. In my ear, Cogge said: 'Bella may not be a witch but she has murdered. This is justice of a sort.'

'It's not the law!' I muttered back. 'There has been no trial!'

'The law is a long way off, in York,' said Cogge shortly. 'And I am more concerned for Mistress Gould's safety than I am for that of Mistress Yates.' And then: 'Dear God, what's this?'

He pointed and I turned to look. As if our situation were not involved enough, a new complication had appeared. A group of horsemen were riding up the hill towards us. 'What on earth . . .?' I said.

'Can't you guess?' asked Cogge.

Others including Rowbotham had now seen the approaching riders. Cogge raised his voice to address the company at large. 'A fine piece of timing!' he observed. He spoke quite coolly, as though the new arrivals were intruding on some ordinary gathering: a family reunion, for instance, or a betrothal party or a tennis match. 'As it happens, Stonemoor has been expecting a group of five guests to arrive at any moment. I think they're here.'

'Who *are* they?' Dale asked him, bemused.

'Why, they're almost certainly the five priests I told you about,' said Cogge, dropping his voice so that the villagers could not hear him. 'Have you really not understood? They will be in this courtyard within a few minutes.'

TWENTY-TWO
Thorby at Bay

'**M**ore guests for Stonemoor? Well, that makes no difference,' said Rowbotham, undisturbed. He moved to meet the new arrivals as they reached the top of the path. They didn't look much like priests. They all wore plain dark travelling cloaks and they were all mounted on hirsute ponies – the local breed seemed to be characteristically shaggy – and looked faintly absurd, with their feet several inches below the ponies' bellies. They reined in uncertainly, looking in astonishment at the extraordinary tableau around Philippa Gould.

'You come at an inopportune moment, my friends, whoever you are,' Rowbotham observed, addressing them. 'We are here to arrest a witch and unfortunately have met with obstructiveness. We have been obliged to use unorthodox methods to quell the resistance. When the sorceress has been apprehended, we will take her away and the other ladies of the house will be free to welcome you. Perhaps you would be good enough to wait until the arrest is accomplished.'

He clearly had no idea who the strangers probably were. No one enlightened him. The quintet, looking dumbfounded, said nothing at all. They simply dismounted and stood holding their ponies' bridles, and waited.

Drury had now let go of Philippa and she had retained her dignity, but she was so very white that I feared she might faint. I myself was conscious of a hammering heart and a desire to break down into tears. Once, I exchanged glances with Philippa, and knew that we were both thinking the same thing. *Thank God we buried that boot last night. If they'd found that, it would have taken some explaining.*

The wait was not very long. Quite soon, Bella was brought out.

It was hateful. I had seen such things before, but the spectacle of any human creature in a state of terror, disintegrated by it, and defenceless in remorseless hands, always horrified me. It is an ugly sight whatever the victim may have done. One thinks: if it were me in those pitiless hands, how would I behave? Would I keep any dignity, would I be the brave, calm heroine I like to think I would be, or would I too collapse, fall apart, pleading and struggling, overcome by animal fear, veil torn off, hair in disorder, tears streaming, bladder and bowels out of control? Bella's were. I saw it.

Bella Yates had murdered two men. I had never met Bernard Hardwicke but he had existed, had a right to his life, and had no doubt been loved by someone. Christopher Spelton had been my friend, and could have been so much more, and perhaps should have been. I ought to rejoice at the arrest of Bella Yates. James Douglas had called Stonemoor a nest of vipers and here indeed was a viper. But all I could see was a terrified peasant woman, struggling in the grasp of a pack of hard-faced men. My gorge rose. The shock on the faces of all my companions except Walter Cogge, plainly showed that they shared my feelings. Will Grimes was tutting and shaking his head and when I looked at him I saw a sickness in his pale eyes.

Rowbotham went forward to meet the search party. 'Bring her down to Thorby,' he said shortly. 'As we planned.'

'What are you going to do with her?' Philippa demanded shrilly.

'We have prepared a gibbet,' said Rowbotham. 'By Butterworth's tavern. All is in readiness. A fitting place for putting an end to the witch who killed him.'

'No!' shouted Philippa. 'You can't do this; it's wrong; she has had no trial . . . where is the law? Where are the High Sheriff's men?'

'In York. Here in Thorby we often have to manage our own affairs,' said Rowbotham, and stepped aside as Bella was dragged past him.

'I didn't kill Master Butterworth, I didn't, I didn't!' Bella wailed. 'I helped him; he was grateful; I never meant harm to him . . . Oh, dear Mother of God, help me now! Don't do this . . .!' Her frantic appeals faded as she was hustled out of the gate and away down the hill. The rest of the villagers, after giving us unfriendly looks, went after them. Two of the women spat on the ground in front of us before they went. Rowbotham turned to the rest of us.

'I suggest you all remain here. Her body will be returned to you for burial if you so wish.'

'I'm going with her!' snapped Philippa. 'She's my sister. Don't dare to hinder me!' Half running, she left us, hastening after the crowd. Will Grimes said, 'Me too,' and scrambling back on to his pony, he followed her. One of the new arrivals, still holding his mount's bridle, said: 'What is going on here? Of all the extraordinary welcomes . . .!'

Angelica Ames had reappeared from the house. 'Gentlemen, I apologize for your unusual reception. Do please come inside. I will act for Mistress Gould, since she has had to leave us. If you will follow me . . . Walter Cogge, perhaps you will help with the ponies . . .'

'I'm going to the village,' said Walter shortly. He looked at us and I said decisively: 'Yes, we must go too. There may be something we can do.' I knew that there was probably nothing of the kind, but in some vague way wanted to offer Philippa – and now, even Bella – some kind of support. What was happening to Bella appalled me; no matter what she had done, it still appalled me, and I was as sure as I could be that she had *not* committed the crime for which she was actually being condemned.

Dale and Sybil nodded their heads and came with me without a word. Brockley and Joseph were ahead of us, with Cogge. We all followed as fast as we could in the footsteps of Philippa and the villagers and the knot of men who were dragging the struggling, weeping Bella down the muddy zigzag path. Will Grimes on his pony had caught the crowd up before it reached the foot of the hill. He plunged into its midst, shouting and expostulating.

In front of the tavern, the crowd halted. When we reached it, we saw that a gibbet had been set up before the doorway, and that there was indeed nothing we could do, for we were far outnumbered. Dozens of people were between us and the gibbet, and some of the men had formed an armed guard in front of it as well. If the village men hadn't brought weapons up the hill with them, they had collected some now. The guard were armed with axes and scythes and billhooks, and in knowledgeable hands, those were weapons as formidable as swords.

The gibbet itself had been obviously assembled from pieces of newly cut wood and been provided with rope and noose, and beneath it was a small cart with a couple of men backing a pony into the shafts. Will Grimes was there, now on foot, and I realized that the pony was his. He must have been dragged off it. Someone had produced some harness and put it on the pony and Will was in furious dispute with the man who was holding the bridle, shouting that the animal belonged to him and he never gave anyone permission to use it, and he'd thank them to get that there harness *off* this minute!

In his fury, he was hopping from one foot to another, an ineffectual hobgoblin, at whom the crowd and the guard were laughing. Someone shouted that the pony had been a bit of luck; they'd thought they'd have to hitch up Butterworth's mule. 'Bloody obstinate beast that is, too, trouble on four legs!'

Philippa Gould was running this way and that on the outskirts of the gathering, crying out to Bella that she was there, that she would try to save her, and calling loudly on God and his saints to come to their aid. The crowd and the guards were laughing at her, too.

The drop-board at the back of the cart had been lowered and two of Bella's captors were heaving her upwards. On the way down the hill, they had evidently tied her hands. She too was crying out prayers for God's help. She too was being laughed at. The noise was both hideous and loud.

'What can we do?' said Brockley. His hand on his sword hilt again but he had not drawn. 'I can't cut my way through all these people!' he said. 'I can't cut down villagers in cold blood and as for those fellows with billhooks and what have you . . .'

'She is guilty,' said Walter Cogge, unmoved. 'Not of witchcraft, perhaps, but certainly of killing.'

Philippa had seen us and now ran to us. 'I heard that! What is wrong with you, Master Cogge? I had my own plans for dealing with Bella! More merciful than this but I would have dealt with her, believe me. But not like this! She is my sister! Why can't you realize? Oh, my God, is there no help anywhere? Why don't you men go to her aid? These village men will give way; they won't use those farm tools; it's only a feint . . .'

'I wouldn't wager much on that,' said Joseph stolidly.

The noise of the crowd surged as the noose was put round Bella's neck. Because of the din, none of us heard the approaching hoof beats as a squad of riders came thudding along the earthen track from the far end of the village. We didn't know they were there until suddenly there were horses beside us, blowing and tossing their manes and jingling their bits and sending up spurts of mud from restless hooves, and men were springing out of their saddles, and a voice . . . a familiar voice! . . . was bellowing: '*Stop this!*'

I spun round. The crowd was shouting to the men in charge of the gibbet to send the cart forward, *Get her swinging, hurry up, quick, quick!* But half a dozen of the new arrivals had their swords out, and Brockley and Joseph, heartened by these sudden reinforcements, had joined them, and all together, they were charging to the rescue, the newcomers on horseback, Brockley and Joseph on foot. And I was staring into the face of the man who had shouted *stop*.

'Good morning, Ursula,' said Christopher Spelton.

He was there. He was real! I had grieved for his death but I hadn't then known how huge and overwhelming my gladness would be when I found he was after all still alive. I threw myself at him, exclaiming for joy.

He had already dismounted, looping the reins of his elegant chestnut horse over his arm. Now he held me gently off so that he could doff his cap with all the graciousness of a man who has just called upon a neighbour and found her peacefully weeding her garden. His balding head gleamed in the winter sunshine and his brown eyes smiled.

'How came you here? What brought you?' I gasped.

'It's a long tale. Briefly, I got to York to find that the High Sheriff had had word that some priests had arrived at a house owned by some people called Brownlow and were expected to come straight on here. You may not know . . .'

'I do know. I know all about that. The priests are at
Stonemoor. They've just arrived.'

'The Brownlows were being watched,' said Christopher.
'Anyway, the news that our quarry had reached the Brownlows'
house caused Sir William Fairfax to send men straight to
Thorby and I came with them. But I didn't expect to find this!'

'These are the High Sheriff's men?' I said.

'Yes. We don't know what's happening here but it's
obviously unlawful. That's Bella Yates on the cart, isn't it?'

'Yes, it is, God help her!'

'I thought so. I've every reason! But even in these out
of the way places, this way of administering justice isn't
allowed . . .'

Dale interrupted us. She had been staring at the scrimmage
between us and the death cart, and now, with an outraged
shriek of '*Roger! Leave him! Let him alone!*' she suddenly
hurled herself in the wake of the rescue squad, which had now
forced its way almost to the gibbet, though not quite, for
though most of the crowd had fallen back from the drawn
swords and charging horses, the self-appointed guardsmen,
shoulder to shoulder, were still brandishing their makeshift
weapons and for the moment still blocked the way for the
horsemen. Bella, her face so distorted with terror that it was
hardly human, was now attached to the gibbet and would have
been swinging already except that Will Grimes was locked in
a kind of wrestling match with the man at the pony's head
and so far had stopped the cart from moving forward. Brockley,
however had somehow got past the guards and was up on the
cart, trying to get the rope off Bella's neck, and simultaneously
using his sword to fend off a hefty man who was trying to
jab him with a knife.

The rescuers' first charge had left a clear path behind them,
through which Dale now tore, skirts flying. I could never
have believed that my conventional, middle-aged Dale could
move so fast. She ran like an athlete from a legend of ancient
Greece. The guards tried to bar her way but they wavered a
little, perhaps not wanting to threaten a respectable-looking
woman with their billhooks and scythes. Dale took the man
immediately in front of her by surprise, striking his right arm

upwards and ducking beneath it. She was past the guards, scrambling on to the cart. Her skirt caught on the side but she tore it free. She sprang behind the knife-wielding villager, seized his ears and twisted.

'God's teeth!' said Christopher admiringly.

The villager tore himself free, twisted round, and caught hold of Dale, with the intention, obviously, of dumping her over the side of the cart. But Brockley's sword point was at the man's throat at once. He let go of Dale, who promptly slapped his face. At that moment, the six sheriff's officers finally burst through the enemy. They formed a protective line, horses plunging and flinging out dangerous hooves, swords flashing as they were brandished in the air. Joseph suddenly emerged from the confusion, dodged between the horses, leapt up on to the cart, and set about releasing Bella. He got her down to the ground. The villagers were enraged but they could do nothing now but give way. The rescue party, sheltered by the armed horsemen, began to make its way towards us.

'I shall have a lively report to make to Sir William,' remarked Walter Cogge, who had stood motionless throughout.

'You will indeed,' said Christopher. 'By the way, we are not merely here to collect five Jesuit priests. We are also here to arrest the woman Bella Yates. You weren't doing very much to preserve her for the law, were you?'

'I meant to ride to York to report the arrival of the priests, and to take Bella Yates with me, except that the villagers intervened,' said Cogge, unmoved. 'No one expected you to reappear. We all thought you were dead.'

'I very nearly was,' said Christopher and would have gone on to say more, except that Philippa Gould, who had been embracing her sister only a few feet away, now broke away and came to us.

'What *is* all this? Where have all these men sprung from? Master Spelton! Bella said . . . Bella told us, but you're alive! Bella didn't kill you! Oh, Bella, my sister . . . whatever she's done . . . whatever she's tried to do . . . Thank God she's off that cart . . . I heard you say something about priests . . .' Philippa was incoherent.

'The guests who arrived just as we were . . . er . . . leaving,' said Cogge, 'are thought to be Jesuit priests, whose purpose in this country is to seek converts and raise money for Mary Stuart. Did you not know who your new guests were? We – the authorities – were waiting for them to arrive here. To fall into a trap set by Sir Francis Walsingham, in fact. We will now proceed to go up the hill and collect them.'

'The authorities . . . *you*?' Philippa looked understandably dazed.

'I am sorry,' said Cogge. He considered her gravely. 'I really am sorry, Mistress Gould, but I have deceived you. I was reared in a Catholic household and I know enough to pass as a priest if I wish. But in truth, I am no priest at all. I am one of Walsingham's men.'

'One of . . .!'

Philippa stood staring at Cogge with such contempt that I half expected him to wither forthwith, like a tree in a forest fire. Then she turned back to the trembling, tearful Bella, and drew her away.

'If they go up to the house, they'll warn the priests!' said Brockley.

'Doesn't matter,' said Christopher calmly. 'Even if the priests run for it they won't get far. Where can they go?'

'And how much time will they have for getting away in?' added Cogge, just as equably. 'They only have little ponies. We have men on long-legged horses. Let them be warned! Master Spelton is right: It won't matter. Ah, yes. I see that Will has got his pony back and Bella has been pushed on to it. He and Mistress Gould are leading it towards the path to the house. We'll soon catch up.'

TWENTY-THREE
Empowered to Bargain

Noise and confusion still raged around us. The sheriff's officers were trying to disperse the crowd, and the crowd itself was shouting and gesticulating. Women were screeching imprecations at the armed men and a couple of small boys were throwing stones at them; also, one group of villagers had started towards the path up to Stonemoor House. They were carrying their axes and scythes and presumably meant to pursue and recapture Bella but while we watched, four of the sheriff's officers were after them on horseback, swords out, had caught them, forced them to surrender their weapons and herded them back to the street, swearing at the tops of their voices.

In the crowd, disagreements had broken out and there were scuffles. But gradually the uproar did begin to subside. Walter Cogge, using his bulk and strength, grabbed the stone-throwing small boys, cuffed them, hauled them away, and said something threatening enough to send them running to their mothers. One of the horsemen who had fetched the villagers back rode over to us. Christopher greeted him with a grin and introduced him.

'This is Sergeant John Hall. He and I are more or less sharing the leadership of this party.' Sergeant Hall, who was young, tanned, and cheerful, raised a respectful hand to his helmet and said: 'That's so.'

'I think, Sergeant,' said Christopher, 'that things are quietening down. Can I suggest that you now proceed up to the house to collect the five Jesuit priests I fancy you will find there. Get them on to their ponies and bring them down under arrest. But leave the women Gould and Yates for the moment. I wish to question them myself. As yet we can't be certain that Mistress Gould actually knows who her five guests are.

Indeed, we're not completely sure ourselves. It shouldn't take long to settle, though. A quick search of their belongings should tell you all you need to know. Look for maps, lists of names, phials of incense, vestments, Popish symbols of any kind. But leave me to deal with Mistress Gould and her sister myself.'

The young sergeant said: 'Sir!' and wheeled his horse away.

'I have a certain amount of authority,' Christopher said. 'I am carrying a document that says so. My original errand included delivering a confidential letter to Scotland and I was provided with the means of asking for help and cooperation from her majesty's enforcers of the law. What happened about that letter, by the way? You know about it?'

'I not only know about it, I delivered it,' I said. 'I went to Scotland first, before coming here to collect the book by John of Evesham.'

'Oh yes, the book. Have you got it? Did Bella Yates bring it back to Stonemoor after she attacked me? You know that she attacked me?'

'Yes, she has confessed. But you didn't actually have the book with you,' I told him. 'She stole it from your luggage before you left Stonemoor and put in a substitute. Then, it seems, she realized that once you got it back to London, the substitution would be discovered and there might be another attempt to buy it. She decided to finish her task by finishing *you*.'

'I see. So it's still at Stonemoor.'

'Well, we don't know. Bella has hidden it, apparently.'

'Well, well. I look forward to a conversation with that charming lady Bella Yates,' said Spelton.

I said: 'Christopher – what happened to you? How did you escape? Bella said she had killed you.'

'She thought she had! I'll tell you all about it, but first . . . ah, there go the squad to collect the priests. I think we should follow them.'

We made our way slowly up the long zigzag. The others were on foot, but Christopher asked me to ride double with him, saying that I looked tired. 'I'll tell all of you all about everything when we're in shelter, beside a nice warm fire in the guest hall. This wind is cold. Brr! It's going to be a long plod up this steep path.'

I was glad of the ride. Christopher's chestnut, which looked like a Barb, since it had slender legs, a short back, and a dish face, was nevertheless strong and seemed to make nothing of its extra load, even on the steep incline to the house. I noticed that its colouring was unusual, a very rich shade of chestnut, with a white mane and tail, and I should have realized at once that this description was familiar, except that I was too tired to do more than wonder why it reminded me of something, only I couldn't remember what.

Halfway up, we had to draw aside to let an ominous procession pass us on its way down. The young sergeant was leading the way, and behind him, the riders were in pairs, each consisting of an officer leading a pony on which, pinioned, sat one of the recent arrivals at Stonemoor. The Jesuits who had walked into Walsingham's trap, I supposed. They were all very quiet and almost expressionless but their eyes were frightened. With good reason, I knew. Walsingham's reputation extended beyond the shores of England.

The gate of Stonemoor House stood wide but when we went through it, we found Philippa Gould, once more white and cold like a marble image, waiting for us in the middle of the courtyard.

'I was upstairs, in Bella's room,' she said. 'It overlooks the path to the village and I saw you approaching. My new guests have been taken away, as you saw. Are you happy with your day's work, Master Spelton, Master Cogge?'

'Very happy,' said Christopher, as we both dismounted. 'And I shall need to talk to you and to Mistress Yates. However, for the moment, we are all tired and chilled by this edged wind and we are splashed with grime from that muddy track. First, we would like to have warm water and a fire in the guest hall and something to eat and drink before we proceed to any further business.'

'*Please!*' said Sybil earnestly. 'Warmth and food and safety! They sound like heaven.'

It wasn't long before we were all, including Cogge and Joseph, in the guest hall, where a fire had been lit. Christopher and Joseph had looked after the chestnut horse but they had wasted no time over it. We had all had a chance to clean our faces and hands, and food had been brought, though Mary Haxby, who brought it, did so sullenly and wouldn't look us in the eye. We were now the enemy, it seemed.

The food wasn't generous this time. Rye bread again, some pieces of cold chicken and a bowl of bean stew, probably heated up. There were two flagons of wine. Brockley, the first to taste it, remarked that it was the sour vintage again. 'Something they keep for putting in gravies, I fancy,' he said disparagingly.

'Never mind. It's warming, anyway,' I said, taking a sip. I looked across the table at Christopher. 'Now!' I said.

'Bella very nearly did kill me,' he said, through a mouthful of the black bread. 'She certainly meant to! That dark-eyed sweetheart caught up with me, riding at a gallop, just as I got near the ford. I turned my head when I heard the hooves and said *hallo* or something, then I saw a knife flash in her hand and she veered her horse round to the other side of me and I felt something hit me between the shoulder blades and everything . . . I hardly know how to describe it. Suddenly, everything was unreal. All the strength seemed to go out of me and I fell out of the saddle, and – this bit is hazy but she seemed to be on top of me and I was trying to get hold of her and then she hit me on the head with something. When I came round, I was in the river and so cold . . . dear God, so cold! I was downstream, by some way . . . I found that out later, of course. The current had pushed me up against an outcrop sticking out of the bank so I was half out of the water and I hadn't drowned. I suppose Bella thought I was dead, but once I'd come round, I found I could move. I can't have been in the river for long though, or the cold would have killed me. As it was, I just managed to crawl out on to the bank. I hurt all over.'

When he began to talk, he did so quite cheerfully, but as he recalled what had happened, his eyes changed. I saw that he was shuddering away from the memory. 'I just lay there,' he said, 'and I fancy I'd have died anyway before long, but a shepherd found me. Or rather, his dog did. I passed out again after I'd dragged myself on to the bank and the next thing I knew, I was waking up because my face was being washed by a warm, wet, canine tongue.'

'A shepherd?' said Cogge with interest. 'There's one lives on his own a couple of miles from here. His actual name is Shepherd – at least, that's what he says. Looks a bit like a sheep himself – curly yellowish white hair and eyes that are almost yellow as well.'

'I think we've met him,' I said. 'He directed us to the bridge when we set out for the Thwaites' farm, yesterday. I remember those yellowish eyes very well. He was rude to us.'

'I fancy he's rude to most people,' said Christopher. 'Not that he meets other people very often. He was out with a dog and a pony, moving his flock, when he found me. He got me on to the pony and took me to his cottage, if you can call it that. It's a tumbledown drystone place with grass growing out of the thatch. There's a ramshackle sort of barn behind it, that he uses to shelter the sheep sometimes. He had them in there during the snow. He keeps a good fire going in his cottage, thank God. He looked after me. I was a mess. I had a hole in my back and a lump on my head and my clothes and the skin of my back were all torn and scraped and my ankles ached and *ached*. I think that woman must have dragged me by them, across rough ground, to get me into the river where it was deep enough to drown me. She must have the strength of an ox!'

'She was brought up on a farm,' I remarked.

'Carrying buckets of pig food and muck for the fields and scything barley?' said Christopher. 'That would account for her muscles, I suppose and muscles she surely had.'

I remembered thinking the same, when Bella crouched at her sister's feet. Her shoulders, surely, were as powerful as a man's.

Christopher leant back, sipping his wine, and now, as he looked back, he had overcome his shudders and once more seemed half amused. I wondered if I would feel amused if the same things had happened to me and was seized with a great surge of admiration for him, for his courage and his gaiety. Sybil said: 'Do go on.'

'Well, this man Shepherd looked after me,' said Christopher, 'though he made it plain enough that I was a nuisance. He was always coming and going, seeing to his sheep, then rushing back to give me drinks of water and ale and feed me on bread soaked in broth and put clean straw under me. He hardly ever spoke to me and he glowered all the time. I told him about me and how Hardwicke had vanished, and what that barbarous woman had done to me, but he just shrugged, said it was nowt to do with him, and hardly seemed interested. Just once, he did bestir himself to talk to me a little and he told me that men from the sheriff in York had twice accosted him out on the moor when he was busy with his sheep. Once they asked if he'd seen anything of Hardwicke and then, the second time – which was while I was with him – they were asking after both of us. But he was annoyed at being bothered and having his time wasted, as he called it, and he wouldn't tell them owt, as he put it. Nobbut pests, that's what he said they were.'

'He denied he'd got you in his cottage?' I said, scandalized.

'He certainly did. He's got no sense at all of civic duty. He wouldn't harm a fellow human being but he hates nearly all of us just the same. He said he'd told the officers, both times, that he knew nothing about any missing men! Just sheer bloody-mindedness, that's what that was! But he *did* give me food and drink and he kept me clean as best he could, and he never left me alone too long. I was in a raging fever for ten days and after that, too weak for a long time to do anything much. I healed, but slowly – at one point, I know he had me crying and cursing while he cleaned pus or something out of my scraped back. He made poultices out of some kind of herb. He had dried herbs in jars in his hut and a herb plot just outside. He seemed to know what he was about, however grumpy he was. I suppose he's had to look after himself, living alone as he does.'

'I wonder why he hates the human race so much,' I said, puzzled.

'He says he prefers sheep. Sheep don't tell lies or stab you in the back, he told me. I think he must have been very badly treated by his fellow men at some point in his life. But he's

honest enough in his own way and his sheep are cared for
better than some men care for their children.'

'He put himself on the wrong side of the law, denying that
he knew where you were,' Cogge said. 'But still . . . he saved
your life. I won't arrange to have him arrested.'

'You had better not!' said Christopher with energy. 'I owe
him my life, you're right about that. Well, eventually, I was
fit to go to York. Luckily, I had a horse. Master Shepherd
wasn't going to lend me his pony but he'd caught a stray,
wandering on the moor, and brought it in. Gave it some of
the winter fodder he keeps for his sheep. He asked me what
to do with it – I was recovering by then and capable of a
sensible conversation – and I said I'd take it to York when
I left.'

'The chestnut with a white mane and tail!' I exclaimed. 'I
knew it reminded me of something. Of course!' Memory had
belatedly flooded back. 'That's the description of the horse
Bernard Hardwicke was riding!'

'Yes, I thought it might be his,' said Christopher. 'Poor
thing, it looked cold and hungry by the time Master Shepherd
found it. He said it came to him, virtually asking to be stabled
and fed!'

'What of its saddle and bridle?' Brockley asked.

'No sign of them,' said Christopher. 'No doubt our dark-
eyed darling took them off and tossed them into the river, like
me! Luckily, my misanthropic host was able to invent a bit
and bridle with some rope, and I rode to York bareback. I
don't know what became of the brown mare I was riding when
Bella accosted me.'

'I think the Thwaites have her,' I said. 'They keep a farm
where we stayed on the way here. They have found a stray
brown mare and at the moment they are looking after her.'

'The Thwaites? I know of them. I'm glad the poor beast
has found shelter in this winter weather. I shall have to go
and inspect her. I shall recognize her at once if she's my mare
– there's a scattering of white hairs round the fetlock on her
off fore and she has a little scar on her near shoulder.'

'You must have been glad to have a horse to get to York
on,' said Sybil. 'It would have been a long trudge on foot.'

I said: 'Christopher, we found your secret sign, chalked on the underside of a seat chest. But if you put the sign there, it must have been because you thought you could be in danger here. What made you think that?'

'I knew that Hardwicke had been here,' said Christopher. 'I knew because of that distinctive chestnut horse. When I was stabling my own mount here, I made some comment or other about a good-looking strawberry roan that was in the next stall and Walter Cogge here happened to mention that there had been a guest not long ago who had been riding something really remarkable – Barb in type, golden chestnut with a white mane and tail and a star and a white sock. I recognized the description. And that made an alarm bell ring in my head. It rang even louder when Mistress Gould told me that Hardwicke had never been here.'

'I had no idea that anything was seriously wrong,' said Cogge contritely. 'As I have already explained, Mistress Gould told me not to mention Hardwicke's visit, because she didn't want anyone to know about her sister's bad behaviour over the John of Evesham book. It wasn't my business and I didn't argue. When the subject of good-looking horses came up, I did describe that chestnut, but I didn't name the rider. I just called him a passing traveller. Careless of me,' he added apologetically. 'There had already been an enquiry after Master Hardwicke, but he was perfectly all right when he left here. So I kept Mistress Gould's counsel as she wished, and the same when the officers came a second time, looking for you, Master Spelton. I had my own secrets to keep.'

'I knew from your description of the horse that Hardwicke must have been here,' said Christopher. 'But Mistress Gould said she had been waiting for someone to call to collect the book. She was very pleased to see me. It sounded as though Hardwicke *hadn't* come after all – yet I was sure he had. So why was she lying? I felt suspicious and . . . I don't know how to describe this sensibly, but there seemed to be a . . . an atmosphere here. A feeling of something dangerous – unpleasant – in the air.'

'Yes,' I said. 'I have felt that too.'

'Did you?' Christopher smiled at me. 'Well, I asked Mistress

Gould outright whether she had seen Hardwicke. She assured me in so many words that he had never come to Stonemoor. I didn't believe her but there was nothing to get hold of. I decided that I would just take the book and report my suspicions in York. The horse had gone from here, so I guessed that Hardwicke had ridden away but I knew he couldn't have got far. He would have gone north, and whatever fate overtook him, it must have done so before he reached the Thwaites. I felt very uneasy indeed and I left my mark . . . just in case.'

'How do you know about the Thwaites?' I asked. 'You can't have been there *yourself.*'

'Through the reports sent in by Fairfax's officers after they had tried to find Hardwicke. I saw those reports before I was sent off to the north, with orders to deliver a letter to Scotland and find Hardwicke if I could. The farm was mentioned. The Thwaites had said that he hadn't been there. So if he'd called at Stonemoor, he either never left it, or vanished before he could reach the Thwaites.'

'This is a horrible story,' said Dale. 'This place, this house full of middle-aged ladies, seems so harmless, and yet . . .!'

'Oh well,' said Christopher. 'I survived Bella's attentions, thanks to Master Shepherd, and I had Hardwicke's beautiful horse to get me to York.'

We digested Christopher's story in silence, until Brockley said: 'What now? What happens to Mistress Gould and Mistress Yates?'

For answer, Walter Cogge picked up the bell, went to the vestibule door, and rang it vigorously. Mary Haxby responded after a moment and stood gazing resentfully at Cogge, who was standing, ready to ring the bell again if there had been no answer.

'Please bring Mistress Gould to us,' said Cogge.

'She's upstairs with Mistress Yates. She can't see you now.'

'Mistress Gould will see me when and where I please. Kindly fetch her at once. If you don't, I will go and get her myself. You have obligingly told me where to look, for which I thank you.'

Mary muttered something that could have been a curse. Then she turned sharply and was gone. How those long blue

skirts could swish! I was reminded of the way in which my
sister Queen Elizabeth sometimes, when provoked, would spin
on her heel and make her skirts hiss across the floor with a
sound like an angry cat.

Mary did do as she was asked, however. Philippa arrived
in a matter of minutes. She held herself well but she was
still very pale. Even Walter Cogge looked at her with some
concern. His wineglass was empty. He filled it and handed
it to her.

'Mistress Gould, you look unwell. You should drink this.
And sit down.'

I rather expected Philippa to brush him and the wineglass
aside but instead she took it and drank the wine, in one long
swallow. A faint colour appeared on her cheekbones. She sat
down as invited. Then she folded her hands in her lap and
raised her chin. She did not speak.

'Were you aware,' said Cogge conversationally, 'that the
five men who, earlier today, arrived here as guests but have
since been removed by officers attached to the sheriff in York,
are Jesuit priests, here on an unlawful mission to raise money
for the enemies of our sovereign lady Elizabeth, and to seek
converts to their heretical faith?'

'No,' said Philippa. 'I didn't know. I am acquainted, though
not closely, with a family called Brownlow, who live twenty
miles east of here. I received word that they wished to pass
some foreign guests on to me. Gentlemen with business in
this country, their message said. They were expected shortly
but it was causing a problem as other, unexpected guests, had
descended on them and were likely to make a long stay. There
was no more room in the Brownlows' house.'

'So that was the tale they told you. But you expect me to
believe that you didn't even suspect the truth?' said Cogge.

'I have told you the truth as far as I knew it. You are a
hateful man.' Philippa's cold remoteness suddenly turned into
scorching contempt. 'You have lived here under false pretences,
making yourself out to be a priest, anxious to offer the comfort
of the Mass and the confessional to a house of women who
love the old faith and would otherwise be deprived of these
blessings. And all the time, you have been spying on us, on

me, and, it seems, holding yourself ready to pounce on my guests like a hawk on a flock of doves . . .'

'Your recent quintet of guests,' said Walter Cogge, 'had their luggage searched before they were arrested. It can't have taken long, because we met them as they were being taken down the hill. I presume that incriminating evidence was easily found. Maps, lists of names – of likely helpers and contributors – and also, no doubt, such things as incense and other Jesuitical toys, such as their priests use in their unseemly rituals.'

'They are not unseemly rituals. They are merely different from yours.'

'We will not argue the point. But the likelihood that you really had no idea that the visitors who came and went today were Jesuit priests is very slender. You surely suspected, even if you didn't know for sure.'

'You can prove nothing.'

'Ah. That is tantamount to an admission. As for the matter of proof, your confession would solve that little difficulty. Believe me, if you are arrested and taken to London and handed over to Walsingham's favourite questioner, whose name is Richard Topcliffe and whose reputation is notorious, that confession would soon be forthcoming.'

'Confessions extracted in such a way are worthless.' Philippa's voice shook, but it was also frigid with disdain. 'I am sure,' she said, 'that in the hands of such as Richard Topcliffe, of whom I have indeed heard, I would say anything he wanted me to say. I would probably say it even before he had tried to extract it.'

'I dare say.' Cogge's voice became soft, almost gentle, and all the more frightening for that. 'Of course, if you do confess, no matter how that comes about, it would mean you have admitted to high treason and that would mean the stake. Don't for a moment consider yourself as a possible martyr. Martyrs like to think of themselves as nobly true to their faith but when the flames are rising round them, most martyrs wish they had been less noble and more self-regarding.'

The colour had once more ebbed from Philippa's face. I myself was frozen with horror. Philippa had done me no harm, and here she was in front of me, a living woman, who might soon . . .

What was it like, to have one's body destroyed while one was still alive inside it?

'But as it happens,' said Cogge smoothly, in that astonishingly cultured voice of his, 'there is a way out, Mistress Gould. I am empowered to make a bargain with you.'

TWENTY-FOUR
The Judgement of Philippa

'**E**mpowered to bargain?' said Philippa.
'With you,' said Cogge. 'Not with Mistress Yates, who has committed murder. She must accompany us to York, where she will probably be tried. But you are somewhat different. There is, shall we say, a possible use for you. I advise you to accept the opportunity. The alternative is so very unpleasant. But you can be left unmolested if you agree to help us.'

'Help you?' Philippa's eyes were those of someone who has been belaboured by too many violent events, too many emotional blows, in too short a time.

'It is known,' said Cogge, 'that in seminaries on the Continent, plans are being laid for what will be virtually an invasion of Jesuit priests into England. The five who have just been arrested under your roof represent the vanguard, as it were.'

'I didn't *know* they were priests! I told you! I only knew that they were guests that some acquaintances of mine, the Brownlows, could not accommodate just now, and who are travelling on into the north of England on business. I am a law-abiding woman! My father always said we should keep Queen Elizabeth's laws; that we wouldn't be kept from following our faith, provided we did that. He didn't think it was wise for the Pope to tell English Catholics that they shouldn't keep Elizabeth's laws. He said it wasn't fair on honest Englishmen,' said Philippa earnestly.

'You may be telling the truth,' said Cogge. 'I can't tell. Nor does it particularly matter. Let us leave that aside. Listen carefully. First, you must swear not to let the Brownlows know that the five men were seized while they were with you. You didn't hesitate to lie when various people asked you if Master

Hardwicke and Master Spelton had stayed here; I suggest you adopt an equally flexible attitude towards the Brownlows. Let word reach them, from you, saying that the five men moved on from here. If the Brownlows come to hear that their erstwhile guests have been caught, let them suppose that it happened after they left you and had nothing to do with you. Encourage them to go on thinking that yours is a safe house.'

'But . . .'

'No buts, please, Mistress Gould. Let me continue. We, the queen's men, will ensure that word is conveyed back to the Continent, to the same effect. We want you to be used as a safe house. We also want you to inform the authorities – by sending word to York – whenever you have Jesuit guests. Try to find out where each of them is going in England, and pass that information along as well. They will be seized *after* they leave you.'

Philippa looked horrified but Cogge appeared not to notice. He continued. 'You will be given a way to transmit your information. It won't be through me. I shall leave you, since you now know that I am not what I seem and so no doubt, do your ladies. You have probably told some of them already.'

'I . . . yes. Yes, I have.'

'A replacement will be provided and you will accept him as genuine. You will assure your ladies that he is. He will have a suitable life history in which you must pretend to believe. But he will be your messenger to York when required. Indeed, he will be well aware himself of all that goes on in this house and will probably perform his duties without your instructions. You will need to do little beyond employing him and appearing to believe in him. With luck, it will be quite a long time before it begins to be realized that when priests pass through Stonemoor, they nearly always get arrested shortly afterwards.'

'You expect me to . . .!'

'You know what the alternative is,' Cogge repeated silkily. 'On the other hand,' he added, 'there are incentives. I believe that this house would welcome extra funds. It would relieve your father from worry as well as you. Sir Francis Walsingham has also empowered me to put that right for you. Given your cooperation.'

There was a long silence. Brockley rose quietly and poured more wine all round. Philippa ignored hers. She was sitting with her eyes lowered, staring down at her hands, which were clasped in her lap and restlessly twitching.

At last she looked up. 'I would be betraying my faith.'

Cogge said: 'In the flames, you might not feel that your faith was so important. You would be feeling something quite different and more forceful. Let me remind you that to assist the supporters of Mary Stuart is to betray England. Your father encouraged you to keep the laws of England, did he not?'

'Yes . . . but I have thought sometimes . . . surely Mary is the rightful queen. She would bring England back to the faith!'

'So that's what has been going on in your mind? You did know, perfectly well, who your five visitors were, didn't you? Mistress Gould, most English people don't want to be brought back to the faith and it's not your business, or Mary Stuart's, to force them. Nor,' said Cogge strongly, 'could they be forced except by *using* force. You do realize that Mary could never take power in this realm without outside help?'

'What do you mean?' Philippa was genuinely puzzled.

Christopher groaned. 'I sometimes think,' he said to me, 'that well-meaning, unworldly people are the most dangerous folk in the world.'

'I mean,' said Cogge, 'that any help she obtained would almost certainly have to come from Philip of Spain. Do you like the idea of a Spanish army marching across England? Bringing the Inquisition along with them?'

Philippa stared at him. 'Mary has let it be known that she would never do that; that she would lead, not compel.'

'Mary wouldn't have any choice,' I snapped. 'Philip of Spain would see to that.'

'And the Inquisition . . .' said Cogge.

His lecture on the known activities of the Inquisition took about fifteen minutes. I will not quote it here. He spoke evenly, in that melodious, educated voice which was so surprising in a man of his appearance. What he said made Dale cry while Sybil at one point stopped her ears. I listened but my skin crawled and my stomach clenched. Philippa listened too, her face tight. At the end, she seized her wineglass and emptied it.

Then she said: 'Very well. I see. I . . . agree.'

'Let's all drink to that,' said Christopher in a cheerful voice, and we did. Thin and sour though the wine was, I was glad to feel it running warmly down my gullet, bringing solace to my shocked and shivering body.

'You are wise,' Cogge said to Philippa. 'Continue to be wise. Don't attempt to cheat. If you are honest with us, we will be honest with you. You will be doing right, do you understand? And you and your ladies will be safe. We will not interfere with your . . . practices here, as long as they remain unobtrusive. Except, of course, that our protection can't extend to Bella Yates. She is guilty of one murder and one attempted murder.'

He too drained his wine. 'Two of the sheriff's officers will return here presently to take her away. Sir William Fairfax will be pleased with this day's events, I think. He's a fine, brisk, upstanding man – even his beard seems to crackle with energy – and he is new to his position, desirous of doing his duties well and leaving a good memory behind him. Capturing five Jesuits and bringing a murderess to justice will make an excellent beginning for him. However, before his officers come back, I want to question her. I want to know all the facts, first hand, and to know her side of it. That's only just. Mistress Gould, will you take me to her?'

Unexpectedly, Philippa smiled. 'I left her locked in her room. But I think she may have gone by now.'

'Gone where?'

'What are you talking about?'

'Gone *how*? Out of a locked room?'

The confused chorus died down after a moment. 'Perhaps,' said Philippa, 'you would all like to follow me.'

I had never seen the topmost storey before. It consisted of one long passage lit by skylights, and with small rooms on either side of it. 'It used to be a series of connected bedchambers,' Philippa said as she led us along it. 'I had them partitioned into small rooms. I told you that, I think.' She took a key from her girdle and inserted it into a lock. 'Here we are.'

It was the smell that hit us first, the reek of vomit and faeces. Bella lay jerking convulsively in a tangle of sheets and coverlet.

She was not yet dead but death was not far off and no one was going to be able to hold it off. A phial lay on the floor. I picked it up. It was empty, but when I sniffed at it, I recognized it and recoiled.

Gladys' unlovely description of this as resembling cats' piss was all too accurate. 'Hemlock,' I said.

'She took that rather than be taken to York,' said Philippa. It was only later that it occurred to me that her remark held an ambiguity. She did not seem shocked or repelled, only sad. 'It was among her potions. She sometimes used a drop or two to relieve pain for people who wanted her help.'

Her tone became defensive. 'I am glad that she did swallow it! I didn't want her dragged to York, any more than she wanted it. She's my sister. She has already come near to being hanged. She has been terrified enough. No, I *didn't* want her held in some filthy prison and tried and then brought to another scaffold. Let her go now. It will soon be over, Bella. Then you can sleep. I wish you'd told me where you hid John of Evesham's book, though.'

Bella's agonized eyes sought her sister's face. She tried to speak, but then craned over the edge of the bed, shaken by a bout of vomiting, though she had already brought up everything that was inside her, and only watery stuff came out. It splashed on to the floor. It was Sybil who stepped compassionately forward and helped her to ease herself back on to the bed.

'Bella,' said Philippa urgently, '*where* is the book?'

Bella's eyes had closed, but they opened again as a convulsion shook her, making her body jerk and twist. The dark eyes were filmed, blurred, and full of tears. She looked piteously at her sister and in the eyes that were now being hazed over by the approach of death, there was surrender. She tried to speak and failed, but raised a feeble hand and pointed, jabbing a forefinger downwards, at the straw pallet on which she was lying. She managed one word.

'M . . . m . . . mattress,' she said.

Cogge marched us all out, except for Philippa, who threw off his hand when he laid it on her arm. 'I will stay until she is gone,' she said, and he let her.

The rest of us went out, and back to the guest hall. Once more, we sat down. I said: 'I've seen hemlock poisoning before. I thought then: those stories they tell of how Socrates died so gently. They're not true. It's a horrible business.'

Sybil said: 'Do you think she took the hemlock herself? Or did Mistress Gould give it to her? Telling her it was better than being arrested and probably hanged successfully next time? Did Mistress Gould pass judgement on her, in a way?'

She took it rather than be taken to York. 'I wonder,' I said. 'Mistress Gould didn't put her back in the cellar, did she? Did our Philippa decide to let her sister die in the comfort of her own room?'

'We'll probably never know,' said Cogge. 'It would be hard to prove, either way.'

We sat there for quite a long time. Mary Haxby came to us again, bringing food, in dishes which she banged down viciously on the table. We thanked her politely, but we couldn't eat much. Then, at last, Philippa came in. In her hands was a box like the one we had been shown in the library. 'It's over,' she said. 'Bella has . . . gone. I have set two of my ladies to clean the room and wash her and lay her out decently. Mistress Angelica Ames is supervising them. I hope my sister can be buried in the church here and that Doctor Rowbotham will agree to preside.'

'He can be ordered to do so. He has encouraged highly unlawful behaviour and would do well to do as he's bid,' said Cogge shortly.

'I have brought the book that caused all this trouble,' Philippa said. She set the box down on the table and opened it. Then she lifted out the volume that was inside

'This is the real one,' she said. 'This is John of Evesham's *Observations of the Heavens.* It was hidden in her mattress, as she said.'

'Did you give your sister the poison? Or talk her into taking it?' Cogge asked, more, I think, from curiosity than in an attempt to solve the mystery. Philippa barely glanced at him. 'She took it of her own choice, rather than face what lay ahead,' she said. 'Do you want to examine the book?'

Ambiguity again. I looked at Cogge, caught his eye and

gave him a small shake of the head. *Don't persist*, that little movement begged him. *Don't pursue this. Let it go.* He stared at me and then returned my signal with a very small nod. I was glad, for it was best.

Philippa had placed the book carefully on the table, in the centre, so that we could all gather round and everyone could see it.

It was so very beautiful. The first book we had been shown was nothing by comparison.

This one was old but it must have been carefully preserved through the centuries because the white leather cover was still white. It was thick, rich leather, the kind that made one's fingertips want to touch it, to feel its cool smoothness and its soft depth. The complex gold-leaf pattern and the title on the front cover were undamaged. I could see the lettering of the title but from where I was standing, it was upside down. I reached out and twitched the book round so that I could see it properly. Archaic though the lettering was, it was also clear-cut and I could understand it perfectly well. *Observations of the Heavens by John of Evesham.* Yes. This was genuine.

There were some small signs of misadventures through the years. There was a brownish smear along the top edge and a blackened corner, as though someone who was injured had at some point handled it and left a trace of blood, and as though the book had at some time been rescued from fire. But they were very tiny blemishes and in a way underlined the book's antiquity.

'Open it,' said Philippa. 'Look inside.'

I did as she asked, and slowly began to turn the pages. Once more, I was smitten with its amazing beauty. So were the others. There were murmurs of admiration.

The stiff vellum pages were a joy to behold. The strong, dark script was enlivened at the start of each section by exquisite pictures, in which the initial letters were embedded. The little pictures were far more perfect than those in the book we had already seen. They were miniature marvels of clear blue and red and green, embellished with gold and silver leaf. Tiny figures gazed in wonder at moon and stars; there were heraldic and mythical beings but not, this time, unicorns or camelopards;

instead, these were to do with the zodiac and the constellations. Here there was a lion, there a pair of scales, on the next page a fish . . . and the man with the club in his hand and a sword at his belt and a dog at heel was surely Orion the mighty hunter of legend.

There were more little drawings in the margins, haphazard ones, without colours, suggesting frivolous moments on the part of the scribes. There was a delightful little picture of a man, seated, dressed in a long robe with stars embroidered on it and a cat curled up on his knee; another, a skittish one, showed a rearing horse and a rider who had fallen off and was tumbled on the ground alongside, arms and legs waving in the air. The detail encompassed in these tiny spaces, at most an inch each way, was incredible.

I couldn't make much of the text and still less of the arithmetical tables which appeared on several pages. But I could appreciate the elegance of the lettering and the numerals and the ornate gold borders, like graceful chains, which surrounded the tables. Then I turned a further page and there, exquisitely drawn, was what I had been looking for, a diagram of the sun, with concentric circles drawn round it and on each circle, a planet, labelled with its name. By looking carefully, I could decipher the names. Closest to the sun was Mercury. Then came Venus, then Earth, then Mars, then Jupiter. The sun was in gold leaf, the planets each a different colour. The Earth was green, like grass.

Then I turned another page and burst out laughing. The others leant close to see what had amused me and all but Philippa, who clicked a disapproving tongue, laughed too. We had found the drawing which the indignant Bella had considered blasphemous.

It was, in fact, very amusing and had a kind of good-humoured charm. Clearly, John of Evesham had regarded the Church's dislike of the theory that the Earth and planets all circled the Sun as unreasonable and had illustrated his opinion in a most entertaining fashion. The picture showed a Pope seated in a chair and using his arms to protect his head from celestial missiles. A golden figure whose face was a flame-crowned sun and whose eyebrows were drawn together in a frown was hurling a golden spear. On a small silver disc, evidently meant to represent the planet Mercury, a silver figure with outspread wings stood poised on one foot. He held a longbow and was aiming a silver arrow at the cowering ecclesiastic below. Venus, more graciously, was robed in a delicate shade of turquoise and held out imploring hands, pleading, it seemed, for the Church to reconsider. The Earth had a green man on top, his body clothed in ivy and his face surrounded by it, just like the inn sign I had seen long ago, hanging above the door of an inn called the Green Man. The maidservant who had told me that he was a forest god would have enjoyed this picture, I thought, for a forest god was just what he was like. He was flourishing a club. On top of a scarlet disc, presumably Mars, stood a martial being with golden breastplate and helmet, brandishing a sword.

I looked at it and suddenly, from the mists of times past, John of Evesham emerged, not any longer as just a name, but as a real man. A man of knowledge. He had known several cultures, he was a scholar, and he was also a man of humour and imagination. I wished I could have known him.

I said: 'John of Evesham was very determined about his theory that the Earth spins round the Sun. And prepared to make fun of anyone who wouldn't accept his ideas. And that is what drove Bella . . .'

'Into a career of madness, trying to protect the world from heresy,' said Philippa miserably. 'Yes. The diagram and that picture are the crucial pages.'

I said: 'This book is a lovely thing. It's worth more than we paid for it. Much more.'

'Is it?' said Philippa. 'I didn't really know what to ask. Ask too much, I thought, and the sale wouldn't go through. I still have the money that Master Hardwicke gave me for it. Bella said she had bought the book back from him and at the time I believed that, but I didn't choose to repay her. Only, I couldn't decide whether I ought to keep the money he had paid me, or not.'

'It's yours,' said Christopher. 'If we can take the book. Mistress Stannard is right. This book is worth far more than you asked.'

Philippa smiled, though sadly. 'Thank you.'

'You will be financially all right in any case,' said Cogge. 'We shall keep our word about that. You can expect another Queen's Messenger in due course, with a purse for you. All you have to do, is keep faith – with us.'

Afterwards, when we were on the road home, Sybil remarked: 'I think that the promise of money did a lot to reconcile Mistress Gould to the idea of betraying any future visits from Jesuits. How money talks!'

'With a loud voice,' Brockley remarked. 'Ah, well. It comes in useful, sometimes.'

TWENTY-FIVE
Consolation Prize

There were several final things to do before we left, of course. Bella Yates was given the funeral that her sister wanted, in the churchyard at Thorby. Walter Cogge and Christopher had had speech with Doctor Rowbotham who was not likely, ever again, to encourage his flock into mob rule. He had a chastened air and agreed – though sulkily – that since no one knew for certain whether Bella had taken her fatal dose herself or been given it, she could be buried in consecrated ground. We attended. So did most of Thorby, and Rowbotham conducted the service.

As we stood by the graveside, cloaked against the cold wind while Rowbotham pronounced the committal, I said to Christopher: 'I am so thankful that all this is over. I've been frightened often enough in the past, but never quite as I have been frightened in Stonemoor. I think I must be past the age for secret assignments now. I've lost my nerve.'

'Have you? Well, it's understandable. As a way of life, yours must come hard on a lady nearing middle life. You don't mind me saying that, I trust?'

'No. Because it's true.'

'All the same,' said Christopher, watching as Rowbotham cast a clod of earth down into the grave, 'in Stonemoor, what probably happened was that you sensed an atmosphere of evil. So did I. It was very strong, and yes, frightening, and all the more so because one couldn't see where the enemy was.'

Brockley, standing on the other side of Christopher, said: 'I don't believe madam will ever lose her nerve. I agree about the sense of evil. I felt it, too.'

I looked down into the grave, at the clod of earth now crumbling on the lid of Bella's coffin, and remembered her terror when the villagers dragged her out of Stonemoor House, and how I had pitied her.

'I don't think Bella was evil to begin with,' I said. 'I suppose she thought she was fighting for her faith. Some people might say that she had a right to do that. Only, she went too far and then . . .'

I thought of Bella, brooding over what she had done, exuding darkness from her mind and filling Stonemoor House with it.

'She let evil in,' said Walter Cogge. 'She didn't have the right to murder people for refusing to agree with her. That's the way the officers of the Inquisition think and *they're* about as evil as it's possible to be. If there were no other reason for keeping Mary Stuart from trying to claim England's throne, and arresting her supporters, that would be enough.'

I didn't want to go on thinking about Bella. The thought of her produced such a muddle in me, of pity, fear, and sheer horror, that I didn't know what to do with it and in my mind, I ran away from it. And not only in my mind. 'I shall be happy to ride away from Thorby,' I said.

'Tomorrow,' said Brockley.

We left Stonemoor the next day, bidding farewell to a subdued, withdrawn Philippa, who since her sister's death had looked every morning as though she had wept in the night. She said farewell in courteous tones but she did not wish us a safe journey, nor, clearly, did she want to clasp our hands in parting. We parted from her with relief, leaving her to the life of deception to which Walter Cogge and Sir Francis Walsingham had condemned her, and hoping earnestly that we would never have to return.

The morning of our departure was grey and cool but we were well into March now, and there were hints of spring, with snowdrops and crocuses in the Stonemoor garden. Christopher Spelton and Walter Cogge were riding with us, bound for the court, to make their report to Sir Francis Walsingham.

As we came to the foot of the hill and within sight of the tavern, we saw Will Grimes, just fastening the top of its half-door back, a sign that the place was open for business. He waved and Christopher and I rode up to him. The dog bounded out of the tavern, barking, but recognized us and skidded to a halt on its haunches, tongue lolling and tail on the wag. Will, grinning, patted its head.

'Master Butterworth left this place to me,' he said. 'I miss him with all my heart, so I do, but I've a living to make and the village wants its alehouse.'

We bade him farewell and gave him our good wishes for the future. 'Grimes looks more like a hobgoblin than ever,' I remarked with amusement as we rode off.

'Or like a good fellow,' said Christopher and everyone laughed.

We were bound first for the Thwaites, to reunite ourselves with our coach. Then we would make for York and return the brown mare and the beautiful chestnut to the remount stable. When we got there, Master Maxton was extremely pleased to see them, though scandalized by their lack of condition. We pointed out that they were barely recovered from being out on the moor in winter, and assured him that they had been well treated since they were rescued. We would need fresh horses, though, for Christopher and Walter Cogge, who had been riding them.

'If you can give me a guarantee that your new mounts won't vanish into thin air first and then be found wandering in the cold on some bloody old moorland where's nowt but frostbitten heather to eat,' said Maxton acidly, hands on hips and looking more like King Henry than ever. 'I'm ashamed to have horses in my stable in the condition these two are in!'

'We promise,' we assured him.

We reached the south of England after two weeks of travelling. Cogge said that we must first go to Hampton Court, where the court was staying, and I demurred. 'Shouldn't we go to Doctor Dee first?' I said. 'To deliver the book. Where does he live?'

'Mortlake,' said Christopher. 'Near Richmond. It's not so far from Hampton Court and we can go on there after we visit the court, but reporting to Sir Francis Walsingham must come first. He is most likely with the court.'

Coming to Hampton Court was so familiar that it almost felt like coming home. We arrived early on a fine afternoon, to see its walls of rosy brick glowing warmly in the sunshine, somehow made even warmer and rosier because of the decorative grey bricks that outlined them. The elaborate chimneys stood tall against a blue sky, with thin plumes of smoke here and there, and the River Thames flowed gently past, with ferries and barges and small pleasure craft afloat on its surface, sails swelling in a soft wind, oars creating ripples that shone gold in the sun.

'It's a lovely palace,' Christopher remarked. 'I have always thought so. Haven't you, Ursula?'

'Yes, indeed. I hope that Walsingham's here, though. This long journey has tired me, and we still have to go to Mortlake!'

Joseph stayed with the horses, but the rest of us all went together to find out if Walsingham could see us. We found that he could, and that we would not after all have to go to Mortlake. 'Doctor Dee is here at court just now. I'll send for him,' said Walsingham, when Cogge, who had unobtrusively taken charge of the proceedings, had explained that we had brought John of Evesham's book and had also, briefly, described the arrest of the priests and the unexpected danger into which Christopher Spelton and Bernard Hardwicke had stumbled at Stonemoor. We had been ushered into the businesslike office that was Walsingham's place of work. He had them in all the Thames-side palaces and they were always the same: plain wood tables and seats, shelves laden with books, maps, deed boxes, piles of files and letters in dusty array, a pervading smell of ink, and a couple of secretaries earnestly busy, heads down. Since the rooms were all in palaces, they always had charming leaded windows, ornate ceilings, and panelling, but the workaday atmosphere that Walsingham created round him made these things almost invisible. I always noticed it. Stools and a bench had been provided so that we could all sit down, and I had taken a window seat. Having heard Walter Cogge out, Walsingham spoke quietly to the nearest secretary, who departed at once to find Dee. I relaxed against the window behind me, glad to be quiet for a while. I really was tired. I was in charge of the *Observations*, in its box, and I now realized how heavy it was. I set it down beside me and while we waited, I looked round the room, thinking yet again about the way Walsingham impressed himself on his surroundings.

And then noticed that here, for once, there was something different. Under a shelf on the opposite side of the room there was a cupboard and its door had been opened and fastened back. I leant forward to see what was inside, and smiled, because the cupboard was occupied by a large black and white cat, lying on a heap of torn-up paper and curled affectionately round some kittens. They were all asleep.

Walsingham saw me looking and he too smiled, which was always a disconcerting sight, since he was such a saturnine man, and his smiles tended to be those of grim satisfaction when he had caught someone out. They were usually widest when the someone in question was headed for the dungeon, the questioner, and very likely the gallows. This time, however, he was only expressing amiable amusement.

'Unusual, in any office of mine,' he said. 'But there are always cats about in these palaces. We need them, if mice and rats are not to overrun us. That cupboard door has always been tiresome; it won't stay shut. I came to my work one morning and found that Lisa had pawed it open and crept inside and produced a family. I have left her there. The kittens are growing fast; they're already old enough to leave her. I sometimes have them tumbling round my feet. Just now, they're asleep because they were fed only a little while ago. I saw the remains of a mouse in there this morning; she's probably started teaching them to hunt. Do you need a cat? Lisa is a good mouser; they may take after her.'

'As it happens, we do,' I said. The remaining secretary and all my companions were laughing and I knew why. This was a most unlikely conversation for Walsingham's office.

'You can take one with you when you go,' Walsingham said. 'Someone will find you a basket. There are two ginger males, one black and white female, and one tabby female. Choose which you want! Ah. Here is Doctor Dee.'

The secretaries were at once banished to the anteroom to sit among the junior clerks, while their master was in conference. They went, I think, with some regret. Doctor

Dee probably intrigued them just as he intrigued me. I looked at him with interest, having wondered what this well-known and controversial character was like.

He was in middle life, not unlike Walsingham to look at, being dark, tall, lean and austere, with a long face and a pointed beard. He had a close fitting black hood on his head and wore a long black velvet gown. I had rather expected him to have a gown with cabalistic signs on it, but his clothing had no decoration. Dee evidently didn't want to draw too much attention to himself. I remembered that according to Cecil, he had chosen not to keep a cat, though he liked them.

'I have been with her majesty,' he said, when the introductions had been completed. 'There are signs in the heavens of a danger averted, which is good news. Have you something to tell me about such a danger, Sir Francis?'

Walsingham looked at Cogge and Spelton, and Cogge said: 'As it happens, we may have. But first, Mistress Stannard here has brought you the book that you wished to buy. She has fetched it from Stonemoor House. There is quite a tale attached to that, but perhaps you would care to see the book first? You will want to be sure it's the one you wanted.'

I took the book to Walsingham's desk and removed it from its box. Dee stooped over it, touching it with long, sensitive fingers, feeling the leather and tracing the gold-leaf pattern on the cover with a fingertip. His nails were short and neatly filed, but there was dirt under them, or perhaps it was ink, for he had ink-stains on his fingers. He opened the book with care, and then sighed with pleasure at the sight of the illustrations and the tables inside.

He turned the pages slowly, pausing at the diagram of the sun and the planets. He fingered the text on the opposite page, obviously reading it with ease, which I had not been able to do, and then turned another page and for a few moments, studied a table of numerals, and then moved on to discover the drawing of the sun and planets aiming missiles at the Pope, and emitted a bark of laughter.

'See this, Sir Francis! Come and share it with me!'

Walsingham went to look over Dee's shoulder and allowed himself a small, tight smile. 'Witty,' he said. 'And also disrespectful. I am not so disrespectful myself. I am too well aware of the danger in Rome.'

'I find this book a joy,' said Dee. 'And there is much knowledge here which I shall delight in studying in detail.'

'You delight in the oddest things,' Walsingham remarked. 'You are very unlike me.'

Dee looked up at him, and I noticed how very keen his deep-set dark eyes were. 'We're more alike than you think, Sir Francis,' he said. 'We both want to *know*. It's just that we seek to know different things. You want to know what her majesty's enemies are planning; I want to know how the universe works. That's the only distinction.'

'Yours is an ambitious plan!' said Walsingham.

'An age-old plan,' said Dee reprovingly. 'And in my opinion, what the human mind is for. However, I am concerned by the trouble that my search for knowledge seems to have caused this time.' Dee's voice was serious. 'I know that two men vanished, who had gone to collect this book for me.' He looked at Christopher. 'One of them was you, was it not? You at least have come back.'

'I was lucky,' said Christopher. 'I was nearly killed. The other man, Bernard Hardwicke, *was* killed.'

'I am sorry for that. Truly sorry. I would never have asked to buy the book, had I known it would bring anyone into danger. I will take good care of it and see that it does no more harm! It is undoubtedly the right book. I thank you, Mistress Stannard. Are there expenses that I should repay to you?'

'We can settle that later,' said Walsingham. 'For the moment, let us tell you the full story of how the book was brought here. Cogge? Please tell Doctor Dee what you have already told me, but perhaps with more detail?'

Cogge once more launched into an account of our adventures, this time adding things that he had omitted when we first arrived. It was a lengthy narrative. It began with the disappearances of Hardwicke and Christopher, went on to the discovery of Christopher's secret sign, to the finding of the boot, to the tricks Bella Yates had played with the book, and then her confession concerning her murderous attacks. He described Christopher's narrow and miraculous escape, went on to the death of

Butterworth, to Bella's own narrow escape from the villagers, to the arrival and arrest of the five priests, and finally to Bella's death at Stonemoor.

'God's teeth!' said Doctor Dee at the end, visibly shocked.

'Do you think she took the hemlock or was given it?' Walsingham asked, at the end.

'We don't know,' said Christopher. 'We suspect that she was perhaps – encouraged to take it.'

'We prefer not to enquire too deeply,' said Cogge. 'Sir Francis, you empowered me to bargain with Mistress Gould. I have done so. She will do as you wish. I felt that we could leave the precise manner of Mistress Yates's death aside.'

'I agree.' Walsingham smiled his old, grim smile. 'And now,' he said, 'since the priests did indeed arrive at Stonemoor and the warning must therefore have been passed to the Brownlows, we know for sure who our traitor is. We had a suspect and fed him with a tale that should cause him to have those Jesuit intruders sent on to Stonemoor for safety. He did so. He is a suspect no longer, but a proven enemy.'

'Who is it?' I asked.

Walsingham's smile dimmed somewhat. 'Who *was* it would be a better question. We will never bring him to justice on earth,' he said. 'If he is arraigned anywhere, it is before the eternal throne. He is dead. It was Bernard Hardwicke. Obligingly removed,' he added, 'by Mistress Bella Yates.'

Before we left, I looked at the kittens and picked out the tabby female. She had a white front and white paws, just as Huntress had had, and I hoped that she would resemble Huntress in being just as good a mouser. She clearly had the right kind of heredity. One of Walsingham's clerks was sent to find a basket from somewhere, and came back with a very good one, with air holes in the front and a lid with a firm latch. The kitten was very sweet and snuggled confidingly into my hands when I picked her up. I settled her in the basket and then it was time to leave.

We could have been accommodated at court that night, had we wished, but we didn't. Christopher had a small house not far away, beside the Thames, and we went there, all of us glad to be, as Dale succinctly put it, somewhere quiet, ma'am, and safe and *normal*.

It was certainly not a big place but it had two good-sized spare rooms upstairs, all the same, and there we slept that night, women in one, men in the other. There was one big bed that I could share with Sybil and Dale, and straw pallets for Walter Cogge, Brockley, and Joseph. Christopher had a caretaker couple, who showed no concern at all over having to arrange supper for us all at short notice. They clearly liked their employer and wanted to please him. From somewhere they produced a meat pie big enough to provide a good slice for us all, with a rich gravy, a vegetable stew, and a tart to follow, made from last year's apples, the woman said, but sweet and tasty with cinnamon and nutmeg. There was ale, too, and a very good dry red wine. It turned into a most enjoyable evening.

Christopher was an amiable host, presiding proudly over the long whitewood table in his dining room, his bald head gleaming in the light of several oil lamps, his brown eyes full of warmth as he watched us eating and drinking and feeling safe under his roof. We were all there, Joseph included. 'We've all shared the same dangers. Joseph will not eat in the kitchen with Annet and Reg. He shares with us,' Christopher said.

I ate and drank and joined in the laughter and talk, but once or twice, I caught Brockley's eye and knew what he was thinking. If, only last year, I had accepted Christopher's proposal, I could have been mistress of this house, as well as of Hawkswood and Withysham. Had I wished, I could have been at Christopher's side, the hostess here, the others my guests as well as his, and I could have been retiring that night, not to share a bed with Sybil and Dale, but to sleep in the main bedchamber, in Christopher's kindly arms.

If he ever asked me again, I thought, I would say yes.

Next day, Walter Cogge said that he was going to his own home, which was in Berkshire. He had asked for and been granted, a well-earned break, before returning to court to take on any new assignment that was on offer.

I asked Christopher what he meant to do. 'If you would

like to come on to Hawkswood with us,' I said, 'and make a stay for a while, you would be so very welcome.'

'That's kind of you, but I think not,' he said. 'I want to have a rest from work, just as Walter does, though it can't be for long. I will be expected back on duty in a week. I want to spend that week putting my garden in order. The new spring growth has started and I've noticed that there's weeding to do. Reg doesn't like gardening much. He's a marvel at mending shutters and hinges, and he looks after my horse and the chicken and pigs that I keep, and he does as much of the cooking as his wife does, but no one is perfect and there it is. He will be very happy if I weed the vegetables.'

'Very well. Then we must say goodbye.' I said it cheerfully. 'But I hope to see you again some time.'

'I expect you will. After a while, I hope to visit the Lakes in their new home and Hawkswood is on the way there, so no doubt I'll call in on you. I shouldn't really go to see Eric and Kate Lake,' Christopher said regretfully. 'I shall have to make some excuse – tell them that *they're* on the way to somewhere or other that I have to visit. Something of that kind. I really just want to see that lovely Kate Lake again. Just once! Do they know that I was missing and supposed to be dead, by the way?'

'No, I never told them. I wanted them to enjoy the first days of their marriage with free minds.'

'That was thoughtful of you. I might tell them myself,' said Christopher. 'Just to bask in their sympathy, especially Kate's. Oh, I shouldn't . . . but I shall do them no harm, I promise. Just visit them and tell them of my adventures, nothing more.' He sighed, a genuinely sad sigh. 'I promoted her marriage to my cousin Eric and began to regret it on the very day they met. You were partly responsible for that.'

'Me?'

'You had taught Kate how to dress, how to present herself! When I saw her that day, arrayed to meet a possible husband, it took me aback. I hadn't paid her much attention before that. I thought of her as just another young girl. But when I saw her that day, I saw a . . . no, not a goddess, but a most beautiful young woman. I thought she was the most delightful, *splendid* lass I had ever set eyes on . . . only it was too late. Eric had come to meet her and they were staring at each other as though they couldn't look away. The pupils of their eyes were all wide and dark. If I had realized sooner . . . if only . . . I would have proposed for her myself! Ah, well. Life isn't always obliging.'

He wasn't going to offer himself to me again. Instead, he was going to yearn after Kate, to dream about her, to give himself up to hopeless love for her. And why not? She was not only a gallant young woman; she was beautiful and far younger than I was. Kate's dark, glossy hair had no grey strands in it as mine now had. Her skin was dewy, her eyes melting. Why would Christopher not prefer her, now that he had seen her clearly? If he had missed his chance, so had I.

Still, I was going home. I was glad enough to see Hawkswood again. Harry came running to greet me: Hawthorn prepared an elaborate supper in welcome, Adam Wilder was eager to give an account of events in the household while I was away.

And the morning after we reached home, I awoke with a migraine.

'I knew it,' said Gladys, stirring a freshly made potion and handing it to me. 'I knew you were going to find trouble. You always do. I told you so.'

'Don't croak, Gladys. What's in this drink you're giving me? It tastes even worse than usual. Have you thought of trying lemons and a little salt?'

'What's lemons?' said Gladys. 'Never heard of them!'

Her potion worked, anyway. I was recovered by midday, though I still wanted to rest. Dale and Brockley came to see me, and brought the tabby kitten with them.

'Hawthorn made her a bed in the kitchen but the poor little thing was crying all night,' Dale said. 'Missing her mother, I expect. Here.'

She put the kitten down beside me. It at once curled into the crook of my right arm, glad, it seemed, to be close to something warm and living and protective.

I had not come home with Master Spelton's betrothal ring on my finger. But I had not come empty handed. Soon, when the kitten had grown a little, we would have a new kitchen cat to keep the mice in order. I supposed it had its funny side. I hadn't got Christopher Spelton; instead, I had a little tabby kitten with a white front and four white paws. She was sleeping now, trustfully settled at my side.

Well, widowed ladies past their youth often found solace in the company of pets. The kitten, I thought wryly, was my consolation prize.

Lightning Source UK Ltd.
Milton Keynes UK
UKHW03f0419270418
321716UK00001B/22/P

9 781780 295749